WATERLINE

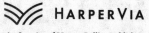

HarperVia

An Imprint of HarperCollins*Publishers*

WATERLINE

a novel

Aram Mrjoian

WATERLINE. Copyright © 2025 by Aram Mrjoian. All rights reserved. Printed in the United States of America. No part of this book may be used or reproduced in any manner whatsoever without written permission except in the case of brief quotations embodied in critical articles and reviews. For information, address HarperCollins Publishers, 195 Broadway, New York, NY 10007.

HarperCollins books may be purchased for educational, business, or sales promotional use. For information, please email the Special Markets Department at SPsales@harpercollins.com.

FIRST EDITION

Designed by Yvonne Chan
Waves illustration © polygraphus/stock.adobe.com

Library of Congress Cataloging-in-Publication Data has been applied for.

ISBN 978-0-06-339352-3

25 26 27 28 29 LBC 5 4 3 2 1

For my family

"In a flash Stephan grasped the fact that no deed is done once and for all, that we always have to begin again at the beginning."

Franz Werfel, *The Forty Days of Musa Dagh*

Gregor Kurkjian
1994

After winning the morning's egg fight, as he did every spring, Gregor Kurkjian allowed an orderly to push his uncomfortable wheelchair to the edge of the brick patio, which overlooked the nursing home lawn, where his two great-granddaughters were patiently waiting, soon nestled in the short grass at his feet, facing him. He had promised them a story. They wore their bright Easter dresses, Mari in custard yellow and Ani in highlighter pink, ready to hear about Gregor's adolescence, details that he had assumed he would never live long enough to tell them. It was the story everyone in his family had heard time and time again. His grandsons could recite most of the details by heart.

"Did you know I was born on a mountain by the sea?" he asked. The girls' eyes went wide with wonder.

"Papa!" Karo, his eldest grandson, shouted from where he stood in listening distance, arguing about sports or politics or any frivolous matter with Edgar. In these moments, on the rare holiday visits from his entire family, Gregor realized how much he missed his wife and son. He never expected to outlive them. His grandsons were too busy these days to find much time for a relic like him. He had lived through so many things only to be left bored and lonely in his final years. Karo continued, "They are too young to hear about that!"

Gregor waved them off. His grandsons' parenting was so different from his own. Always hovering. They were too touchy about what children could handle, and on this occasion Gregor was well rehearsed, it was the perfect opportunity. Every few months, another graduate student would drive from Ann Arbor or Detroit or East Lansing to the old folks homes in Dearborn to hear the remembered horrors of the few remaining survivors. Not a week ago some young woman pursuing her PhD in Armenian studies had shown up and spent an hour taking notes while he regaled her. There were so many excellent documentarians, but he was convinced no one truly listened. If anyone paid attention, the world would look different.

"There is a lot to this story," Gregor said, wagging a finger at his great-granddaughters. "You must be patient and listen closely." Mari nodded at him. Even though she was barely five years old, Gregor was certain she was destined to be the brightest of them all. Ani, wanting to impress her older cousin, sat quietly even though she would rather be running around with the other children. Gregor calmed his breathing until he was certain he had their undivided attention.

Gregor was the best marksman in his village. His father taught him to fire a rifle when he was eight years old. By his twelfth

birthday, his father boasted that Gregor could pit an apricot resting atop a fence post at thirty paces. It was something of a local
legend, and it was good for business, as Gregor's father sold furs.
The boy with eyes like binoculars; a behemoth, a head taller than
any of his elders. He was lanky in his early years, but as Gregor
reached adolescence, he built brawn from mornings out hunt-
ing, days of hard labor around his family's farm, and evenings
showing off his strength playing games with other boys on the
steep, uneven terrain. Gregor, the firstborn son, the pride and
joy of the Kurkjian family. He never complained when his father
worked him an extra hour before supper. He was never bothered
by the simplicity of his provincial upbringing. And for years, Gregor imagined he would take over the household when his father
grew too old.

Musa Dagh towered over them, both near and far. At sixteen
years old, Gregor loaded his family's stores of food, water, and a
few valuables in canvas saddlebags across their mule's back to
carry up the mountain. Thousands of Armenians from the six
villages at the base of Musa Dagh ascended to the summit in
defiance of the Ottoman government. They refused to be moved
from their land and murdered in the desert. Gregor helped con-
struct their ramshackle camp. He dug trenches to his chest. Their
backs were protected by the Mediterranean Sea, where Gregor
was told his ancestors sailed merchant ships centuries ago. The
water spanned far past the horizon. Gregor stood by as the elders
took stock of their resources, counting their arsenal of rifles and
ammunition. They quickly built a sanctuary from the turmoil
below.

Gregor was given a Mauser and a ration of bullets. Later that evening, his father snuck a few extra rounds and a lump of chocolate in his son's pack. No one could deny Gregor would make better use of the ammunition than the other boys. Yes, it was primarily a matter of precision, but a true shot required steadiness that went beyond a good eye. His father was confident the other boys would follow Gregor's lead. As with the men, they too needed a leader. No one on the mountain held illusions about what was coming. If they were to face death, they would go down fighting.

When Turkish soldiers arrived, Gregor's father sat him down and explained that he could not blame himself if he killed the men trying to exterminate them. There was no more time for shooting at rotten fruit and small animals, now it was a matter of life and death. Survival. The Ottoman government was not there to negotiate. *God will forgive you*, his father said, *for what else can you do?*

The Mauser remained steady at Gregor's side. He cradled it to his chest when he stole an hour or two of sleep, the barrel rising and falling with his breathing. He slept very little and ate sporadically. Any commotion was enough to rouse him. Each day, smaller rations were distributed. Each meal was a dwindling blessing, every bite as sacred as a prayer.

"You're more poetic with every telling," Edgar interrupted. Gregor's grandsons had come closer at some point, now intently listening behind their daughters. A few of the other children had wandered over too, no longer distracted by their yard games.

Gregor sighed. "Some respect, please." Even in his old age,

Gregor lost himself in the scene, still full of that thunderous adrenaline—Musa Dagh was their last stand.

Edgar raised his hands in an exaggerated apology.

Days turned into weeks, and soon more than a month had gone by. Gregor thought the hunger was the worst of it. A lingering, painful way to die. He distracted himself by peering through the crosshairs of the rifle, vigilantly on the lookout for fire from the scattered groups of soldiers below. The Ottomans knew it was a matter of waiting. Time had never moved so fast and so slow. He listened as the older men gathered and discussed their next move, only to realize there was nothing for them to do.

After fifty days had passed, the Armenians on Musa Dagh had to face that their remaining time for rescue was limited. In the moments Gregor was not holding his position on the front lines, he wrapped his mother and younger sisters in his burly arms, though his limbs were skinnier now, even gaunt, since they'd first ascended the mountain. His family felt small and bony in his embrace. Starvation, Gregor told the small crowd, ignoring the concerned expressions of a few parents, was what for decades his people would become known for.

Each night, Gregor stayed awake for more hours so that his father could rest. Once a crack shot himself, his father's eyes weren't what they used to be. Gregor was now the marksman in the family.

"Not a bullet could be spared," Karo whispered before his grandfather reached his next line. Mari turned and glared at him in disappointment. She turned back, eyes full of wonder, and hung on to every word.

Soon, the Armenian stores were fully depleted. No rations to offer even the children. Thousands of hungry bellies. An army of undernourished souls. Six villages' worth of desperation. The mountain was barren. The mountain was all they had. The mountain was nothing more than a pile of rocks lifting them a step closer to what awaited after their ultimate earthly demise.

But Gregor would not give up. His father, too weak to stand, curled among coarse wool blankets with his family, the furs long since abandoned. They had so little left. Gregor reeked of soil, grass, gunpowder, perspiration. The fat and muscle had melted from his body. In private, he counted the lines of his meatless rib bones, the bulges of his weary knuckles, the veins in his neck and forearms. Many of their neighbors succumbed to fever and starvation in the night.

In one last, desperate plea, the camp hoisted two banners facing the water. A white flag, beckoning for help from the sea. And like a prophetic miracle, a warship appeared in the distance, charging toward the shore. The survivors were weak, too fatigued and feeble to paddle against the salty tides, but upon hearing the distant Klaxons, Gregor left his position and volunteered to race to the vessel. He was young, revitalized, unconcerned by the dark and choppy waters or the purifying salt burning against the cut and bruised landscape of his body.

It had felt like a dream. All these decades later, with his great-granddaughters as his captive audience, he prayed they understood. Shedding the soiled shirt glued to his skin. How the damp beach was like ice on his mangled bare toes. How even in the direst of circumstances, he wriggled his feet in the cold wet sand and felt the grit rub his raw, blistered soles, a blissful sensation that erupted through his whole body, so that by the time he had waded to his waist and dove into the frigid brine, his lean, unfed muscles pulsed with heat.

Gregor couldn't afford to expend his energy too quickly. Each stroke was purposeful, each breath a reminder that he was still alive. Two other young men swam through the sea on either side of him. The trio couldn't help but laugh when they met a rowboat of Frenchmen at the stern of the massive warship. Gregor could not speak the language, but one of the other swimmers could and translated in fierce spurts with the European soldiers. They vowed they wouldn't leave the Christian resistance of Musa Dagh faced with certain death. Allies were soon on the way, a fleet to carry the helpless refugees to safety. The people of the mountain were saved.

Gregor swam to the shore as fast as he could, propelled back toward land by the foaming waves. Returning to the beach made him feel like a new person altogether, a creature leaving the water for the first time. Masses awaited him on the beach. *To the boats!* A delayed reaction, hundreds of hopeless men, women, and children too weak to move, until they realized they were rescued and leapt into action, their weary bodies renewed. Gregor retrieved the Mauser from his febrile father, kissed each member of his family on the forehead, and shooed them toward the sea.

To buy time, Gregor stayed behind and steadied the rifle at the burst of advancing Ottoman soldiers who did not want the Armenian resistance to escape. He waited as long as he could before opening fire. Only a handful of the other men remained with him, defending their position. The sun warmed Gregor's face. He was calm, each shot calculated and patient. There was no way Gregor would allow the camp to be overtaken in their moment of salvation.

Anyone without a gun rushed to the incoming ships. Then, one by one, the remaining men sprinted down to the hulking, beckoning blue. Gregor waited until bullets whizzed past his shoulders. No one else remained on the mountain; he was the last to flee. Gregor lowered the rifle, slung the strap over his shoulder, and sloshed into the shallows, lifeboats awaiting.

"I had no other option," he told the horrified crowd. "There was no choice." So much of life was outside of our control, Gregor thought. After he left his home, nowhere else ever felt safe again. Anywhere could become hostile. Every place was at risk. This is what haunted Gregor whenever he thought about leaving Musa Dagh behind.

PART ONE: 2018

Edgar Kurkjian

Edgar Kurkjian slid the kitchen window above the sink to a close and wiped the drenched sill with a paper towel, wondering why he paid an arm and a leg to blast the air conditioning when his wife and children so insistently allowed the cold to seep out of the house. He rinsed red and green bell peppers and left them to dry on a scrap of cheesecloth on the counter. He smashed garlic beneath the broadside of a chef's knife. He chopped white onions until tears welled behind his glasses. He hadn't grilled shish kebab since his mother died. When she was in her final years, they always made these elaborate meals together. If his mother were standing next to him at the counter now, she would scold his lack of seasoning, demand another full bulb of garlic, sprigs of fresh mint and rosemary from her long-abandoned herb garden, flecks of black peppercorn crushed from the grinder, instead of the weak powder pummeled fine as sugar Edgar shook from a McCormick's tin.

Chicken broth came to a boil on the stove, rice and egg noodles swimming to the surface. The smell of butter in the air. The scent of his childhood. A side of pilaf with every meal. He had wanted to grill the shish kebab in the backyard, a frigid tallboy of Bell's Two Hearted in hand, slick with condensation in the July sun, but the thunderstorm had entered its second unrelenting day, dousing the state from Lake Michigan to Lake Huron. The driveway was flooded; the yard, waterlogged. He might have waited for the weather to cooperate if he wasn't feeling guilty for all the time he was spending out of the house. On a sunny day, the scent of charcoal and seared lamb would have sent his brother and sister-in-law lumbering over from next door with a bottle of wine. They would FaceTime his eldest daughter, Ani, and his niece, Mari. They could sit on the back patio together, a family, enjoying a meal alfresco. Instead, Edgar set the oven to broil and lined up two rows of flimsy, damp wood skewers, like giant toothpicks, on a cookie sheet doused with olive oil. He was determined to make the meal spectacular, regardless of the torrential downpour.

A fork of lightning, there then gone, in the window. Everyone had left the office early on the eve of the Fourth of July holiday. It was rare Edgar found the house empty after returning from work. For once, he could make a mess of the kitchen without tripping over his family. Where were they? Little did they expect they would arrive home to a weeknight feast like the ones his mother used to pull together with ease. It was as if she could stretch time and complete a half-day's preparation in an hour. Her timing was impeccable, honed over decades spent in front of a hissing stove. Everything always landed on the table at once, steaming, elegantly plated, demanding to be consumed. Edgar was already out of sync. The pilaf would be ready before he managed to get the lamb in the oven. He needed to text Karo and Hova before they started planning their own dinner.

Not a clean inch of workspace remained. The kitchen's redone granite countertops opened into a small dining area, and the hardwood stretched far past the table into a living room, with its large sectional sofa and easy chair facing a television nestled in the center of two floor-to-ceiling bookshelves. Beyond that, there was the laundry room exiting out into the garage. He turned on the television and it came to life in the distance. The screen illuminated in the middle of a commercial for one of the many regional car dealerships. Grosse Ile might as well have been a tolled-off extension of the Motor City. His family had surely spent a small fortune crossing over the toll bridge in the many decades they'd lived on the island. Edgar wanted to listen to the weather report, worried that if the rain kept coming, the city would cancel tomorrow's fireworks on the river.

Skewers soaked, Edgar alternated between protein and vegetables: lamb, pepper, onion, lamb, pepper, onion, and tried not to prick his finger. The car commercial faded into the evening news. Edgar attempted to wipe away his oniony tears with his wrists, but the water clung to his eyelids and blurred his vision. The local anchor's austere face emerged, whatever oncoming tragedy he was about to deliver in a practiced somber tone poised to burst from his mouth, but then, like thunder, there was a banging at the front door.

Edgar dropped a skewer and scrubbed the meat and oil from his palms with dish soap. His eyes itched in irritation. The banging at the door came again, unflinching and relentless. His phone buzzed to life on the countertop, glowing with a smiling photo of his wife, but the knocking did not stop. He wiped his smeared glasses on his white undershirt and walked into the front foyer. Even though no one was home, Edgar couldn't help but look down the other hallway to see if anyone else would hustle from one of the three bedrooms to get the door. He unclicked the lock and found his brother on the front porch, dripping with rain. The cul-de-sac behind Karo was as dark and wet as if they were aboard a sinking ship surrounded by rough waters. Karo leaned into Edgar's chest. The two years between them had seemingly aged his elder brother a decade more. Gray hairs overran Karo's sideburns and rough beard. His thin nose pointed like an arrow toward the ground. Karo was defeated and wayworn, there was nowhere else to go. Outside, the storm pressed on, indifferent.

Edgar pulled him into the house. Karo shivered and dripped all over the floor. Edgar grabbed him by the nape of his damp neck and forced him to look up. They never liked making eye contact, always reaching each other at an angle, but Edgar waited for his brother to speak.

"Mari's gone," Karo gasped out a sob. "In the lake. She's gone."

Edgar drove. Karo collapsed in the passenger seat of Edgar's black Ford Explorer and spoke briefly on the phone with Hova. Karo had refused to wait for her. Six hours to Milwaukee if they hit no traffic and the rain let up. With all the cars on the road for the holiday, Edgar wasn't optimistic about either possibility. After they drove across the toll bridge, the Detroit River a dark abyss beneath them, and off the island, through the mess of 275, and merged onto I-94, they were met by an endless row of taillights glowing red. The ditch on the side of the highway was filled with standing water. Windshield wipers heaved back and forth. On the shoulder, a dead doe tilted its head back toward the forest, as if wishing to go home, the white of its belly sopped with mud. Edgar fumbled with the radio. All the baseball games were rained out. He landed on a classic rock station that would stay with them as far as Kalamazoo.

"Stop," Karo groaned, an hour into the drive. They had not even passed Ann Arbor. Edgar pulled over. They were crawling at a snail's pace anyway, down to one lane in seasonal construction, orange traffic cones spaced every ten yards for miles. Karo got out and waddled to the shoulder, where he vomited onto the verdant mat of wet grass. Drenched immediately, he fell back into the car. He buckled his seatbelt and glared at Edgar. "Drive."

Edgar's phone buzzed in his pocket and he ignored it. After Karo arrived at the door, Edgar had turned off the oven and stovetop. He left the food out, the kitchen a disaster of dishes and food scraps. His frantic note to his wife, left in its usual spot on a notepad at the center of the kitchen table, read, *Call Hova. Don't tell the kids anything yet.* He hoped Hannah would be the one to find it. Edgar didn't want to break the news that his niece was dead until they were certain.

"It might not be Mari," Edgar proposed. His voice was scratchy. They had driven in silence for so long. At this rate, they would arrive around the time the bars closed.

"It's her. They mentioned the flag tattoos on her ankles."

"Maybe they got it wrong." Edgar was reaching for anything. Not many people were familiar with the Armenian flag. "Her

15

phone might be out of battery," he added, knowing better than to use the word *dead*.

"Stop being a fucking idiot!" Karo barked. "It's her, Ed."

Karo's hands were cracked with age, pale at the knuckles with chill. Edgar turned on the heat even though it was warm outside. His phone continued its litany of buzzing. He removed the device from his pocket and read a text message from Hannah: *Hova is driving to meet you. She's a couple hours behind.*

"Hova's on the road."

"Goddamn it." Karo rubbed his hands together. "We have to beat her to the station. I don't want her to see the body."

After one last break at a rest stop near the Michigan–Indiana border, they drove around Chicago to circumvent downtown traffic and continued north in the dark, zooming through the wet night until the lights of the Milwaukee skyline sparkled in the Explorer's rain-spattered windows.

They spent longer than Edgar anticipated waiting to be escorted to the hospital's morgue. White sterile walls, bright fluorescent lighting, the lingering scent of bleach, those damn freezing chrome chairs with turquoise and purple cushions. A medical examiner met them with a manila folder that contained Mari's postmortem photo. "Are you kidding me?" Edgar pushed away the folder before the examiner could remove the image from its sheath. "No photos. Take us to the body."

"It's protocol."

"We didn't drive eight damn hours for protocol."

They followed a police officer and the medical examiner around labyrinthine hallways through half a dozen locked doors. At each checkpoint, the medical examiner scanned her ID attached to the breast pocket of her scrubs like it was a nuisance. Karo hunched with his hands knotted together at his chest while he prepared to identify his daughter's body. Edgar stood at his side, trying to remain strong for his brother. The coroner flipped back the sheet at the neck.

Karo's body shook like he would freeze to death. Snot dripped over Edgar's lips. He couldn't breathe. The police officer excused herself from the room while they stood there, clinging to one another.

An hour later, in the blue haze of dawn, they met Hova in the lobby of a La Quinta Inn on the north side of Milwaukee. For half the morning, Edgar fell in and out of sleep on a chair in the corner of the room, then left his brother and sister-in-law, devastated and supine on a pair of firm queen beds, to make the necessary arrangements and phone calls. They had paperwork to fill out and sign, a locksmith to call so they could access Mari's condo. She'd never remembered to make them a copy of her key. Edgar could sense when he was no longer wanted. He could attend to the other arrangements at home.

The Fourth of July was sunny and hot, all signs of the past days' storm evaporated. Edgar drove from one block of traffic to the next, making a pit stop in Chicago to pick up Ani, who lived in a cramped studio apartment in a tall building in Lincoln Park. It had already taken Edgar a lengthy phone call to coax Ani out of riding the train to Milwaukee earlier that morning. Ani exited her building in black leggings despite the heat, a Michigan State tank top, her black hair loose under a plain navy baseball cap, and a clunky duffel bag over each shoulder. They sat through hour after hour of stop and go, the road bumper to bumper in both directions. "Indiana, the crossroads of America," Edgar joked as they left Illinois, but he didn't provide the tired punchline. *Because no one wants to stay here.* Ani didn't laugh. It was a recycled family joke Ed or Karo dragged out on every road trip. Edgar was sure there were beautiful parts of Indiana, and he enjoyed the Indiana Dunes, but the forty-mile stretch they drove between Illinois and Michigan was half industrial ports and half barren stretches of dead grass and desiccated trees. It felt like a transitional space. A term Edgar hated—a flyover state. The Cubs made an easy feat of the Tigers while they listened in on the radio.

Edgar pulled into the driveway. The sun was low, the sky littered with thumping fireworks in all directions. Inside, Hannah and the twins were sprawled across the couch. Hannah rose to hug them. She felt small and stiff in Edgar's arms, muscled from all the hours she had been spending in spin class at the gym. Her long brown hair caught in his beard stubble. Joseph and Talin hid together under the musty patterned blankets Edgar's mother had crocheted decades ago. They looked so young, though they were now sixteen. Ani folded between them and the three huddled into a ball. Joseph wrapped his long arms around his two sisters. Edgar had never seen his children look so helpless and defeated.

He walked to the refrigerator, thirsty from the drive, in search of grape juice or orange juice, something sweet and sugary and painfully cold. He opened the door and shivered from the expulsion of frigid air. On the center shelf his shish kebab and pilaf were cooked and packaged neatly in a stack of Tupperware containers. Hannah was always cleaning up his messes.

At Mari's memorial service, Edgar played host to their family and friends. Many of their parents' remaining acquaintances were in attendance. Edgar struggled to place most of them, having not seen many since his young adulthood. Cocktail parties and neighborhood barbecues, basement card games (poker, euchre, pinochle), summer days when his father would man the grill for hours while people mingled across the lawn under the walnut trees. Karo drank Ararat brandy out of a flask and kept to himself, even as Hova tried to coax him from his grief long enough to fulfill his duties as the family patriarch. Karo had not stopped drinking since he returned home from Milwaukee. Mari's body was to be cremated later in the week. Edgar's phone had buzzed all morning with condolences, though he had also hung up on two reporters trying to reach the family for comment. He checked the time and found another sympathetic text from Iris—one of the accountants at his firm, who had sent a massive arrangement of white lilies. He would have to ignore her for at least a few more days.

Ani refused to give any kind of speech at the memorial, even though the family had expected her to. Edgar's eldest daughter and Mari were like sisters. In a long black dress Hannah had ripped the tags from that morning, Ani stood in line with him, head down, fidgety, hugging the seemingly endless parade of perfumed, ancient Armenian women.

Hannah held Edgar's hand and reintroduced herself to many of his parents' friends they had not seen since their wedding. Her black dress was longer than Ani's and Edgar kept stepping on the hem as he shuffled his feet to shake the stiffness from his knees. She asked him, "Why do they keep grimacing at me?"

"You have to remember how their generation is," Edgar whispered, his upper lip nearly caressed her pearl earring. "They think I should have married within the community."

"I know that," Hannah sighed. "I just thought they'd set it aside, at least for today."

Hannah's phone vibrated. "Please stop calling," she demanded into it, before hanging up and releasing a sigh. "Do they think if they keep harassing us we'll change our minds into giving a statement?"

Hova approached them. She wore black heels so that she stood level with Hannah. Edgar's sister-in-law was more on par with what the older women expected: a younger version of themselves, or a daughter, a niece, a neighbor.

"Ed," she sighed, more composed than he would have expected. "You're going to need to give the eulogy. Ani won't, I can't, and I won't let Karo go up there blotto."

"Give me a minute." Edgar squeezed Hannah's fingers between his own and looked at her. "Fuck." He tried to collect his thoughts, but he was exhausted, having slept so little over the past few days, nights squinting under his desk lamp as he perused his niece's finances and voided life insurance policy for his brother. Mari had left instructions for her savings, but Karo wouldn't let Edgar read the note. He wasn't sure he wanted to. Mari was always the most articulate in their family, and he was certain her parting words would stick with him. He, on the other hand, was a terrible orator, now stuck in the position of doing the impossible. There was nothing he could say off the cuff about his niece that would meet his older brother's expectations. Even if he'd had the chance to prepare, anything he said would inevitably fall short.

Hannah dropped her head and leaned against his chest, the scent of her hair spray in his face. An old receipt crinkled in the vest pocket of his suit coat. "Say whatever comes to mind. You'll do great."

Edgar left the main funeral parlor and found an unlocked annex filled with empty silver coat racks and extra chairs precariously stacked higher than his head. Plastic hangers pell-mell, a yellowed phone book in the corner on the stiff carpet. The room was wallpapered in a chartreuse hexagonal pattern that reminded Edgar of the hideous designs that used to cover every inch of his childhood home, before Karo moved in and stripped it all away and repainted. Pacing the room, he ran through several versions of what he could say about Mari.

Six months ago, at his mother's funeral, in the same parlor with many of the same people, he had not even realized this room existed. For that occasion, Karo had stepped up, both during their mother's final days in the hospital and with the funeral arrangements, and Edgar had done nothing but grieve in silence. A passionate eulogy delivered by the eldest son, written with aplomb and grace. Not a dry eye in the house. But this was different. For someone his age, the death of a parent was tragic, but anticipated. The death of a daughter—an explosion, a shattering. Edgar thought about what his father or grandfather would say in his position. He had never been good with words.

After he constructed a mental outline and rehearsed a few times, Edgar exited the storage room and stumbled down the center aisle of the main parlor, through the circles of mourners conversing in the corners of the room or waiting in line to stand next to Mari's body to say goodbye.

Among large bouquets at the front of the room, he stood behind the wooden dais, grateful that it hid his shaky legs. His whole body quivered. There was no microphone. He had no notes. His family sat down in the front row—Hannah, Ani, Talin, and Joseph, all in a line, his son towering among the women—but they felt light-years away. Hova walked Karo to the front row on the other side of the center aisle, where they could sit alone and undisturbed. Everyone caught the cue and found their seats.

"Well," Edgar started, but his voice was muffled by a string of saliva gathering at the back of his throat. He coughed. A large, unfamiliar group stood with their hands in their pockets against the back wall. Many of Mari's former students and colleagues had rented a bus and made the long drive from Wisconsin to pay their respects. Mari taught freshman and sophomore English, so most of them must have been only fourteen or fifteen years old, even younger than Joseph and Talin.

Unsure of how best to begin, Edgar relied on chronology. He told stories of Mari's childhood, how proud he was as an uncle watching her grow up and excel in school, how her contagious confidence helped his own children become strong and kind individuals. He talked about how much she enjoyed teaching English, her infectious love for history and books and movies. He felt his eyes tearing and worried he would break, but he continued on and on, slouched at the shoulders, staring at the back wall as the crowd grew bored and drifted away from him. He wanted to be out of the spotlight and sit down with his family, but the words just kept tumbling out, the right conclusion eluding him.

After he finally sat down, Hannah dropped her face onto the shoulder of his jacket. "You did so well," she soothed. "I love you."

His kids bent forward in their seats, messy with tears, nodding in agreement. The whole room was disorderly with sniffles. His words were better than nothing. Edgar leaned over to peer down the row, and he found his older brother, craned forward, head to his knees, hands behind his neck in a position that reminded Edgar of the duck-and-cover bomb drills they'd done in grade school. Hova rubbed circles over Karo's back, nodding to Edgar with a mouthed *thank you.*

In the parking lot, Edgar received loose handshakes and overbearing hugs, hands curled over his shoulder blades, caresses on his cheeks from the older women. There was to be tea at his house after the ceremony. Hannah had offered to relieve the burden from her in-laws, and so the house waited, stocked with pastries and refreshments. Photos of their niece covered a corkboard in the entryway, below it a thick leather notebook where people could document their condolences. Mostly out of respect for Karo and Edgar's parents, women from the church had insisted on handling the majority of the food. Old school.

Edgar noticed a photographer lingering at the edge of the parking lot, so he offered Joseph a hundred dollars to get rid of the guy. "I got it," Talin interrupted, immediately storming away. The whole family was tired of the constant speculation. Edgar watched his daughter storm away and wondered when the media would finally grow tired of asking the family about Mari and what she did or didn't do. He shook his head.

Cars shifted in all directions. The sun was unbearable, and by the time he ran through all of his thank-yous and goodbyes, Edgar's black suit was sopped in a film of sweat and felt heavy on his frame. If he waited too long, the cul-de-sac would be crowded with mourners before he reached home. There was an hour gap between the events, but half those attending didn't live on the island and had nowhere else to go.

"You reminded me of your father up there," Dr. Magarian said, his hairy-knuckled fingers heavy as they sandwiched Edgar's hands. He had delivered Karo and Edgar, and even Mari so many years later, but retired months afterward, before Ani was born. Magarian was in his late eighties. Edgar felt the lack of steadiness in his hands, the tiny, frail earthquakes of growing old. He was stunted with age, low to the ground and wavering in the heat. A black fisherman's cap sat snug on his head to block the sun. Edgar wondered if he was bald now. A gray-and-white beard covered most of the doctor's blotchy face. Edgar had not thought about it much until that moment, the infinite variations in hair color between black and white. His father and grandfather were all salt and pepper, sharp juxtaposition like a checkerboard, and here was a man aged enough that even his grays were losing the scrap of color they had left. Magarian's suit was loose on his shoulders and arms, crumpled from the areas of excess material, revealing the man he used to be.

"It sounds morbid to say, but I'm glad Dad isn't here."

The doctor nodded. "Hayk was always tough on the outside. He loved you boys and his grandchildren. We were in the same school together growing up. I was three years ahead of your father. He was even serious as a kid. Never emotional, all business. The first time I saw him cry was after I delivered your brother."

"He could be a rough old man."

Dr. Magarian wagged a gold-ringed finger. "He was always trying to live up to your grandfather. The family legend."

Edgar laughed. "No one can live up to that."

Dr. Magarian lifted his arm and shook his hand free from the hem of his coat sleeve to inspect his wristwatch. Edgar was surprised to see it was one of the overpriced, faux-luxury models assembled in Detroit now, even if the parts were still manufactured in Switzerland. It was a stylish timepiece with its leather band and a face larger than a half-dollar, but a bit gaudy, nonetheless. He'd expected something more antiquated, classic. The doctor's cheeks glistened with perspiration.

"I imagine you need to get going." Dr. Magarian sighed. "I will stop by the house to pay my respects to the rest of the family."

Edgar patted the doctor's shoulder. "There are enough sweets to feed a village."

The old man waddled back toward his boat of a black Lincoln Town Car. Edgar's grandfather used to have a car just like it before moving into the nursing home. Nearby, his family had gathered in a line, staring out at the busy road. Joseph stood a head above his mother and sisters, the four of them with their backs to Edgar, varying in height like a dark, jagged mountain range; forlorn, staggered peaks in the distance.

A week later, with his morning cup of coffee and a sudoku in the newspaper, Edgar sat on the opposite end of the L-shaped couch from his slumbering eldest daughter. His wife had left earlier for her routine morning at the gym—what felt like several hours ago. Ani slept night and day in front of the unending glow of the television blaring *Law & Order* and all of its procedural variations. She arose only to go to the bathroom or change into a fresh pair of sweatpants. Edgar tried to clear one of his errors, but the eraser of his pencil was at its nub, and it left one of the squares smudged dark gray, illegible.

Accrued vacation time allowed Edgar to log nearly two weeks of bereavement leave, but in the days after the memorial service, his many hours around the house were restless. He found so many excuses to bury himself in numbers. Accounting always added up. He appreciated the balance, the simple answers math provided no matter what else was going on in the world. There was an endless stream of money to keep track of. He was hopeless without his spreadsheets, his emails, forms to explain, reports to send. He felt cooped up, and he'd nearly forgotten what it was like to have all three of his children home for more than a weekend or holiday.

Joseph and Talin had both passed their drivers' tests at the beginning of the summer and appeared to be making a sport of putting miles on Ani's hand-me-down Ford Focus. The car was on its last legs, edging the two hundred-thousand-mile marker. When the sun rose over the driveway and warmed the car's interior, Edgar didn't even need to open the door for the odorous funk of weed and cigarettes to emanate. The past few mornings the twins slept well past noon, wandered into the living room in yesterday's clothes, un-showered and sluggish with hangovers, asked for gas money, and played rock-paper-scissors to see who would earn the privilege of driving across the island to drink away the evening in whichever dank and empty basement occupied their friends. Meanwhile, his eldest had made camp on the couch and refused to emerge from its embrace of throw pillows and crocheted blankets.

When Edgar was left with nothing but tepid dregs at the bottom of his coffee mug, he wandered down the hall to the bathroom. Days of dense stubble poked down his neck. His eyebrows, a bushy bridge traversing the valley of his nose. He needed a haircut. His gray hair was not coming in as much as Karo's yet, but he had the same permanent bags under his eyes, the same thin nose heavy with blackheads. The mole on his forehead was pink from scratching at it restlessly in the night. He returned to the kitchen to pour another cup from their cheap French press. The seal was worn away and his coffee was always littered with grounds. He had not walked next door to see Karo and Hova—who'd left him and Hannah to clean up the disaster area of their house after the mourners had come through—since before the funeral. They needed time alone.

"Can you make more coffee?" Joseph emerged from the hall at the kitchen threshold. He was awake surprisingly early, perhaps a sign that at least one of his children was in the process of getting better.

Joseph, uncharacteristically tall and lanky for their family, scratched at the edge of his hairline. Joseph's hair was nearly long enough to reach his shoulders and swooped outward at the end like he was one of the Beatles. His shirt rose over the hem of his basketball shorts and revealed a circular welt the size of a golf ball near his belly button.

"What's that?" Edgar nodded.

Joseph feigned unawareness, but reached directly for the wound. "Oh yeah, one of the guys on the hockey team gave me twenty bucks to take a paintball to the stomach."

Edgar walked over to the stove to refill the stainless-steel tea-kettle. He was about to fill the pot with water in the sink when he thought twice about it. "Why don't you make your own coffee?"

"I can never figure that thing out." Joseph pointed at the French press. "Talin and I usually just stop at the Starbucks in Kroger."

"So you're risking bodily harm to fund an exorbitant latte habit. It's about time I teach you how to make a budget."

"You sound like one of those viral articles. 'Be a millionaire by skipping out on this everyday item' or 'stop eating avocado toast and do this.' Buying coffee isn't going to be what breaks the bank," Joseph scoffed. He moseyed over to the sink and nudged Edgar out of the way so he could dunk his head to drink from the faucet's downward stream. Joseph's hair fell to the side and revealed a hickey high on his neck.

"That's not from a paintball." Edgar flicked his son on the ear.

Joseph shot up. "Shit."

"What do I care?" Edgar grinned. "Good for you."

"Don't tell Mom. I don't want her asking me who I'm dating or getting all in my business."

Edgar laughed. "Your mother knows everything that goes on in this house. I won't have to tell her a thing."

Joseph wiped water away from his mouth and moved on to the refrigerator, opened the door, and stared into the cavernous light as he assessed the array of memorial leftovers, the brick of Edgar's abandoned pilaf, wilting fruits and vegetables galore. He lugged out a gallon of skim milk with a capital J written in black marker atop the pink cap. Joseph was trying to bulk up and drank milk multiple times a day for the protein. At any time, the top shelf of the fridge was cluttered with at least two plastic jugs set aside just for him. Edgar thought at this rate his son would drain his college fund on beverages alone. Joseph uncapped the milk and lifted the large bottle to his lips.

"Give me some of that," Edgar demanded, grabbing the gallon. "I'll show you how to make the coffee."

It was certain to be a tough few weeks after their loss, but Edgar felt a nostalgic sense of excitement and hope for his youngest children. Joseph and Talin were reaching the age where the island felt its most magical. Communal fifths passed around roaring bonfires, joints smoked on languorous boat rides at the mouth of Lake Erie. Edgar's high school prom had been at the Grosse Ile Yacht Club. Gregor slipped him a hundred-dollar bill in the driveway to pay for dinner and a bottle. While the dance was at its peak, Edgar lost his virginity on a canvas tarp in an unlocked boathouse. That was nearly three years before he met Hannah.

Edgar scrubbed the pile of foreign Tupperware accumulating in the sink. He glanced over at Ani on the couch and wondered how she could sleep through all of their clatter. The kettle whistled and billowed with steam and Joseph removed it from the burner, the thin purple lightning of veins in his arms bulging. Edgar directed him to pour the scalding water over the fresh grounds.

"How's the weightlifting going?" Edgar asked.

"I can't gain any weight at all. I get stronger, but no bigger."

"That's in your genes, I guess. Give it time and age. You're the tallest person in our family in a couple generations. Your great-grandfather was as tall as you, and he had biceps like you wouldn't believe."

Joseph poured more milk into his mug and waited for the coffee to steep. Edgar was surprised his son did not get sick from drinking so much dairy. Joseph bent a slice of toast in half around a pat of butter and shoved the whole thing in his mouth. Crumbs cascaded to the tile.

Joseph filled his mug then walked over to the bookshelves by the television. He removed a massive gray hardcover with a black spine. The two hollow thumps of a judge's gavel echoed. It took Edgar a moment to recognize his grandfather's weathered copy of *The Forty Days of Musa Dagh*.

"What are you doing with that old doorstop?" Edgar asked. He remembered Gregor standing over Karo's shoulder when they were home one winter for Christmas break during college. Their grandfather would point to a passage Karo was reading and say, *This part is important* or *Werfel is well intentioned here, but that's not how it happened.*

"Ani told me to read it." Joseph nodded at the lump of her hair, all that was visible of his older sister since one of the couch cushions was draped over her head. "She said a lot of our family history is in here."

"Well," Edgar sighed. He sat down on the other end of the couch. "It's not exactly about our family, but your great-grandfather Gregor was there. On the mountain."

"You never talk about them."

"It's hard to talk about," Edgar began. "My mother's parents died around the time your uncle Karo was born. My dad's mom, your great-grandmother Mara, refused to talk about her childhood at all. She died when I was a teenager, Karo was in college. The only reason we have any account of her life is because right before she passed a professor from the University of Michigan showed up recording stories from all the Armenians who fled the Genocide. He couldn't even convince her, but his insistence made your uncle realize we would lose her history if no one wrote it down." Edgar scoffed, "Your great-grandfather, on the other hand, talked the professor's ear off. We could tell his story inside and out, every detail and embellishment. He loved mythologizing himself."

"What was he like?" Joseph asked. "I've only ever seen pictures."

Edgar didn't have any idea where to begin. He was not a good storyteller and hated trying to recount his grandfather's legend. It was like an enormous generational game of telephone. He could provide the details well enough, but building up the narrative, keeping everything in order, reciting the historical facts he had memorized in his youth, was exhausting. He was fatigued by the onus of having to tell the same story so many times through-out his life, to clients, coworkers, acquaintances, friends—so few people remembered the Armenian Genocide. Still, he understood he must pass on the weight so that the import of their people's history was not erased.

Ironically, Hannah could probably do a better job. She'd read the official family accounts and was forced to endure other old family stories time and time again throughout the course of their relationship. While Edgar's grandfather was always supportive of their dating, it was not easy for Hannah to gain the approval of his parents, so she never interrupted or stopped listening, even if they had told her the same story half a dozen times before. His grandfather had witnessed enough pain to not deny anyone hap-piness, but Edgar always thought his parents wanted to uphold the values of the church and their social circles, which came with strong ideas about marriage within the community.

"I'll muck it all up. Why don't you just finish the book?"

"This will take me all summer!"

"Ani read it in a week." Edgar peeked at his daughter to see if she stirred. He lowered his voice. "Mari spent a whole summer reading it before sixth grade and couldn't stop talking about it. Your sister wanted to catch up, but it's nearly nine hundred pages, and not exactly a fast read. Your mother and I thought Ani would give up after a day or two of trying to slog through it. Instead, she finished it in a week! Truth be told I haven't even read the whole thing. I skimmed it after I graduated college, but mostly paid attention to all the passages your uncle Karo had underlined."

Joseph swallowed and stared at the floor. Edgar was trying to avoid Mari's name as much as possible for the time being, certain a glancing mention would send his kids in a downward spiral, but it proved difficult given the closeness of their family. Sometimes Edgar wondered if living next door to his brother caused social problems for his children. They might as well have grown up with two sets of parents, especially Ani. Joseph set the book down on the coffee table. "So, basically you're giving me homework?"

Joseph walked back into the kitchen and overloaded his empty plate with grilled chicken thighs and pilaf and lahmajoon. Edgar thought about the jailing of journalists and violent rhetoric from Turkey. The assassination of Hrant Dink. Artsakh. The reality that things could get worse again at any time. There were always talks of fixing relations, but history was stubborn. The burden would soon be Joseph's to carry too.

He took stock of his hungover son. He remembered a time Mari called their home phone in the middle of the night when she was in high school. She had drunk too much at a party and gotten in a fight with her friends, so they left without her. A boy would not leave her alone and kept commenting on her figure. She felt unsafe, unsure of what to do, but she didn't want her parents to punish her, so it was Edgar who had risen from bed and driven across the island to pick her up.

"What were you drinking?" Edgar had asked her.

"Stroh's." Mari grimaced.

Edgar had laughed. "I guess the island doesn't change. We'll tell your dad you decided to come home but forgot your house keys."

Edgar had accepted it was an imperfect alibi. Mari was too meticulous to leave anything behind. But the nighttime logic of how she made it to Edgar's couch would make sense. Karo, cautious and untrusting, refused to leave out a spare, whereas Edgar hid one on the back deck beneath the bottom stair. Mari knew well where to find it when she wanted to get in.

Joseph inhaled a folded, lukewarm piece of lahmajoon.

"I can't give you a story that's not mine," Edgar said. Joseph's phone rested face down on the countertop. It was the first time in months Edgar could think of where one of his family members was not fiddling with their phone while they spoke. He was a bad example. He spent too much time on his own phone responding to emails and text messages from his clients and coworkers.

"I guess I'll read it."

"Take your time."

"I have some now. I need to wait for Talin to wake up to drive to the gym or she'll yell at me for taking the car."

"Take mine," Edgar offered. "I'm not going anywhere today. My keys are on the hook."

"Thanks, Dad." Joseph disappeared down the hall and Edgar returned to his sudoku puzzle at the kitchen table. He sat scribbling small numbers in pencil for another ten minutes before

Joseph reemerged in different clothes carrying a water bottle and tromped out the back door.

After Edgar solved the puzzle, he grew bored with the paper and rejoined Ani in the living room. He never liked *Law & Order*. He thought it glamorized a corrupt policing and justice system. Growing up, his father, Hayk, like much of the Armenian community, had inherited a distrust in law enforcement. *There's no such thing as a good cop*, his father once warned while Edgar and Karo watched an old detective show on television. This was a trait passed down from his grandfather, who remembered well what could happen when lawmen and soldiers showed up at the door. But Ani liked *Law & Order* for the predictability. There was a formula down to the commercial breaks. It wasn't a program that required too much attention. The answers were always spelled out.

He leaned over the coffee table and placed his fingers atop the cover of Werfel's fraying book. Their family copy, a first edition, was first translated and published in English in the 1930s. Edgar flipped through the yellowed pages until he found one of Karo's meticulous notes written in the margins. *Hard to distinguish this scene from Grandpa's stories. Which one accurate? Review resources at Shapiro.* His older brother devoted so much attention to every book or blueprint, but for Edgar the line between Werfel's fiction and his family history was hazy. His grandfather's version and the version in the novel melded together in his memory, so many important details lost.

The half acre separating Edgar from his brother felt infinite and hazardous. He could walk from the sliding glass door on the side of his house to the mirroring one of his childhood home in less than a minute whenever he pleased, but covering that distance was impossible now. He could not bear to see his older brother so hopeless and depressed. Hova kept texting Hannah to say he should come over, and Hannah would hold her phone up to his face as they ate dinner or read in bed, Hova's name glowing atop the messages and FaceTime calls.

Edgar didn't want to go over empty-handed. He thought of the countless times Karo drove the girls when they were kids to the A&W in Trenton for smushed-flat bacon cheeseburgers and overflowing sleeves of curly fries and frosty mugs of fountain pop. Edgar could not remember how many years it had been since his last root beer float, but the A&W was closed now. Coney Island would have to do.

Edgar called ahead and ordered three cheeseburgers and Coney dogs and sides of chili-cheese fries to go. The drive south was short enough that it felt silly to not have walked. He entered the diner and paid in cash, tempted to buy a slice of banana cream pie as he glanced at the illuminated desserts under the glass counter. The white paper bag heavy with Styrofoam containers sat warm on his lap as he circled back into the neighborhood. He should have sent Joseph next door first as a scout. His son's sudden interest in *Musa Dagh* would've made an easy excuse. *Ask your uncle, he's kept better track of our family history,* Edgar could have said. Karo might even relish the opportunity for a distraction. Edgar accepted that Joseph often went to Karo for advice when he didn't want to talk with him or Hannah.

He turned into the cul-de-sac and parked in the corner driveway behind his sister-in-law's black Ford Fusion hybrid. The stop felt like coming to the end of a tortuous journey, even if his destination was only one house over. The home he grew up in. His childhood bedroom had become Mari's bedroom, but now was a shrine. The invisible barrier across their lawns had been evaded, the flat stretch of grass where they played soccer and baseball and freeze tag as kids. Three generations of his family had occupied that damn house. He went to the front door and rang the bell like a guest.

"Edgar," Hova voiced with surprise. "Why not just walk in?"

"I brought some food." He lifted the bag. The grease shined through the bottom of the grayed paper. The color reminded Edgar of springtime, when the snow thaws and reveals gravel on the side of the road.

"That smells lovely. I'm getting tired of leftovers and halva. Every time I start to clear out the fridge someone else stops by with food and condolences."

"I asked for no mustard on one of the hot dogs for you," Edgar told her. "There's one with chili on the side for Karo. He's always dipped his like a heathen."

Hova chuckled, but her face dropped. "He's not eating, Ed. I try to bring food down for him, but it's just Ararat all day and night."

Their father's brandy, Edgar thought. He was never without a case or two of Ararat in the storage room of the basement. Those unopened bottles must have been older than the twins. When he was a kid, Edgar thought the basement was eerie. It was unfinished, a floor of concrete with a drain in the middle and metal poles they would spin around until they were dizzy. It was dark and damp. A cave at the heart of a mountain. Edgar's father never bothered to fix it up, but when Karo and Hova moved in to take care of their mother the first time she fought breast cancer, a mere six months after their father passed away, Karo installed drywall and thin, cheap carpet and nestled a desk into one of the corners by his drafting boards, turning the space into a home office. It was a fluke that Edgar moved next door three years later. A joke, at first, that he would even consider a home in such close proximity. They went to an open house mostly out of curiosity, their parents having never been that close to the next-door neighbors—in their youth, an old cantankerous couple Edgar always suspected was racist and secretly called his family dirty foreigners, and then once Karo had moved in, a busy young family with ties high up in GM, so that they quickly outgrew what they always imagined as a starter home. Once Edgar and Hannah had walked around, Mari and Ani had their hearts set on the idea of being neighbors. In the end, Edgar and Karo couldn't say no.

Edgar set the bag of food down on the kitchen table and gave Hova a timid hug. He was never certain how much intimacy to show after a tragedy, even with his family. They hugged all the time, but now the meaning of such gestures had changed. At most, he would give Karo a pat on the shoulder, a brotherly, collegial sign that he was there for him. Hova went to the kitchen, slid a stack of three plates from the cupboard left of the stove. The same shelves where his mother once stored them. Everything in its right place. The house looked so different and yet nothing had changed. Hova divvied the food, portioning not nearly enough for herself. Half her hot dog, a sparse smatter of fries Edgar could count on his fingers.

"Can you carry both plates down the stairs?" she asked.

"Did you forget I used to wait tables at the Peanut Barrel?"

"Thirty years ago, sure," Hova jibed. "When you still had some muscle."

Edgar grinned. He stacked the plates up his left arm so he could open the basement door. He grabbed the greasy bag, fat with leftover chili-cheese fries. "I could still lug a keg from the cellar if I needed to. We weren't all trapped in the library like you nerds in Ann Arbor."

Hova halfheartedly feigned a laugh. She sat in front of her meal and Edgar left her alone, descending into his brother's subterranean fortress.

The basement emanated the funk of brandy. Edgar hated walking down the stairs when Karo was working; his brother was at a vantage point where he could see Edgar coming before Edgar could see him. Uncharacteristically, there was no music on the record player. Karo usually listened to his vinyl collection while he worked, anything from Sam Cooke to the Rolling Stones to the A Tribe Called Quest record Mari bought him one Christmas as a joke about her father's dated taste. *The Low End Theory*. Karo fell in love with it. Edgar knew which floorboards were creaky, every peculiarity of the house now a matter of muscle memory, but he did not make an effort to avoid them, especially carrying his precarious load, the bag at his side and plates tucked at chest level. The plates rattled against one another and for a moment he worried the one balanced on his arm would fall. He was not as steady on his feet as he had thought.

When Karo came into view, Edgar could see the trouble was worse than expected. His brother was unshaven, oily, eyes a dehydrated tumult of pink and red, sweaty hair clinging to him as if he had emerged minutes ago from the depths of a great ocean.

The overhead lights were at their dimmest setting, which exacerbated the bulges of sickly blue under Karo's eyes. His drafting boards were overflowing with curling blueprints and sketches. Karo, the elder, the naval architect. Designer of ships. Master of the sea. Carrying on the ancient family trade. A half-empty bottle of Ararat rested at the desk's center. The label was turned away from Edgar, but he could recognize the profile of the brandy bottle anywhere. The aroma of warm fries brought new life to the stale air of the cavernous space.

"I brought us a meal. Hova keeps telling Hannah you've been working night and day. I figured you would be hungry."

Karo leaned against his desk chair. It was a stern schoolhouse model, stained wood with a straight back and a thin cushion on the seat.

"We have a fridge full of leftovers," Karo complained. "More kibbeh than we can figure out what to do with."

Edgar found a spot without papers on the desk and set down the bag and plates. Karo's stomach gurgled audibly. Edgar turned to the storage room, looking for a folding chair. While he searched, he shouted back, "You would choose french fries over pilaf any day."

In the back corner, Edgar found a set of squeaky metal chairs that matched a card table they no longer owned, sparing a glance at their grandfather's canvas rifle case nearby. He hoisted the closest chair, returned to the office, and jammed the hinge open to take a seat. Karo reluctantly plucked a fry and shoved it in his mouth, but Edgar couldn't see past his brother's vacant expression. After a minute, Edgar bit into his cheeseburger first, a concession that he was younger and weaker, less disciplined, but

Karo remained hesitant. His first bite barely broke the bun. Edgar waited for Karo's brain to signal the need for nutrition. Soon, they were both gnashing ravenously, but Edgar worried if his brother ate too fast he wouldn't be able to keep his food down.

"You shouldn't worry about designing boats for tech bros at a time like this," Edgar mumbled through a mouthful of meat and bread and tasteless iceberg lettuce. Karo wavered in his chair, pickled through, Edgar thought, but the food appeared to be doing him some good. Edgar decided then and there that he would visit Karo every evening until his brother spun back out of his despair. He had been a negligent brother, hiding idly next door while Karo lost himself in grief. No longer.

"It's nothing," Karo assured him in a hoarse whisper, swallowing. "Some consulting work." A partial omission, no doubt. Throughout his career, Karo had built a prominent reputation around his ecofriendly designs, so that any consultation he provided was certain to be for a big-name client. He had advised on sensitive military projects, designed green sailboats for hip-hop moguls, and even digitally reconstructed Norse wooden ships based on splintered fragments provided by Scandinavian archaeologists. The truth was that Karo could have afforded one of the enormous gaudy mansions on the island. Edgar knew his brother made much more money than he ever talked about, it was easy to see based on his line of work. Behind his desk, Karo had framed photos standing dockside with celebrities and billionaires. Little did they recognize Karo disdained them; he only consulted with the hope of mitigating the damage they caused to the planet. Time and time again Karo complained to Edgar about the catastrophic waste caused by a single cruise ship, how the ocean would someday swallow them up for their mistreatment of it. *I'm a piece of chewed gum trying to seal a cracked dam,* Karo once told him. If it were up to his older brother, any vessel reliant on gasoline would never again barrel across the water.

"That looks complicated, like a floating mansion."

"That's called a yacht, Ed."

"Who in the world can afford a yacht like that?"

"You know as well as I do that there are people on this earth who can afford anything."

Edgar removed a clump of napkins from the bag and meticulously wiped cheese and grease away from his hands, finger by finger. Even so, as he perused Karo's plans, the spirals of his smudged fingerprints darkened the corners of the papers. Karo's stomach gurgled again as it settled. He belched loudly. The cheeseburger was gone, but the hot dog and fries remained untouched for now. Edgar's own plate was sopped clean, a few swirled lines of dried-out chili near the rim.

Karo wiped his brow. "There's pilaf upstairs if you're still hungry."

"Hova's pilaf?"

"No, one of Dad's old friends."

"That's fine. No one makes pilaf like Mom did anyway."

"Your wife makes pilaf like Mom," Karo argued. "She knows not to be shy with the butter."

Edgar continued browsing the drafts. "This isn't military is it? We're not going to get locked up when they pull my fingerprints off of these?"

"I only take military contracts when I like the administration."

Edgar laughed. Karo was being serious, but it was the closest thing he could expect to good humor.

Edgar coughed. "I see the Mauser is still in its spot."

"Yes." Karo nibbled at his fries. "I've been thinking about do-nating it though, to the museum at St. John's."

Edgar scoffed. "It's our family history. Papa would roll over in his grave if we got rid of it."

"Do you remember what he was like in the end?" Karo mused. "In the nursing home, when his mind started to go? On bad days, he was always scared the Ottomans were coming for him. He hoarded cookies because he remembered nearly starving. He probably associates that gun with the worst time in his life, even if he loved telling that story. There's a reason he had us keep it buried down here in the basement."

"I just don't think we should be so quick to get rid of some-thing so close to where we come from."

Karo sighed. "It's a gun. We're certainly not using it. Junk is still junk even if it once meant something."

Edgar nodded. There was no point in arguing further. Like all his parents' possessions that had passed to Karo along with the house, the Mauser probably wouldn't be leaving the basement anytime soon.

After it became evident Karo wanted to be left alone again, Edgar cleared their plates and bussed them back upstairs. He felt as if he was rising from a cabin deep within a ship, returning to the fresh air above deck. Upstairs, he found Hova reading a slim novel at the kitchen table. Her food was picked over, but nearly all of it remained. Edgar shook Karo's leftovers into a messy pile atop hers.

"You need to eat too."

"I'll be fine," she said. "Did he eat?"

"More than you."

"Send Joseph over for some."

"He's reading Werfel."

Hova kept her eyes on her book. "I hope he doesn't get too tangled up in all of Karo's notes. When I met your brother, he was in the campus library trying to locate missing accounts from other Musa Dagh survivors. Most of them ended up in the same place, probably even your great-great-grandparents."

"I know both of those stories well."

"I'm lucky my family immigrated before all that." Hova's family had fled after the Hamidian massacres, having decided the Ottoman Empire was no longer safe for Armenians, nearly twenty years before the stand at Musa Dagh.

"They left for the same reason though. It doesn't mean you don't share the burden."

Edgar patted his sister-in-law on both shoulders in his traditional farewell. Once in his car, Edgar reread the text messages that had been sitting in his phone all day. He suppressed the urge to reply once more and pocketed his phone. The driveway of his house was crowded with cars when he arrived. Everyone was home. He pulled in behind his wife's black Fusion.

The aroma of pizza had drifted into the laundry room. Ani and Hannah were shouting in the kitchen. Edgar lumbered into the living area, where Joseph was sprawled on the couch with a pizza box on his lap, eyes like aquarium glass, stoned, watching *Jeopardy*. For the moment, his son's blatant inebriation was not worth a fight. Talin was the only one not to be found. Ani and Hannah stood opposite one another across the dining table, which was crowded with camping supplies. Among them were a brand-new turquoise thermal sleeping bag; Ani's orange two-person tent, bagged up, caked in dust after being excavated from its resting place in the basement; a red, rust-pocked, one-burner camp stove; and a miscellany of collapsible bowls, mugs, and plastic silverware. Bags from the supermarket and REI littered the floor.

"What's all this?" he asked.

The women turned, shook from their argument. Ani spoke first. "Dad, is my hiking backpack still around here somewhere? I couldn't find it in the basement."

Edgar was dazed. "Are you going camping?"

"Ed," Hannah said, "please come talk some sense into your oldest daughter."

"What's wrong?" he asked. He walked into the kitchen and assessed the stockpile scattered across the table. Now that he was closer, he perused the abundance of dry goods. White rice, oatmeal packets, protein bars, instant coffee. Bagged meals of dehydrated lamb stew, chicken and dumplings, and pasta primavera. Trail mix of every variety. Dried fruit. Hannah folded her arms and waited for Ani to explain. His daughter composed herself, ready to give a lecture.

"Don't worry, the apricots aren't from Turkey," Ani replied lightheartedly.

Edgar was pretty sure where the conversation was going. For years, Ani and Mari had been planning a summerlong road trip to stay in as many national parks as they could visit. With Mari's teaching schedule and Ani's willingness to skip out on whatever bartending gig she held, they could travel for weeks without worrying about returning to work, but something always fell through. Last year, Mari had purchased a condo and the cost of moving set her back, so she tutored over the summer. The year before, Ani fractured her foot training for the Chicago Rock 'n' Roll half-marathon, making days of hiking unrealistic while she recovered. They had been patiently stowing away money together, waiting for their chance to explore the country, and now that patience was wasted.

"Dad," Ani began. "You've heard well enough about the trip Mari and me always planned on taking. I've been thinking a lot. She would want me to go."

"And so what?" Edgar asked. "You're going to run out into the wilderness all by yourself?" The idea of his daughter and niece roaming unknown remote areas filled him with natural parental anxiety, but the reality of Ani out there alone inundated him with a new kind of unshakable fear. Anything could happen out on the road. And he had to admit, Mari had always been the more responsible and resourceful of the two of them. They needed one another, yes, but Mari was the true architect of the trip. Ani would be lost without her. Hannah looked poised to jump in, clearly waiting for him to put the kibosh on the whole thing.

"Don't you think that's dangerous, Ani?" Edgar asked. "It won't be the same as you imagined when you're out there all alone."

"This is the same way you guys acted when I moved to Chicago. There's danger everywhere, Dad." Hannah rolled her eyes. Edgar thought it wasn't the first time his daughter used this line. It sounded so familiar. Rehearsed. She continued, "With all that's happened, isn't that obvious by now?"

Edgar sighed. "I'm not as much of an old fart as you think, and I'm not naïve. I recognize the realities you and your cousin deal with as women living in the world. That doesn't mean you should voluntarily trek off into the woods where anything can happen to you."

"You think Chicago is safer than the woods?"

"That's a bullshit argument and you know it. Don't contradict yourself. You can't have it both ways."

Joseph slunk past them holding his empty pizza box. They waited in silence until he had walked down the hall and his bedroom door shut. Ani argued, "You don't get to pretend to be enlightened all of a sudden to bolster your argument."

"You don't even have a car," Edgar shouted. "I suppose you're going to hitchhike? Hop trains like Jack fucking Kerouac?"

"I'm going to ask Aunt Hov and Uncle Karo if they'll let me take Mari's car."

Edgar's mind flashed to the olive-green Outback sitting in the driveway next door. He had arranged for a service to drive it to the island from Milwaukee. He never understood his niece's purchase. They had A-plan discounts with Ford and still she bought a Subaru.

"They could say no," Edgar countered.

"Or they might say yes."

"And what about your job?" Hannah asked. Edgar was grateful for her interjection. The conversation was getting away from him. "No restaurant in Chicago is going to let its bar manager take off half the summer."

"I quit this morning." Ani shifted her weight from one leg to the other. "I called and asked for the time. They said no, so I quit. There's nothing you can do to stop me from going."

Hannah sat down at the table, flummoxed. They had reached

an impasse. Edgar had expected the conversation would eventually take this turn. His children were old enough now that he knew better than to believe he had any control over their decisions. At the very least, Ani was well equipped and prepared. She had been planning this trip with Mari for years. Edgar had seen their methodical spreadsheets. Color-coded columns listing emergency supplies, the average variations in the cost of gasoline by state, the weight of each item in their backpacks. They'd inherited a familial sense for organization that Edgar always lacked outside of his workday. Always plan, always keep a record. Last Christmas, Karo bought them matching survival manuals and a canister of bear spray. He was the one who loved the camping trips they took as a family when the girls were young. Edgar never found comfort in the great outdoors—the perpetual state of cold and damp, the tiresome process of preparing bland, soupy meals over a camp stove, the ceaseless packing and unpacking— but he made the best of it.

Edgar sat down next to his wife. He reached for her hand, and she grabbed his like she was clinging to a life raft.

"You're right," Edgar agreed. "I can't stop you, so let's hear your plan."

Ani dug her laptop from her duffel bag of dirty clothes and pulled up the notes on highway routes, camping destinations, and finances that she and Mari had compiled, all the miniscule details organized with precision. Edgar read the nutritional facts on a box of protein bars while he listened. He wondered how much of the stagnant time that his daughter had spent on the couch was devoted to thinking through this trip. How would it be the same without Mari? Mari had even compiled guides on how to handle unexpected interactions with aggressive wild animals. It was night and day compared to when he and Karo used to toss a bunch of backpacks and loose groceries into their cars and drive their families to the nearest state forest, hoping it wouldn't rain. While Edgar was worried about his daughter, he was also filled with a profound sense of pride. What a wondrous young woman he had raised: practical, ambitious, undeterred, and now, for Ani to have faced such loss, to be dealing with her cousin's absence and still wanting to go, how difficult it must be to carry that weight. They had been an inseparable team for so much of their lives. Now, Ani was alone, but somehow no less determined. Hannah's combative expression slowly eroded into one of defeat. His fingers were falling asleep in her tight grip.

"Dad," Ani pleaded. "I do need your help with something, though."

"What is it?"

Ani glanced at Hannah then back to him. "I need you to talk to Uncle Karo and Aunt Hova for me. I'll go to see them myself tomorrow, but it would help if you brought the idea to them first."

"The car?"

"Not the car."

Hannah let go of Edgar's hand and he pulled on his wedding ring.

"I want to take some of Mari's ashes with me. We always were going to make this trip together. I've thought about it a lot and I think it's what Mari would want."

Edgar grunted. It would be difficult to convince his brother and sister-in-law to part with any of the remains of their daughter. He pulled the wedding ring from below his knuckle, an old habit from his youth when the band of gold still felt foreign around his finger. He lost hold of it, and the ring chimed against the kitchen floor, rolling under the table toward Ani. Ani picked it up, considered it for a moment, and spun it like a coin across the wood.

After a slice of lukewarm pizza, Edgar returned to see his brother so he could pitch Ani's request before she went over there the next day. Hova was surprised to see him back so soon. The rest of her food was still untouched, cold and stiff, on the table. Edgar was short and to the point.

Upon returning home, the twins' car was gone, Hannah was reading in bed, and Ani had returned to her spot on the couch in front of the television. Edgar lumbered to the mini fridge he once purchased for Ani's freshman dorm, where he now stashed extra beer in the garage. He dug out two orange tallboys of Bell's Two Hearted. Edgar found his canvas green Michigan State chair next to Hannah's car in the garage and carried it to the back deck, where the crickets and other insects took up their nightly racket. He nestled a can in each cupholder. The television next door flickered, Hova zoned out in front of some sitcom or the nightly news alone while Karo drank in the basement. He wondered if either of them was getting any sleep.

The air was muggy, but cool enough that Edgar craved the hug of a thick sweatshirt. He could hear cars whooshing around the edge of the neighborhood and imagined the distant shush of the river. A few of the brightest stars penetrated the light pollution from the city, and a slice of moon was low in the sky. Every few minutes, green walnuts thumped against the ground. Edgar dug his phone out of his pocket and scrolled through more of his unread texts, smirking.

The side door slid open and Ani came outside to join him. She carried two beers for herself, having long ago learned this trick from her father. She drank from the one in her hand, and the other sagged in the front pocket of her green Michigan State hoodie. Edgar remembered how excited he'd been when Ani chose his and Hannah's alma mater. For those four years, when they made the drive to East Lansing for move-ins and homecoming weekends and fall tailgates, it was like entering little windows into his college days all over again.

"How'd it go?" she asked.

"The car is yours." Edgar sighed. "But the ashes? I'd say fifty-fifty."

"Those aren't bad odds."

"Are you sure you can handle this?"

"I'm as prepared as I'll ever be."

"I don't mean the camping part," Edgar clarified. He finished the backwash at the bottom of his beer, then wiggled the metal tab back and forth until it broke free. "It's going to hurt to leave her behind. I'm sure a therapist could extrapolate on how painful finding closure can be, or something."

"You'd be a terrible therapist."

"The solution to every problem is to hold it in forever. Repress."

Ani scowled at his sarcasm. "I think it's what she would have wanted, Dad. To be part of the wilderness. She loved nature. There was nothing she enjoyed more."

"Do you think that's what she was trying to do in the lake?" Edgar asked. It was an unfair question, but he couldn't stop wondering about it. He thought he had known his niece. He thought he understood the kind of woman she had become: stubborn, motivated, caring. She was like another daughter, even if older and more distant. She had been an integral part of his world since the day she was born. But he could not imagine the version of Mari who would end her own life.

He dug the sharp nub of the can tab into the dead skin along his thumbnail. With a snap, he sent the small piece of metal spinning off into the darkness, a trick he learned during his own time at Michigan State. He thought about what Karo would say and swore he would clean it up from the lawn in the morning.

"No." Ani had caught up with him and cracked open her second can of beer. "Mari would have done the research to be sure the tide would carry her back to shore. I think she thought it was poetic. There are so many uglier ways to die."

"I'm sorry for bringing it up." He never would have been so inquisitive if he was sober.

"We don't need to talk," Ani told him. "Let's just sit for a while."

Edgar nodded. The neighborhood was unusually quiet, no restless dogs or feral teenagers causing a ruckus. He pretended he could hear the rush of water in the distance. The river, in constant movement, surrounding them on all sides, making its way out to the great lake, flowing anywhere the earth would allow.

⸻

Two mornings later, Edgar stood beside Hannah in the driveway while Ani finished packing the car for the lengthy trip ahead. A mason jar with some of Mari's ashes rested in the cupholder.

"They gave me a third," Ani had told Edgar. He appreciated the math of their decision. "An equal share."

The trunk of the green Outback was full, the backseat flooded past the windows with Ani's belongings. Dawn rose brisk and dew stained as listless birds whistled from the walnut trees. In another hour it would be a scorcher. Ani squeezed them, Edgar first and then Hannah, having already hugged Joseph and Talin goodbye in their bedrooms when she first woke up so they could go back to sleep. They'd come in well past midnight curfew again. Ani backed out of the driveway and crept toward the exit of the cul-de-sac. Edgar wrapped an arm around Hannah's shoulders, holding her to him until long after the car was out of sight.

Hannah cried into his chest. She was dressed for the gym and would work out for most of the morning to relieve her anxiety. Edgar had two days of bereavement leave left but was heading into the office anyway.

Hannah peeled her face from his body. "She'll be okay, right?"

"National parks are practically resorts these days," Edgar assured her. "They have cabins and hotels and gas stations."

"I love you." Hannah coughed, closing her eyes and letting out a whoosh of breath.

"I love you too." Edgar wrapped up his wife and let her go. If he waited too long to leave, he would get stuck in traffic. Hannah seemed to read his mind. She quickly wiped the lingering tears from her face and kissed him on the cheek.

"I should get to the gym before it gets crowded."

She left him alone and walked back inside to retrieve her keys and water bottle from the kitchen counter. Edgar unlocked his Explorer and settled in for the drive before he could find a reason to stay. The island was quiet, but a line of cars was stalled on the toll bridge. The sun reflected off the river and welcomed the day.

He drove through Lincoln Park and River Rouge and Mexican-town until he arrived in Midtown and pulled into the parking lot of the Greektown Casino Hotel. He scanned the area quickly for anyone from the press that may have followed him; they mostly stopped bothering the family about Mari, but some were especially persistent. He tossed his keys to the valet and walked through the gold doors into the lobby. Even early in the morning, the floor was busy with people eating continental breakfast at the slot machines. For a moment, Edgar stood still and listened to the din of noisy contraptions and music and employees laughing in the lull before the day's energy caught hold. He rode silently in the elevator to the twenty-second floor then made his way down the hall to the familiar door; the room number never changed.

He knocked three times, holding his fist against the door on the final wrap. His body felt heavy. His hand fell to his side as the door moved away and bonked the rubber stopper on the wall. Iris reached for his face and rubbed her thumb across his cheek, her black hair wet and shiny, sprawled over the white expanse of a hotel robe. The robe was fuzzy and clean with the Greektown logo over her heart. An aura of warmth radiated from her as if the steam had followed her from the shower. Edgar's head fell. He ogled her tan calves poking from beneath the fluffy hem and felt part of himself fall away.

Guilt bubbled inside him, but he pushed it away. Falling for a younger Armenian woman in the months following his mother's death, with both his parents and familial pressure now gone. The irony wasn't lost on him.

"Are you okay?" she asked, her thick brows furrowed. "I've been so worried."

"Later," he told her. "We'll talk about it later."

Iris stepped aside to make space for him to enter the room. The bed was made, a shiny and creaseless comforter, unbothered, white sheets still tucked in, pillows stacked three deep against the dark wood headboard. The television played the weather channel, a fog of oranges and reds with temperatures scattered across the state. The beige curtains were pulled back to welcome the low rays of sunlight, and the central tower of GM's headquarters glistened in the window, a city of its own within the city by the river, prominent in the skyline. An enormous mirror ball of a building. The room's massive windows were streaked from a dirty squeegee. Even at this height, the streets were loud with traffic, and Edgar could hear the impatient car horns conversing above the soft grumble of the air conditioner. He walked toward the large windows so he could enjoy this ephemeral view. He thought about his grandfather atop the mountain overlooking the sea, how different it would be to feel trapped at the summit with nowhere to go. How lucky Edgar was to look out over so much safe and familiar space, the landscape below stretching for miles. He nearly didn't hear the click of Iris latching the door behind them.

Talin Kurkjian

In the dim light of her desk lamp, across the hall from her brother, Talin knelt on the carpet in front of the full-length mirror hanging from the back of her door. She applied foundation and curled her eyelashes, straightened her curly black hair. Talin was not so much in the mood to party, but she needed to get out of the house. Gwen's mom and dad were up north in Petoskey for an extended weekend vacation, and Gwen never passed up the opportunity to open their space for a good time. Years ago, Mari and Ani had taught Talin how to get ready for a night out. There was no reason to put in too much effort, they said, even as they spent an hour or more in front of the mirror. Talin's hamper was overflowing with dirty laundry, and she could smell the funk from her accumulating gym clothes. It could wait until morning. Her phone dinged from somewhere in the pile of blue-and-white throw pillows crowding her twin bed. Out the window, night had arrived as fast as a flood.

Talin slid into the hall, past the perpetual subwoofer of Joseph's bedroom. The well-trodden carpet in the hallway never felt as soft as it did in her room. There was leftover pizza in the fridge, and she needed a slice or two if she expected to drink anything later in the evening. The women in her family were notorious lightweights. Her father stood at the counter with his hand cupped around a can of Bell's Two Hearted. Talin always wondered what that name was in reference to, if it had anything to do with the gray grumpy fish that curved around the label. On the handful of occasions Talin had consumed alcohol, the gap between her body and mind made her feel as if she also had two hearts. Her pulse would multiply and wash over her, then pull back like riptide.

"Tal," her father sighed. "Your car is a mess."

She passed him and released the light from the refrigerator. "Sorry, Dad."

"Driving is a privilege." He tilted the lid of the can in her direction. "You two need to respect what you're given. No more gas money until it is clean."

"I'll vacuum and wash it tomorrow," she promised. There were three slices of sausage and a lone shriveled square of veggie supreme left in the flat orange pizza box. Talin placed the veggie on a plate and clanked it into the microwave. She was tired of red meat. Everything was loaded with lamb and beef.

Her father drank his beer. "Make your brother help."

"I'll try."

"He won't help." Edgar sighed. "And when he doesn't, don't let him have any of the money I give you. I'll throw in an extra twenty if you mow the lawn."

"Thanks, Dad."

The microwave dinged, and Talin pulled the hot plate out onto the counter to cool.

"Joseph needs you right now," her father told her, leaning toward her for a hug. She snapped her arms around him and could feel the blooming bulge of his stomach in contrast to his taut back muscles. When they were little, she and Joseph had clung to each of their father's biceps, like they'd been told Mari and Ani had years before they were born. He would crouch in the middle of the yard for them to grab hold, then stand tall and spin in circles until they couldn't keep their grip. She remembered her fingers slipping away from the curving peak of muscle as he whipped her and Joseph round and round until they were all dizzy. A familiar motion, she thought, embedded in the memory. "Don't let him do anything stupid tonight."

"I'll try."

"And don't drive if you can't. It's okay to admit that. We won't penalize you for it. You can always call."

"I know."

Talin cautiously grabbed her plate of pizza and left him staring out the sliding glass door on the side of the house, hands clasped behind his back in contemplation. Her father spent a lot of time there lately, peering over at her uncle's house. Talin wondered where her mother was hiding. Maybe she was next door with Aunt Hova. Talin folded the pizza and knocked on Joseph's door with her elbow.

"Tal?"

"Yeah!"

"Come in."

She closed the door as soon as she entered the room. Clothes were scattered across the floor, leaving hardly anywhere to stand. Old movie posters, thumbtacked in each corner, covered the walls. Joseph's friend Cal worked at a chain movie theater, so he had his choice of the old posters they discarded. The wall of sound created by Joseph's music—the same recycled playlist he'd shuffled on repeat all summer—was impenetrable. Myopic taste, Talin thought. Too much Eminem, Machine Gun Kelly. All subpar rap and angry electropop. Atop his dresser, an uncapped plastic fifth of cherry Burnett's stood surrounded by a mess of baseball caps, crumpled receipts, BIC pens, and cheap sunglasses. Joseph fussed with a constellation of pimples on his chin. Baggy cargo shorts past his knees, an oversized rugby shirt that tented out at his midsection. The heat had barely dissipated in the night. Why couldn't he dress more sensibly? He looked at her with reddened, distant eyes.

He asked, "Can you drive?"

"Well you can't," she retorted. Maybe her father was right— maybe Joseph did need her. He grabbed the nearly empty bottle by the neck and raised it until its bottom faced the sky. He brought it back down and shivered like a bothered cat, then twisted the cap as tight as it would go and slid the bottle like a curling stone beneath the bed.

They wandered to the laundry room to find their shoes. Edgar had migrated from the window to his chair on the back deck. He was smoking a cigar, a rare habit Talin had never seen him do alone. Cigars were a shared pastime between her father and her uncle. They sat down together, in celebration or mourning, or sometimes simply for a good Big Ten football game, and enjoyed this vice together. She was told her great-grandfather had loved cigars, among other indulgences. He had already cheated death, her father once told her. What was a bit of tar in his lungs every now and again?

Fireflies grazed the front lawn. Talin could see the lights on in her aunt and uncle's living room, the blue subterranean glow from the basement windows at the base of the house. Clouds resembling old, thin bed sheets drifted across the night sky. She unlocked the car and fell into the driver seat. A king-size Twix wrapper crinkled under her foot. Half a dozen empty Vernors cans and empty bottles of Faygo Rock & Rye clanked beneath Joseph's seat. The center cupholders were stuffed with wadded receipts, paper bracelets from the public pool, and the program from Mari's memorial service. Talin's backpack was still in the backseat from her trip last week to the public library. Her father was right about the car, too—it was disgusting. A cricket thumped against the windshield and hopped away.

During the ride, Joseph flopped his head out the window in line with the side mirror and let his long hair fly back in a dark mane. Talin preferred AC, but Joseph wanted fresh air and for his music to be heard, so the windows remained down. It wasn't worth the argument.

Joseph's phone was connected to an old cassette converter, and every time he turned the music up another notch, the sound crackled and the quality deteriorated. He sat with one leg outstretched on the dash and turned on System of a Down, an unexpectedly pleasant change of pace. Talin was worried about bringing him along to Gwen's party. He had been out of control: drinking and fighting, that damn paintball crater on his stomach like a badge of honor. She wasn't sure what to do about it.

Talin adjusted the rearview mirror as they drove along the coast. "Dad says we need to clean the car."

"Does it really matter?"

"He'll take away our gas money."

"That's bullshit," Joseph snapped. He bobbed his head along and tapped his knuckles on the dashboard. The song ended and went right back to Eminem. He flipped his hair back. "Let's just take it to the car wash."

"Dad will say that's not the point." Talin shifted in her seat. "Why do you listen to so much Eminem?"

"Mari and Ani used to play him all the time."

"And then they stopped." Talin accidentally hit the brake hard as they rolled up to a stop sign. It was like she had planned it, punctuating her point. "They realized he was a homophobic asshole and moved on. All you have to do is listen to the lyrics and then it becomes terrible."

The intersection was empty. No one seemed to be out on the road. Joseph sighed. "So what are you saying?"

"I'm saying we don't always need to listen to some angry violent white boy just because he's from the same state as us."

"C'mon, Tal." Joseph threw his hands up. "It's not like I believe those things just because I hear them in music."

"But you know it bothers me."

Joseph crossed his arms in front of him. End of conversation. They continued in silence, Joseph still bobbing to the beat. Talin's whole family still owned Fords, except for Mari. Her great-grandfather had worked the line at Ford for more than thirty-five years. "Lots of close calls, but never an accident," Uncle Karo always bragged. "He was too careful."

Talin crawled down Bayview looking for a spot on the street that wouldn't block anyone's driveway. Gwen had told Talin to park a couple blocks away so there wouldn't be a line of cars outside of her parents' house to draw suspicion from the neighbors.

Talin turned down the music. Joseph was tipsy and kept singing anyway. A few houses were illuminated, but half of these homes were seasonal.

Talin parked on the gravel shoulder in front of a dark house, no lights or cars, as good a find as any. She slouched, tired, and momentarily regretted leaving the house at all. Opportunity cost, she thought, remembering the economics unit from math class last spring. She imagined the freezer full of Bagel Bites, Netflix on her laptop, and the scent of blood-orange essential oil circulating throughout her bedroom. The fear of missing out never made much sense to her.

"What's the plan for tonight?" Talin asked, knowing that their conversation about Eminem likely already put Joseph in a surly mood. He scrolled and changed the song again even though they were parked. For all Talin cared, they could sit in the car all night if it made her brother feel better.

"You fucking sound like Mom and Dad all the time now," he eventually said. He thumbed more at his phone. Talin dug her own phone out from the nest of center console detritus to see if Gwen had texted. Nothing. Talin's legs stuck to the leather seat.

"If someone mentions Mari, just walk away."

"I'll be fine," Joseph grumbled. He shouldered the door open and dug a blue BIC lighter from his pocket to ignite a spliff. He had smoked every day since the memorial service. Another new habit. He was walking down the road before she had even un-buckled her seatbelt. A gentle bump of her hip to shut the door. Talin took a moment to fix her hair in the shadowy reflection of the window. She jogged down the quiet road to catch up with her brother.

"Do you want some?" Joseph asked, offering the spliff once she fell in line with his pace.

"I'm okay." Talin didn't like to smoke before she drank. She found that when she mixed weed and booze, the spins were un-bearable and endless. She could never come down. It was like being lost in a dark shaking room, worse than seasickness. Talin hoped Gwen hadn't found anyone to buy a keg. Joseph was a menace with a red Solo cup. He would drink until the keg was cashed. At home, she would have to gather him from the car and surreptitiously lug him back into the house without waking their parents. He wouldn't be as fast to crash if he was forced to buy loose cans and bottles off of friends.

No streetlights, the whole neighborhood serene. The trees stood ominous and foreboding, their expansive branches sprawled above a handful of houses. In seventh grade, Talin's first kiss was on the lawn in Hickory Island Park after she and Gwen snuck out to meet two boys in the middle of the night. Matthew, the one she was paired with, had moved to Windsor a year later. Talin kissed him timidly, only after she had first kissed Gwen on a dare. The boys had been in awe, but Talin al-ways thought it was better that way, more intimate and honest, to share such a significant and memorable moment with her best friend, someone she held true affection for, a kiss that held palpable electricity, even if her and Gwen grew more distant with each passing year of high school. No kiss since then had been as special.

"I have more if you want some later," Joseph offered. He inhaled a long drag and flicked the roach off onto the shoulder of the road.

"We need to take a left to get to Gwen's," Talin pointed out.

"Oh, right." Joseph nodded, pretending not to remember the directions. Over the years, Joseph had been in the car enough times when their parents dropped Talin off at the Morrises' house for him to memorize the route.

Talin sped ahead of her brother. Gwen's dark house sat at the very end, the back looking out over the water into the mouth of Lake Erie. The gate stood ajar and gas lanterns illuminated the posts on either side.

As they walked up the circle drive, Talin could hear music and people laughing. The house was grandiose. Talin never ceased to be impressed by its size. A wall of red brick towered two stories along the side that faced the street, its dramatically steep peaks reaching even higher in the sky. A massive oak door stood in a covered entryway with two wicker rocking chairs safely protected from the months of rain and snow. The deck on the back of the house led straight to the water, their boat docked and ready at a moment's notice until winter came. Gwen's bedroom had a private balcony where they used to camp out as kids in forts of blankets to keep the wind away. Now, when Talin stayed the night, they gave her one of the three guest bedrooms and her own bathroom for privacy.

"Do we ring the doorbell?" Joseph asked.

"Gwen texted to go through the garage," Talin answered.

They veered to the four-car garage on the side of the house. Light pooled beneath the door. Ping-Pong balls clopped against plastic cups. As they walked in, Talin thought again about her warm bed at home. A few rising seniors hovered beside Mr. Morris's 1966 red Tempest GTO, a car Talin had only been allowed in for one lap around the island on a cloudless summer day after she and Gwen finished their freshman year of high school. She was surprised the blue cover was off, scrunched on the concrete floor like an abandoned oversize fitted sheet. One of these assholes probably slipped it off to get a peek, she thought.

Her favorite car was beneath its black mesh in the back corner—a jet-black 1920 Cadillac Model 59 Victoria with whitewall tires. The era of car her great-grandfather would have worked on, but not for GM. Talin loved that car. She dreamed of riding it off Grosse Ile and through Detroit and far out into rural Michigan farmland, down the crumbling nameless state roads surrounded by cornfields or cherry orchards on both sides, nothing tarnishing the landscape except the occasional rundown gas station at an odd intersection. She would hide out and eat fast food next to dilapidated barns and muddy ponds. Ani had left and Talin wished she had asked to go on the road trip with her sister. They could have camped, kept one another safe, and explored the vastness of the country together.

Gwen's new white Malibu was nearest them, mud spattered and in need of a wash. Back in April, the first time Gwen pulled her birthday present into Talin's driveway, Edgar had given it one glance and griped, *Why would anyone get a white car in Michigan?*

Two of Joseph's friends from the track team, Cal and Eric, leaned on the hood. They were playing beer pong against two rising sophomore girls across the table. Talin couldn't think of the girls' names—only that boys in their grade would be labeled too young to be there and kicked out, but that same standard didn't apply.

"Hey, Tal," Connor said. He was one of the older guys admiring the GTO, a wiry stick figure who rock climbed and ran the two-mile on the track team. All seasons he dressed like he was interviewing for a job in middle management. Pastel gingham shirts and khaki pants, dark brown boat shoes from DSW, his matching dark brown hair combed and parted to the left. The group Connor hung with had all been hitting on Talin and Gwen since they were freshman, when they were first invited to parties. Talin ignored him.

Joseph grumbled to Talin, "That cheesy fucker looks like the balding, middle-aged manager of a Buffalo Wild Wings." Talin held a frown. Joseph had made similar jokes about Connor before, but they used to be less mean spirited.

"Joe." Cal shrugged himself from the bumper of Gwen's car and gave Joseph a quick fist bump. His clothes were too big for his short frame, and his red hair reminded Talin of overripe apricots. The sleeves of his blue V-neck T-shirt widened around his arms like the erumpent mouths of trumpets muted by his pasty white appendages. Talin liked Cal though. He was a good friend to her brother, a calming force, the voice of reason. Cal smiled at them both. "Get a beer and come play."

Joseph nodded. He briefly grabbed Cal by the shoulders and walked on. It was a gesture of affection parroted from their father, a kind of distant hug. Talin let him walk in front of her through the back door into the laundry room.

A silver keg, slick with condensation, a sleeve of red cups

upside down stacked on its brim, was nestled in a blue plastic tub full of ice. Gwen never asked anyone to pay. Talin knew right away it was going to be a long night.

A dozen people stood around the massive marble island at the kitchen's center. The island was bigger than the dining table in Talin's house. Their classmates were lined up to play flip cup and Gwen was on the end. She squealed and ran over to Talin.

So much had happened. Talin had not seen her best friend in a month. The Morrises attended family camp up north together every summer and had been out of town for the weeks around Mari's memorial service. Gwen had texted nonstop, but they had not had an opportunity to talk in person yet.

"I missed you," Gwen cooed with a hug. Her eyes shined, tipsy. They were glacier blue and matched the sharp Nordic features of her face. Talin was nearly a head shorter than Gwen, but she was used to being the shortest person in the room. Gwen sniffed her hair. "I'll tell everyone to get the fuck out if you want."

Talin shook her head no against Gwen's shoulder. It felt nice to be held and consoled. Gwen smelled like vanilla vodka and her father's cigars. Talin wondered if she'd taken out the pontoon by herself and used her fake ID to purchase Cubans at the nebulous aquatic line of the Canadian border, even if there was no need to buy her own, of course. Mr. Morris had a full humidor in his study and he never noticed if one or two went missing.

The Morrises' custom speedboat with the wakeboard tower stayed at their cabin up north on Torch Lake, the cabin near as big as their house on the island. In comparison, the pontoon was bare bones. A twenty-seven-foot Avalon Ambassador with a top-of-the-line Bose speaker system. Mr. Morris never spared any expense on sound quality. Out on the water, he always blasted the Talking Heads and Led Zeppelin and Bob Seger, but tonight the Bose speakers surreptitiously installed throughout the kitchen and living room blared Frank Ocean. *Channel Orange.* "Super Rich Kids." Predictable, Talin thought.

"Do you want an espresso?" Gwen asked. "You look tired."

"I'm good. Did you go out and sunbathe today?"

"I needed peace and quiet." Gwen lifted her forearm up against Talin's to compare the color. "Look, I'm almost as tan as you are now!"

Talin's dark arm hairs spindled together between her wrists and elbows in contrast to the translucent blond ones hiding across Gwen's reddened skin. Gwen was tan, nearly burnt, but Talin could tell it was fleeting. The color would be gone in a week or two if she didn't keep baking in the sun. In the winter, Gwen would be pale again and Talin would remain the same.

"Darn." Gwen sighed at the realization she was still ashen in comparison. "A couple more days out and I'll catch up."

"Don't get skin cancer on my account," Talin deadpanned. Across the room, Joseph had found a handle of Jack Daniels on the counter and downed two shots in quick succession. He kept peeking in their direction. Joseph had crushed on her best friend for years, and Talin tried her best to ignore how much it bugged her.

Gwen slapped Talin on the shoulder. "Don't joke about that. You know I wear sunscreen."

"Sorry."

"Sorry for not being here." Gwen hugged Talin again.

Joseph snuck past them back toward the keg. He would be

shit-faced next time she went out into the garage. He drank fast and with abandon. Across the marble island, her other friends, really Gwen's friends, Bonnie and Madison, were taking selfies. They looked like siblings, both tall and thin and angular, thick brown hair down to their waists, long tan legs from summer conditioning for the soccer team. Someone dragged out a wolf whistle. The whole kitchen was sticky, the smooth surfaces filmy and sweet and soaked in booze. She was glad Gwen had contained them to the kitchen and garage. A group of boys Talin recognized passed a joint around on the back deck. The hockey team never missed a party.

Talin accepted a shot of whipped cream vodka and joined the game of flip cup. She played a few rounds until her stomach bulged and her throat felt raspy. Beer always filled her up, a fact she learned her first night drinking green cans of Rolling Rock at Mari's apartment in Milwaukee when they drove with Ani to visit. That night, Talin had felt safe drinking as much as she wanted on the couch in her cousin's condo, surrounded by the people she loved, with no fear over her well-being, no one caring if she fell asleep or threw up or demanded a pyramid of microwave taquitos—but now, she never drank to excess. The next day, when they were hungover, they had spent an afternoon at the downtown art museum by the lake and caught an early movie.

It was impossible to rebuild those ideal circumstances. At the last party they'd attended, trying to impress Gwen, her brother took a paintball to the stomach at near point-blank range to show off his six pack.

While Gwen posed for more photos with the other girls, Talin snuck out onto the back deck, now vacant. The group of guys who were congregated there had migrated around the house back to the garage. Outside, it was cooler than Talin thought as gusts dragged toward the house off the water. The pontoon boat clunked once against the dock during a burst of chop. To the right, the lights of boats drifted in the distance, hanging in an even plane above the surface, a mirror reflecting the stars above. Across the river, some Canadians were having a bonfire, faint as the end of a matchstick. A wisp of smoke drifted above the pontoon boat and the dark silhouette of a boy standing behind the steering wheel, as if cruising full speed ahead.

A glass shattered inside. Talin hated when people took advantage of Gwen's generosity. Everyone was always fucking up her house. Still, Talin ignored the noise and descended from the deck to the beach. In the sand, Mr. Morris had dug a bonfire pit lined with chunky gray bricks. Two burnt orange kayaks were tied together around a birch tree so they would not drift off in high tide. Talin slid off her tennis shoes and removed her socks. Her feet felt cold and sensitive against the wet white plastic grooves of the dock.

"What are you doing?" she asked when she reached the boat. Zack had tugged a hooded black sweatshirt over his head to block the wind. She did not really know him well, but knew of him. He was tall and broad, muscled from the weight room and drills on the ice. Even though he hadn't moved to the island until high school, it didn't take long for his hockey skills to get noticed. An MLive article she had recently read called Zack "an anachronistic player in the spirit of Darren McCarty." Talin had to google that word, and realized this was a polite way of saying he liked to fight. Even so, Zack had already been offered full scholarships to play in Ann Arbor and East Lansing. Earlier in the spring, when the team made a run at the state title, and they had attended the games, Edgar and Karo speculated over Zack's draft stock and argued about where he should play in college. It was always a rivalry with them, her father with a chip on his shoulder. Her mother once suggested that Talin's grandparents had made no effort to hide the fact that Karo was their favorite son.

Zack turned around. "Tal," he greeted her with a smile. She immediately thought his casual hello was presumptuous. Most people used her full name. He was wearing old-man glasses, rounded tortoiseshells that dipped low enough to rest on his sharp cheekbones. His ruddy facial hair was thick and short, the playoff beard long gone. He wore tight dark jeans and flimsy black flip-flops. A joint hung between his front teeth. He was likely the one who had secured the keg. Zack could walk into any liquor store off the island, those places across the river where he would not be recognized, and any cashier would not bother to ID him because he could pass for thirty.

"What are you doing out here?" she asked.

"Same as you I guess."

Talin stepped onto the boat and found a seat across from him. She crossed her legs and arms to stay warm. A whiff of rotten fish came and went, a nearby bass or carp or bluegill decomposing. Zack kept one hand on the wheel like he was holding their course. They could unknot themselves from the dock and drift away. Talin wondered if he was waiting for her or any other girl, hoping some company would roam outside tipsy and bored and decide to see why he was brooding alone. He held the joint in Talin's direction without taking his eyes from the water ahead of him. She was buzzed from the beer, but more dizzy than drunk. She shook her head to decline the joint, unwilling to compromise her self-control.

"Weed not your thing?"

"Not when I'm driving."

"I'd try to compliment you for being responsible *and* pretty, but my guess is you'd roll your eyes."

Talin felt her cheeks warm in the dark. "What are you doing out here?" she repeated.

"I told you already."

"But you don't know the reason I'm out here."

"I do." Zack flicked the end of the joint off into the water. Talin's stomach felt hollow enough to collapse in on itself. Whenever she decided to return to the kitchen, she would dig through Gwen's freezer for ice cream. The Morrises were reliable with a half-gallon of Mackinac Island Fudge or Michigan Mud.

Talin thought of Mari swimming with abandon out into the lake. The brief note in a tattered hardcover of Kate Chopin's *The Awakening* that only her aunt and uncle had read. Before the memorial, she had quietly lingered in the hallway one of those indistinguishable days or nights listening to the adults talk and overheard the details. Earlier that week, Talin had dropped Joseph at home after they left the gym and circled back to the public library so she could check out a copy of the novel. The librarian produced a tattered black paperback with a woman disrobing on the front cover. The book was now hidden in the bottom of her backpack, sandwiched between two magazines, so no one in her family would see it, but every time she found a moment to herself, she could not even find the courage to take it out of the car. The thought of reading it caused her to shiver, she wasn't sure what she would learn from the novel about her cousin, and so it remained unread.

"Is it hard to look at the water?" Zack asked, as if reading her thoughts.

"Seriously?" she shot back, defensive.

"Sorry." He raised him arms in apology. "Sometimes I think it's better to ask the question than dance around it. It's the same with hockey." He put on a weird Russian accent. "Too much dangle dangle. At some point you just have to take a fucking shot on net."

Talin actually rolled her eyes this time. Zack was letting the weed talk for him. She hated stoner philosophy. She sighed. "I try not to think about the water. If I did, it would be difficult to stay on the island."

"You're surrounded."

"I never notice until I notice."

"I get what you mean."

He sat down on the bench seat opposite her and leaned his elbows on his thighs. Spread out, he took up more space than anyone else Talin had ever met. He removed his hood and his messy blond hair flipped out. Zack's hair was long like her brother's, but not as thick or dark. In a few more years he would probably be making millions in the NHL. If he was lucky—or unlucky, depending on how you looked at it—he might even play for the Red Wings someday. She imagined it didn't matter to him that they hadn't been real contenders for the cup in years. For most of the hockey boys, wearing red and white was still the dream. Even though Talin was born after Detroit's golden era in the nineties, she grew up immersed in its lore. Every Michigan kid had heard the stories. Uncle Karo had signed pucks displayed all over his office, and her father kept a framed poster of Steve Yzerman hung in the garage. Water sloshed against the dock.

"I realize people say this shit all the time," Zack started, breaking the silence, "but I understand what you're going through." A noisy gust of wind barraged them and Talin shook. Zack pulled his sweatshirt over his head and Talin could glimpse his abs where his T-shirt rose. Zack tossed the hoodie to her and it felt warm in her arms when she caught it. He continued while she dove into his sweatshirt. "I never talk about it, but we only moved to the island because my mom died. My dad couldn't bear being in Holland after that. Too many memories of her in that place I guess."

The hoodie was long enough to drape over Talin's knees. She tucked her arms into the middle like she was under a blanket, and the sleeves hung vacant and deflated at her sides. It was so big it reminded her of elementary-school gym period when the whole class would lift a multicolored parachute over their heads in unison and run underneath it. The parachute would remain full of stale air and they'd sit on the edge so that it made a big canvas igloo for all of them. She always felt safe and warm in there, even if after a minute the air turned hot and stuffy and took on an odor of dirty socks. Talin ran into Zack a lot in passing, but she had never realized his mother was dead.

"How'd she die?"

"Pancreatic cancer."

"That's awful. I'm sorry."

"It's okay." He kicked at her feet. "The shock wears off eventually, even if you never really recover."

Talin was curious how often he brought out this sob story with girls at parties. She ignored the urge to go comfort him. Zack swatted mosquitos nipping at his bare arms. Talin could hear the insects zooming around even if they were invisible in the dark. These pests never bothered attacking Talin. A matter of the blood. She was genetically undesirable to them. That's what Ani and Mari always said when they spent time in the outdoors. Once, the three of them had gone camping near Ludington without the rest of the family, and Mari taught her how to preportion food and pitch the tent and start a fire. The trip was much more organized than when they went with their parents. Talin's thoughts flicked again to her sister on the road, her cousin's ashes beside her, and hoped Ani was safe wherever she'd stopped for the night.

Standing, Talin realized how cold and numb her feet were. She found her legs and stepped across the boat to sit at Zack's side. He wrapped an arm around her, and she tucked her knees into his sweatshirt, leaning against him in a lump under the black fabric.

"This doesn't mean shit. I'm just cold."

"Clearly frigid."

They both laughed.

After a pause, he murmured, "My dad sent me to a therapist after my mom died."

"Did it work?"

"No," he answered. "Every time we talked it felt like I was being evaluated in terms of progress, like a kind of physical conditioning for grief. We were just running through the motions. It was so fake. I never felt comfortable there."

"My family just doesn't talk," Talin told him. "We all orbit around one another, waiting for something to get better."

Waterline

"What about your brother? You guys seem pretty close."

Her brow furrowed. "How would you know?"

Zack shrugged. "You're twins. And it's a small island."

People always assumed she and Joseph were close, that they must have some sort of freak connection, but Talin felt more distant from him every day. When they were little it was all cute matching outfits and protecting one another at school. They learned to ride bikes together, confessed first crushes, teamed up on difficult homework, but now he was so angry and stubborn all the time. He pushed her away. She coughed. "He's probably blacked out by now."

"Oh." Zack looked down and swatted more bugs. He squeezed her shoulder apologetically.

"It's nothing. He's an idiot. Let's just sit for a minute."

Talin wanted to kiss Zack, but didn't want to waste her time. Enough girls around school already treated him like royalty. *Puck fucks*, Joseph told her once, was what the other guys called the hockey groupies. Talin had socked him in the arm after that and was happy the next day when a bruise blossomed where his bicep met his shoulder. There were too many women in Joseph's life for him to grow up to be another misogynist asshole. She wanted to believe he was smarter than that, but maybe she was wrong. Maybe she was wrong about most of her family.

"Tal!" Gwen's voice shouted from the back deck. Talin turned to the door and her eyes adjusted to the light coming from inside. Gwen was smoking a cigar. The cherry illuminated and pulsed like a firefly as she puffed on it. All of this damn *Great Gatsby* shit, Talin thought. It was the only book they had read last year that Gwen enjoyed. Gwen resembled a kingpin surveying her empire. *I'll tell everyone to get the fuck out if you want.* Gwen had meant it when she said it, not because she wanted to spend time together alone, but because there was a thrill in exercising her power. For Gwen it would be that easy. A snap of the fingers and they would all leave.

Zack leaned away from her and they both stood. He held her hand as she stepped off the boat and she could feel the calluses across his palms from his gloves. He languorously followed her up the dock.

"I'm here if you want to talk more," he offered.

"I'll get your number from Gwen."

At the beach, Talin found her socks and shoes and pulled them over her numb feet while Zack helped her balance. They ascended to the back deck. Zack nodded at Gwen, she dismissed him with a wave, and he meandered back into the kitchen. Talin wasn't sure how late it was, but there were fewer people inside. The music trickled out, Kendrick Lamar now, pools full of liquor. Gwen pinched the cigar by its middle and handed it to Talin. Talin received the gift and sniffed along the top, careful not to slide the burning end too close to her nose. She hated the taste, but loved the aroma. It reminded her of boat rides, Sundays when the men around the neighborhood sat outside after mowing their lawns, the barbecues her father and uncle used to have in the backyard on Labor Day weekend.

"Your brother is fucked up."

"Don't I know it."

"Seriously though." Gwen sighed. Talin returned her smoke. "I can't find him, but earlier he looked about ready to puke and pass out."

"Shit. I'll go look for him."

"Can you stop by and help me clean up tomorrow?" Gwen asked. "We can go out on the boat after."

"Sure." Talin couldn't imagine what the state of the house would be in the morning, but she wanted to go out on the boat, even if she also wanted to escape the water. "He's not in the garage?"

"No. I didn't see him on this floor at all, and I put the dog gate in front of the upstairs with tape on it," Gwen said. "It doesn't look moved, so I don't think he wandered up there." The dog gate was for Ralphie, the Morris family's geriatric golden retriever, but Gwen used it at parties like a red velvet rope outside a VIP section. No one was allowed upstairs without permission. Talin was mortified. She pictured Joseph blacked out in Gwen's bedroom, fumbling through her belongings. She couldn't imagine what else Joseph had done while she was out on the boat with Zack.

As if on cue, Ralphie poked his nose against the glass door behind them and barked. His hair was white and stringy with age, his back legs splayed wide as he struggled to remain standing on the hardwood. Most nights, Gwen's parents left Ralphie holed up in their bedroom on his own Tempur-Pedic mattress with a menagerie of soft toys resembling critters he used to chase in the park: googly-eyed squirrels and striped raccoons and toothy possums, a fluff of white cotton innards surrounding him like he was king of the hunt.

Talin left Gwen on the porch, feeling like she had received her marching orders from a mob boss. She snuck by the stragglers eating and canoodling in the kitchen and made her way down the hall. The basement door sighed ajar, so Talin turned on the stairwell light and descended. The stairs were carpeted, the walls lined with framed photos of Mr. Morris with stunt drivers and auto industry bigwigs and a few professional athletes. In one, Mr. Morris stood with his arm around several former Detroit Pistons on a private golf course in Birmingham, a verdant expanse of fairway behind them, matching blue polo shirts and crisp charcoal chinos for a charity scramble. It was the summer after the Pistons won the NBA championship. Talin had heard the story more times than she could count.

Suddenly—the clap of liquid against the floor. She rushed down the stairs. The lights in the basement were on their dimmest setting, but she could make out the dark shape of Joseph, shorts and underwear scrunched below his knees, spraying piss into a growing puddle on the carpet near the back sofa in front of Mr. Morris's movie projector. According to the neon GTO wall clock, it wasn't as late as she had feared. Not even midnight yet, well before curfew.

"Joe!"

The clatter of urine stopped. He hauled his pants up and fumbled with his belt. He turned to her bewildered. "Where the fuck am I?"

Talin was furious, but if she acted upset, he would only get worse. She walked over to him and adjusted his shirt, which was tucked halfway into his shorts. He'd somehow managed not to splash a drop on any of his clothes. His vacant face held a sickly glow in the green neon of the clock. The fuzz on his upper lip took on the color so that the hair resembled little sprouts of grass on a Chia Pet. Ani used to have one in her room shaped like Garfield, the year before she moved next door.

"You're in the basement at Gwen's house."

"I'm in the bathroom."

"Why don't you lie down on the sofa? I'll get you a blanket."

Talin guided her brother to the cushions, where he fell onto his side and curled into a ball. Talin picked up a navy throw pillow with gigantic wooden buttons sewn to its center and pushed it hard into her face. She didn't yell. The fabric was cool on her eyes and smelled like flowery air freshener. She hit Joseph on the shoulder with it and he didn't move. He was already out. There was nothing to do but clean up his mess. More than once Talin had helped Gwen with her chores so they could go out on the boat, so she knew where to find cleaning supplies. In the basement closet, she dug out a roll of paper towels and pet spray for when Ralphie had accidents. Thank goodness there was a pair of yellow rubber gloves. Then she was on her bare knees, chilled again in the damp basement, Zack's oversized sweatshirt sleeves rolled up past her elbows, wiping away any evidence of her brother's idiocy. Every minute or two, Joseph grunted and wheezed. She felt utterly alone.

It would take time to wake Joseph and guide him back to the car. She thought of leaving him behind, but he would get in trouble. Their parents were flexible, but not indifferent. Talin wished she was still sitting next to Zack and looking out over the mouth of the river. Her family had always had a thing about the water. How many times had they told her Gregor's legend, about the elder she had never met who loomed large in her imagination, swimming out to meet the French navy? Lake Erie was hardly the Mediterranean, puny even compared to Lake Michigan, but the water was deep, unfathomable, polluted.

Talin couldn't imagine what the lake held beneath its surface. She didn't want to think about being submerged.

Talin woke early the next morning heavy with sweat. Her throat was dry and tasted like mushrooms. Sheets and blankets were scrunched at her feet, and the low bluish sun sluiced through the blinds and left a ladder of sunny lines as thick as pencils across her mattress. Her phone, charging on the nightstand, showed two messages on the home screen.

The first, an unfamiliar number: *Decided to ask Gwen for your number first. Hope we can hang out soon. Maybe I can get my sweatshirt back. ;) –Z.*

The second was from Gwen. *Don't worry about coming over early. I cleaned up the rest of the house last night after everyone left. Boat this afternoon! No one found out about JoJo. YOU OWE ME though.*

Talin changed from her damp T-shirt and shorts into clothes for the gym. Her body felt heavy, stiff, dehydrated. She sent an abrupt text to Ani—*Wish you were here. Where are you?*—and tromped to the bathroom, washed her face, and brushed her teeth. Her mother was clanking around in the kitchen, the only other person in the house who could possibly be up at this hour. Most mornings, Talin's mom went to the gym before anyone else was awake and remained there until midday. Talin found her at the kitchen table drinking one of her green juices.

"You're up early." Hannah, dressed for the gym, leaned back in her chair. Talin couldn't believe her mom was turning fifty next spring. She was in better shape than most people her age. While Talin noticed her father soften over the years, her mom was more fit and toned than ever. "I heard you get home last night a while after curfew."

"Sorry for being loud."

"It didn't sound like you were the problem."

"Um . . ."

"You don't have to cover for him," Hannah told her. "We were young once. We know what goes on."

"He's just struggling with everything," Talin tried as an excuse, her face hot as she went to the kitchen and poured a glass of water from the tap. She stood at the counter and gulped half of it down. It hurt her dry throat. "It helps for him to let loose I think."

"Your brother can afford to. He doesn't have to worry the same way you do."

"What do you mean?"

"Women can't let loose in those situations," her mother explained.

Talin rolled her eyes. "Is this going to be a talk?"

"I'm just saying, don't trust drunk boys at parties."

Talin finished her water and refilled it. Mari and Ani had already lectured her about a million different scenarios when it came to drunk boys and high boys and old men and being alone with men in general. She asked her mom, "Are you doing the seven o'clock spin class?"

"Yes."

"Can I go with you?"

Hannah's eyebrows rose in surprise. "You bet, but you must be exhausted."

"I can nap later."

"Don't think you've managed to avoid this conversation," her mother cautioned.

"Ani warned me it would come."

"Well, your sister is more like your brother. I was too late to have the conversation with her. She caused a lot of trouble before she moved out."

"I remember."

"Which part?"

Talin thought for a moment. "Enough of it."

Hannah sighed. "It drives me crazy thinking about her out there on the road by herself. I have no idea what's gotten into her."

Talin thought about how nice it was when the three of them were curled up in a tent together telling jokes and listening for wildlife. "She's always wanted to go."

"With Mari, sure," her mother conceded. "I understood that idea."

Sweat beaded on Talin's brow. Her hair was oily and frizzed. She would tie it back in a ponytail and throw a baseball cap over it for the gym. "It's still them out there together."

"Oh, sweetie," Hannah croaked and stood to embrace her in a tight hug. Talin hated to see her mom get emotional. It broke her down too. There was no one in the family it was harder for Talin to see upset. Hannah finished her juice and avoided Talin's eye contact. The bottom of the pint glass was coated in translucent slime, a spatter of filmy kale and spinach refuse. "You should fill up a water bottle," Hannah advised, regaining her composure. "The classroom gets hot and there's no easy way to leave halfway through."

Talin placed her glass in the sink and went back down the hall for her faded Tigers hat and Nalgene. Her brother's door was closed. He would sleep off his hangover for a few more hours. She turned the knob slowly enough that the latch did not click and nudged the door open. The hinges creaked, but Joseph didn't stir. The room was stale and reeked of alcohol. She could see the back of his head and waited for his body to rise and fall with his breath under the covers several times. Still alive, she thought, and closed the door with the quiet grace of a storm cloud eclipsing the sun.

For the next several days, Talin woke every morning for spin class, but the following Monday she decided to go on a long bike ride around the island instead. Spin class was nice, she told her mom, and she adored the instructor, but it was dark and crowded and a couple of the regulars gave her the creeps, so now she wanted open road and fresh air. None of this was untrue, even if her real motive was to meet up with Zack.

They had been texting back and forth all week. He understood the nuances of when to send a paragraph-long response and when to send one or two terse words and when to not respond at all so they could both take a break from carrying on the conversation. She found herself waking up in the middle of the night to check her messages, wanting to see him again. Joseph had been too far gone that night to even remember Talin was wearing Zack's sweatshirt, which she hadn't yet returned. Zack lived in a condo with his dad on the west side of the island. Pedaling over would take no time at all.

Talin waited until late in the morning, after her mom was at the gym and her father was off to work. The sun was high and hot and she was sweating by the time she rolled her bike out of the garage and wiped it off with an old dishrag, pumped up the tires, and greased the gears. In the few weeks since she'd passed her driver's test, she hadn't ridden anywhere. The driveway felt warm enough to melt the white rubber soles of her black Nike cross trainers. She dressed in frayed jean shorts and a loose gray tank top over a black sports bra. It wasn't exactly something to wear on a date, but she didn't want to show up in gym clothes. If she took the car, Joseph would want to tag along. Talin filled her drawstring backpack with makeup, deodorant, a fresh tank top, Zack's sweatshirt, and a water bottle. Zack could wait for her to clean up when she got there.

Her helmet was bulky and cumbersome over her thick black hair, which she hadn't bothered to straighten. Joseph always made fun of her for wearing a helmet, but she never worried about looking cool if it was a risk to her safety. She walked her bike out of the garage and hopped on. Talin's father had cut the overgrown grass that weekend and chunks of clippings remained in little dried-out cakes on the edges of the driveway. The skunky smell of rotten walnuts reminded her of weed. Her father had cut her uncle's lawn, too, for continuity. Standing outside, everything appeared normal—another well-kept house in a row of well-kept houses in an idyllic, grassy neighborhood. There were no signs of her aunt and uncle's despair.

She circled the cul-de-sac and coasted back to the garage. Her front tire could use more air.

"You doing a lap?" Joseph asked as he stomped out of the house.

"Maybe a couple," Talin ad-libbed; she'd never been great at lying, and they had never ridden around the island more than once in a day. She unclicked her helmet strap. "I was hoping for a better workout."

Joseph was shirtless and wore glossy, baggy red basketball shorts with white stripes down the side and a pair of dirtied white high-top Chucks, his usual uniform for when he rotated between the heavy bag and speed bag in the basement. The gym didn't have boxing equipment. He removed a thin black jump rope from the top shelf of dirtied PVC units abutting the garage wall. Joseph had to jump rope outside because the basement ceiling was too low. He turned the music up on his phone, some moody rapper from Minnesota who dragged out his syllables, and set it on the shelf. Talin flipped her bike upside down. She dug through an old laundry basket to retrieve the bike pump, then uncapped the air valve.

"Early movie later?" Joseph asked. "This heat is too much."

"Let me think about it."

"You got your phone?" Joseph pranced by her and brought the rope in a swooping arc beneath his feet. In a split second he had sped up and the rope whistled with each rotation as he frantically danced from one foot to the other. Talin could see the veins rhythmically pulse in his forearms. It was a surprisingly elegant movement, much different from when she and Gwen had to shoulder him out of the basement after everyone else had either left or passed out in one of the guest rooms. It amazed her how quickly his body bounced back after drinking so much.

"Yeah." They used to share their locations with one another, but they realized as they got older that it was a mutual invasion of privacy. Tire inflated, she removed the hose from the valve with a satisfying hiss and righted the bike on its wheels. She tossed the pump back in the bin and flung a leg over her bike, finding her balance. The seat could be raised, but she'd deal with it later.

"Call me if you want to get picked up," Joseph offered. "We can fit your bike in the car if we put the backseat down."

"Thanks." She gave him a soft smile. As little as he'd seemed to care about inconveniencing her last week, he could be considerate when he wanted to be. It must have been difficult for him to grow up around so many girls, but she was convinced that aspect of his childhood had resulted in the few good habits among all his bad ones.

Talin kicked off down the driveway and leaned to turn into the street. The harsh whoosh of the jump rope intensified as she pedaled away. Joseph would be there for half an hour, three minutes on with thirty-second rests, same as a boxing match. They were all creatures of routine.

Talin navigated out of the neighborhood and headed toward the coast. Even with a breeze in the air, the humidity was unbearable. It was too late in the day for anyone to be fishing on the beach.

At first, Talin thought about cutting south until she arrived at Zack's condo, a straight shot, but she decided to loop north and take the scenic route so she could enjoy some alone time, when the roads and houses were still quiet. What Talin remembered most about camping with Mari and Ani were the mornings. Mari insisted sunrise was superior to sunset, so they woke early, shivering as they slithered out of their sleeping bags, to appreciate the coming day. Talin had wanted to stay tucked in, but she would rise at her cousin's urging, even though she was stiff and cold. "This," Mari had exclaimed, "is when the world feels most alive."

The condos Zack lived in looked out of place in their spot on the island. A row of units, two stories tall, with floor-to-ceiling windows facing the water. On either side Talin could see the gaudy mansions drawn farther back from the road. She wrapped her helmet strap around the handlebars, walked her bike down the sidewalk, and knocked on the glass sliding door. En route she had ridden slowly enough to avoid sweating clean through her shirt, but upon reaching her destination, her body wouldn't stop its flow of perspiration. She regretted taking such a round-about path.

Zack came into view, a green Michigan State tank top loose around his frame. Talin peeked at the bulk of his arms, the twin valleys where his biceps met his shoulders. The ridge of his collarbone above his chest. He opened the door and smiled. "You made it."

"Did you choose State?" Talin asked.

"Not yet, but my dad went there. I grew up a fan."

"Makes your decision easy then, doesn't it?" She lay her bike down on the porch, and Zack moved out of the way so she could come inside. The air conditioning was overwhelming and sent goose bumps down her arms and legs. The living room was covered in beige carpet, so Talin slid off her shoes. The condo reminded her of Ani's apartment in Chicago, except it was much larger. The cabinets and appliances didn't have much character, and the white walls were bare. A black leather sofa with recliners on either end rested across from an enormous flat screen television. It was the biggest TV Talin had ever seen in someone's home, other than the projector in Gwen's basement. The ceiling fan whirred above her and she could feel the sweat down her back cool.

"Do you have a bathroom where I can get ready?"

"Are we going somewhere?"

"No." Talin felt her face redden. "I just wouldn't usually show up sweaty and gross for a date."

He smiled. "Is this a date?"

"Maybe."

"I'm still in my pajamas. It's no big deal."

"It's not the same."

Zack nodded in sluggish comprehension. He gave her a quick tour of the first floor and showed her to the bathroom. The mirror was spattered with white flecks of dried toothpaste. A plug-in air freshener glowed in the outlet above the sink next to a dispenser of orange liquid soap. He found her a poorly folded shower towel, laundered to the point where it had lost its fluff.

"I'll find us a movie or something."

Talin stood on her tiptoes and kissed him as he stood at the threshold. He grinned and closed the door. She could tell he hadn't been expecting it. Despite his reputation, he seemed kind and soft spoken and patient, but maybe that was all part of an act. She wanted to be careful and didn't want to be careful at all. She never did anything this reckless, alone in a house with a guy she didn't know all that well. But she could take her time getting ready now. He would wait.

They spent the rest of the morning making out on the couch and watching a bootlegged download of the newest *Jurassic Park* movie. Talin wrapped herself in his sweatshirt again to mitigate the arctic blast of air conditioning. When the movie ended, Talin arose from the sticky embrace of the leather cushions and put on her helmet. The plastic visor made it difficult for Zack to kiss her goodbye and she laughed while he tried to navigate around it.

At home, Talin showered and found a box of microwave lasagna in the freezer for a late lunch. It was impossible to warm without burning the cheese and sauce in one corner. When they babysat, Mari and Ani used to always heat the lasagna in the oven, the four of them sitting at the table like adults with place settings and their grandma's cloth napkins, but Talin didn't have the patience to wait that long. She gnashed on the gooey mess right out of the black plastic tray, even though there was grease and water inundating the bottom. The sauce was still icy in the middle. Joseph wandered into the kitchen.

"Still up for a movie?" His bare feet clapped heavy on the kitchen floor. He opened the fridge and found his gallon of milk, uncapped the jug, and tilted it back. His Adam's apple bobbed up and down with each swallow. He looked skinnier than ever. "We still haven't seen *Jurassic World*."

"Oh, I just . . ." Talin caught her error. She took a bite of lasagna to buy time, but the edge was scorching and the pale cheese clung to the roof of her mouth. She coughed and spat the glob back into the tray.

"Attractive."

"Maybe we should skip the theater today," Talin proposed. "It's hot, but why waste the afternoon inside?"

"What do you want to do?"

Talin thought while she used the edge of her fork to hack up the large noodles.

They could drive into the city or to the beach, even to Ann Arbor to walk around campus and downtown like they used to as a family when Mari was in school, scarfing free samples of sour candies and chocolate-covered fruit in the cherry shop and fancy hot dogs in the Diag, playing air hockey in the basement arcade, throwing coins in the fountain of King Triton. Uncle Karo used to buy football tickets for everyone and they'd cram into the blue bench seats near the top of the Big House and eat nachos with cold gelatinous cheese and oversalted jumbo pretzels. Her dad and uncle would go together during rivalry weekend, whether in East Lansing or Ann Arbor, but they took those trips alone, too invested in the game to deal with distractions or snacks or niceties. They didn't want to bother anyone else with their sibling bickering. Even though it was a short drive, Ann Arbor felt far away now. A forbidden city full of family ghosts. What was she thinking? There was no way they could go there.

"What if we went to the zoo?"

"Which one?"

"Toledo," Talin pitched, ad-libbing again. The Detroit Zoo would have been easier. "We could see the polar bears."

"Let me check and see if we have enough gas." Joseph tromped toward the garage. They had visited the Detroit Zoo a few days before last Christmas, when Mari and Ani were both home for the holidays, to see the lights, alternating every year between the colorful displays in Michigan and Ohio. It was an annual tradition, but Talin wasn't sure they would go again now that Mari was gone. Outside of the holidays, she couldn't remember the last time they'd visited the animals, who always looked so lethargic and unhappy in their manufactured habits. But she thought they might be safer enclosed than off in the deteriorating wilderness, the places they called home melting and burning and being cut down. Maybe there was nowhere else for them to go. Maybe they were safest where the same species that preyed on them and destroyed their environments marveled at them and tried to keep them alive, even if they were the last of their kind. Everything was endangered these days.

The zoo turned out to be the best afternoon Talin had had since before finding out Mari died. She was still floating from her morning with Zack. Joseph was energetic and sober, in a joking and generous mood for once, so they walked around and bought tall slushies that turned their tongues blue and shriveled yellow popcorn that left them chugging water from the public drinking fountains. It was like old times, except now they were on their own, unworried about having to make conversation with their parents or arguing over the car radio. Before they left, Joseph even bought Talin an overpriced gray T-shirt with an image of a smiling hippo on it in the gift shop. Despite their father's protest, Edgar kept giving her brother money, no matter that he flaked out on his chores. Her father was avoiding an inevitable fight, sure, but he was also acting strange, giving them more leeway than normal. And he was home less often, always working or next door. They all agreed Joseph was out of control, but every dollar her dad threw their way kicked the can of conflict farther down the road.

The next day, Talin was wearing the new T-shirt when she arrived at Zack's condo.

"Hippos, huh?" Zack remarked.

"We went to the zoo yesterday." Talin smiled. She grabbed

the T-shirt at her sides and stretched out the image so it lay flat. "They're my favorite."

"I've always been more of a cheetah guy."

"That's predictable." Talin laughed. She unclipped her helmet and held it upside down at her hip. "Because they're fast and dangerous, right?"

"Well now I just sound like a cliché."

"All boys are a cliché."

He laughed and cupped his palm on the small of her back. They walked inside. When he closed the door all the noise of the island went silent, replaced by the whir of the air conditioner.

Talin biked to see Zack every day for the rest of the week, late enough in the mornings so that his father would have already left for his job at Comerica Park downtown. Zack's dad managed food and drink orders for the home games and other events throughout the year. As she learned the layout of the condo, Talin realized random corners were filled with Bud Light golf bags and Jameson poker chips and piles of Little Caesars stress balls, all sorts of vendor freebies and leftover swag. Zack told Talin his dad used to be the head chef for a brewery on the west side of the state, where he was kind of a big deal and even a finalist for a James Beard Award, but he never went into the specifics of his dad's job. Every morning Zack offered her water or juice or Gatorade, but she wanted to look inside their refrigerator, curious to see what fancy ingredients his dad might have stashed away.

They fell into a pattern. Each day began with them turning on a movie on the couch as a pretense before moving to Zack's bedroom. It was harmless fooling around on the sofa that first morning, but Talin, desperate for a distraction, allowed things to progress quickly. By the fourth morning they were both naked and Talin asked him to find a condom. Zack produced one from an open pack in the drawer of his nightstand, and Talin wondered if he had lived the whole summer this way, waiting for different girls to come over while he had the place to himself. He was eager to unwrap the slick latex and accidentally tried to unroll it on himself upside down before he fixed it. He chuckled and tried to shrug it off.

Even though she had talked with Mari and Ani about sex, she was unprepared for how clunky and ungraceful the experience was, the weight and mechanics difficult to manage, his body heavy and immovable above her. Zack did not possess the pacing or control she desired. He moved fast and came before she found her bearings. He fell to the other side of the bed and they rested side by side.

She was surprised when he reached for her hand. She thought the whole experience was okay, having listened to the awkward virginity stories from Mari and Ani and Gwen. They had all told her it would get better. After the first time, it wasn't good or bad for her, pleasant in moments and uncomfortable in others, simply something to do to escape her loneliness and frustration, even if only for a few minutes at a time. She wished Ani was around so she could ask her questions. Who knew if she had cell service where she was, and sex was something Talin wanted to discuss face to face anyway.

The next Friday, after briefly fooling around and running through the motions, their most satisfying attempt for Talin thus far, they lay in bed and ate microwave breakfast burritos. Talin was tired and hungry and couldn't decide whether she was excited to spend the weekend away from Zack—he was traveling for a hockey tournament out of town—or disappointed that she would have to figure out something else to do to clear her mind. Gwen, her parents now back in town, had invited her to go out on the pontoon the following afternoon, and if Talin went, she would tell her best friend everything. It was easy for her to conceal things via text, but in person, Talin was an open book, and Gwen would want the details of what was keeping her so busy during an otherwise listless second half of the summer. As always, the condo was freezing, and she curled under the comforter next to Zack. Her T-shirt was loose and malodorous from the bike ride. She had stopped fussing over how she looked during their time together.

"Was it weird growing up next door to family?" he asked. He picked at a callus on the palm of his hand.

She pulled the comforter farther over her shoulders. "I can't really imagine what it's like any other way."

"I guess there's a pretty big gap between you and your brother and your older sister and cousin."

Talin wanted to fall asleep. "Joseph and I kind of grew up in their shadows."

"What do you mean?"

Talin couldn't explain. Her cousin used to be the gold standard for her parents. Confident, intelligent, driven, they envisioned Mari as a model for Talin. Mari did well in school, had lots of hobbies and friends, and never got into trouble even when she was causing it. Ani, on the other hand, in their view, was unmotivated and rebellious. Sometimes Talin imagined them as two sides of the same coin. They were the best women in her life, even though they were so different.

By the time she and Joseph entered middle school, her sister and cousin were both gone, off living adult lives, only home for birthdays and holidays. When Ani was a senior in high school, she had lived with their aunt and uncle so Talin could finally have her own bedroom. At least, that was the excuse they fell back on, even though, in truth, her parents were on their last nerve after shooing one of Ani's boyfriends out of the house in the middle of the night.

"We had to live up to them. You get it?"

"Not really." Zack had no siblings.

"Is it weird being an only child?"

"I guess," Zack said. "My parents wanted more kids, but then my mom got sick."

"That sucks."

"We all got our shit," he mused. "I mean, look at your cousin."

"Excuse me?" Talin sat up and shook the creases from her T-shirt.

"The revenge porn and everything. What a cowardly fucker."

She could not understand everyone's fascination with the circumstances of Mari's death. There were so many conspiracy theories, so much misinformation and gossip. Who knew what lies Zack had heard? Talin was on the edge of the bed because Zack took up so much space. His hair hung in front of his eyes, and his forehead was pocked with acne. It had taken her two days to brush his bangs aside and find the greasy blotches beneath. Was she making the same mistake as her cousin? She wanted to trust Zack, but he could have easily taken pictures of her on his phone. What had he told his friends? Why had she been so careless?

"What do you know about it?" Talin asked.

"Tal, everyone knows about it. It was in the news."

Talin felt nauseated. She stood up and found her shorts and socks. She turned to him. "But what do *you* know about it?"

He scoffed, "Some guys on the team were watching it on the bus coming home from a tournament. They made me watch it too. There was nowhere I could go. I was trapped."

"Oh, I see, you let other people tell you what to do." Talin leaned over and punched him hard in the arm, knuckles cracking on impact, but her fist wouldn't leave a mark the way it had on her brother. Zack didn't pretend to be hurt. She left the bedroom. The mattress squeaked in relief behind her. She scampered down the stairs and found her helmet on the kitchen table.

"Wait." He stood shirtless in the living room. His shoulders were pale and littered with stray, spiraling hairs. "I tried to stop them, I swear. But they ignored me. They're just assholes. It's how guys are. They thought it was like the video of Kim Kardashian or something."

"Fuck you."

"Tal."

"Fuck off!"

Talin slid open the glass door and Zack didn't try to stop her. Her body ached and felt itchy in the heat. All she wanted to do was bike home as fast as possible. She pedaled away without looking back at him and accelerated until the warm wind cut across her cheeks and caused her eyes to water. She refused to stop moving. Every rotation of the tires brought her farther away from Zack.

No one in her family would watch the video. The police had explained what was on it and why they could not arrest the man who had released it and that there was nothing they could do to guarantee it was removed from the internet, where it was free and available for the entire world to see. Her cousin's body on permanent display for horny, violent men. It was beyond their control. No one could destroy it now. What they really meant was that no justice would be done.

Talin turned full speed into the cul-de-sac and coasted into the front yard. She tossed her bike down in the grass. Her car was the only one in the driveway. Joseph was wrapping up his jump rope in the garage. Talin tried to walk past him nonchalantly, but he blocked her way.

"What's wrong?"

"Nothing." She pushed by, but he scrambled in front of the door to the laundry room and grabbed the knob. He was so much taller than she was. She hurled a limp fist into his stomach. He didn't flinch.

"Who is he?" Joseph asked. "I'll fucking kill him."

"You have no idea what you're talking about."

"C'mon," he groaned, "no one goes on a three- or four-hour bike ride every day."

"Let me by!"

"Who is it?"

Talin began to cry. Joseph reached out to comfort her and she ducked under his arms and ran into the house. She left her shoes on and beelined to her room. Robotically, Talin slammed and locked her door. She fell to the rug. All she wanted to do was hide on the bedroom floor. The carpet fibers poked through her shirt and irritated her back. The funk of Zack's bedroom clung to her clothes. She had not realized how sore and tired her body was.

She held her phone above her and thought about texting Ani, but decided against it.

Joseph's footsteps thumped down the hallway until his bedroom door cracked into its frame with enough force to shake the house. A moment later, the low bass of his music vibrated through the walls. They were only a door apart from one another, but it might as well have been a voyage spanning the Atlantic, a distant and torturous expanse. They were miles and miles away.

Hannah Kurkjian (née Williams)

These men know nothing of grief, Hannah thought as she pedaled through her morning spin class. She missed Talin, but was also grateful to no longer worry about the middle-aged and senior men ogling her daughter. The room was blistering. The black walls of an oven. Every time the young woman on the neighboring bike rose from her seat, Hannah was misted with cool sweat.

The bikes were arranged in a tight, two-row semicircle around the instructor. The church of spin facing its high priestess, Denise, a seasonal coach home for the summer from the University of Wisconsin where she was studying dietetics. Denise always wore tight spandex shorts and a pastel crop top, fashionable athletic wear, her dark brown hair in a high ponytail that arched free from the back of her neck. She reminded Hannah of the instructors on the infomercials for subscription home cycling programs: intense, taut, glowing with sweat, unblemished, curvy, incapable of fatigue. Denise's music choices matched Hannah's vision, a whump of techno that flowed together into one endless song. Of the various instructors' preferences, these selections were Hannah's least favorite, thumping beats with laser beams and no lyrics except for DJs shouting catchphrases. She would almost prefer Joseph's obnoxious rap.

Under the black light, Hannah felt both more and less herself. The dim glow helped define the slim profile of her body, was kind to her stomach and legs, but it made her skin appear gray and scaly. She sometimes wondered why each morning she put herself through this hour in hell before the rest of her workout. The class was full, and the heat was unbearable. It was crowded, stinky, excruciatingly loud. Hannah could feel the rivulets dribbling down her back to the hem of her yoga pants.

Denise commanded them to stand and sit and stand again, increase resistance, increase more, decrease, dial it up until they could barely move, like trying to push their calves through bottomless sludge. In the penultimate stretch, they sped up until Hannah was certain her legs could not move any faster. The bike's stationary momentum lurched her a couple inches forward. When Hannah felt ready to collapse, Denise told them to rest. They had reached the cooldown. It was in these final minutes that Hannah remembered why she rose from bed early and didn't snooze her alarm. *I do this for me.* She smiled. *This time is mine.*

The Armenian family Hannah had married into was subconsciously taught from birth to hold their angst and depression somewhere deep inside of them, but she hadn't been raised that way. Her parents had never paid much attention to their lineage. *From London or Cambridge or one of those fancy old towns,* her father always said. Her mother claimed her great-grandparents were

Dutch but wasn't certain. They had flown in hours before the memorial service and gone back to Tallahassee—where they moved in their retirement—two days later. While polite and affectionate, Hannah's parents had never quite connected to Edgar's on a deep level, so after spending some time with their grandchildren, they didn't want to overstay their welcome.

Whether it was from nature or nurture, Hannah believed there were healthy ways to mitigate stress: diet, exercise, meditation. She bought into a lifestyle and aesthetic that Talin once referred to as *basic*, and she was okay with that. She pressed the button on her smart watch that ended her workout. Six hundred and ninety calories burned.

Her husband was cheating. How he could be so foolish, Hannah wasn't sure. She wiped down her bike, having completed the routine too many times to be embarrassed by the streaks of sweat she left behind. He must have suspected she would eventually figure it out. The moment she came home to that damn half-finished meal the night Edgar drove Karo to Milwaukee. Edgar was terrible in the kitchen. Cooking was his tell, the way he tried to apologize whenever something went awry in their marriage. When he totaled their minivan skidding out on a patch of black ice; the year the Spartans made it to the national championship game during March Madness and got train wrecked by UNC, and Edgar got so drunk that Hannah and Ani had to drive into the crowded mayhem of angry fans outside Ford Field to retrieve him and drive his car home; no matter the infraction he'd committed, there was always an elaborate meal waiting for her in the following days. Mostly, Hannah was embarrassed it had taken her this long to realize what was going on. His late nights at the firm made sense during tax season, but he had continued to keep unusual hours well after the April deadline.

The classroom was nearly empty by the time Hannah finished cleaning the seat, handlebars, resistance knob, and frame. Most of the regulars were awful about decontaminating the equipment. A quick spray and they fled. Soon, it was just her and Denise. Denise had changed the music to something soft and doleful, a female vocalist lamenting the loss of youth over a static blur of electric guitars.

"Why don't you ever play anything like this in class?" Hannah asked.

Denise laughed. She was responsible for wiping down all of the bikes her students ignored. "And depress you while we're working out? This is breakup music. I got into this album after I found out my ex cheated."

"Don't you still exercise when you're sad?"

"I exercise more when I'm sad."

"Me too," Hannah said. Awkwardly, she turned to follow Denise around the room from dirty bike to dirty bike. The gym had been her sole release in the weeks since her niece had died. Hannah didn't usually spend much time talking to the instructors or staff, but she suddenly felt chatty. There was no one to talk to at home. With the overhead lights on, the room appeared overcrowded with equipment. It was a sterile and stuffy space, like one of the closet-sized gyms buried next to the lobby in a cheap hotel, thick with a miasma of body odor. Her eyes passed over Denise's perfect legs, the toned calves arcing out like tanned crescent moons. Youth. She tilted her water bottle above her lips before remembering it was empty. The most eventful part of her day was over. On to the weight room, the treadmill, the sauna, maybe even the juice bar, listening to her podcast all the while, in isolation.

Denise tossed a wad of wet wipes into the trash can. Hannah's legs were wobbly and unbalanced from all the rotations on the bike. For a moment, the black rubber floor left Hannah feeling like she was standing at the center of an enormous chasm, a cartoon character who would free-fall the moment she glanced down. She coughed. "I'll see you Friday."

"It'll be my last class before I move back to campus for the fall."

"I'll make sure to be here then." Hannah smiled, as if she would be anywhere else. This routine was the closest thing she had to a church service.

On Friday, Denise's final class was uneventful, predictable, familiar. It was a breeze. Hannah wondered if any of the other regulars realized they would soon have someone new drilling them. She doubted it; they moved in and out of class like they were allergic to socializing.

Again, Hannah lingered while Denise cleaned up and offered to take her out for breakfast. She needed an excuse to talk with someone outside of her family. Denise had another class to teach, but asked if Hannah would mind waiting. Hannah lifted weights and kept an eye on the clock. They met in the locker room afterward.

At a chic eatery masquerading as a diner, they ordered the same dish: egg-white omelets with asparagus, zucchini, spinach, onions, and mushrooms, a medley of vegetables too bloated with water weight, so that the plates were soggy the moment they cut into the middle. They split a bowl of fresh fruit and a carafe of black iced coffee between them.

"Maybe the new instructor will play sad music for you," Denise quipped.

"It won't be the same." Hannah sighed. "I'll just associate it with you and your boyfriend breaking up."

"Girlfriend."

Hannah poked at a halved stalk of flaccid asparagus that had fallen free from its envelope of eggs. "I'm sorry. I shouldn't have assumed."

"That's okay. Most women your age do."

"Isn't that an assumption too?" Hannah tried to joke.

Denise poured herself more coffee. "More an observation."

"I have become a relic."

"There's always more time to learn," Denise offered. "I'm sure Talin can catch you up. I was bummed she wasn't in class this week."

Hannah's mind flashed unbidden to an image of Talin and Denise holding hands. They were only a few years apart in age, but she became immediately frustrated at herself for jumping to this conclusion. Her earlier assumption might have been an honest mistake, but now her own biases took over her train of thought. She hated that she'd grown up so traditional—conservative parents, a white flight suburb outside Detroit, taught to believe in civility—with everyone in her family trying to ingrain their prejudices into her head. Outside of her mom and dad, she didn't speak with the rest of her relatives much anymore. It wasn't worth the trouble or embarrassment.

"I was surprised Tal came with me at all in the first place," Hannah admitted, trying to segue. "I feel like we barely talk anymore. We're so distant. My other daughter was the same way before she moved out."

"I was like that too." Denise's plate was wiped clean. Hannah had no idea how she'd consumed her food so fast. "Sometimes it takes leaving for a while before you realize how good it is to be back home."

"Are you excited to go back to school?"

"Yeah," Denise replied, smiling. "It doesn't actually start for a couple more weeks, but I'm moving into a house with some friends, so we're all heading back early. It'll be nice to have our own place for senior year. Being home has been fun, but it feels like an interruption. I'm used to living on my own schedule."

Hannah remembered Ani's last two years in East Lansing, the dilapidated house with the bonfire pit and rusted charcoal grill in the backyard off Albert Street where her daughter lived with three other girls. The living room a perennial coalescence of hookah smoke, mildew, and cheap, fruity vodka. The dishes were never clean, pots and pans cornered with rust and soap scum. The tops of their kitchen cabinets were lined with empty bottles of alcohol that had been refilled with water and dissolved Jolly Ranchers, backlit by a string of white Christmas lights so that they glowed different colors: watermelon pink, sour apple green, blue raspberry. Ani's room had a window that opened out onto their roof.

Edgar had driven there one weekend to scoop out the gutters so the basement wouldn't flood. By then, Hannah had made peace with her daughter over the boys and the drugs and the flag tattoos Ani and Mari got together when Ani was still underage. Ani's senior year, after she moved into the spare bedroom next door, Hannah worried her firstborn would never return. Hannah had always moved between her house and her in-laws without thinking about it, but that final year before Ani left for college, every trip across the lawn was at risk of turning volatile.

"Are you okay?" Denise asked. "You're giving your plate a death stare."

"Sorry, I got lost in the past for a moment."

"Don't we all."

When Hannah returned home, she could feel something was amiss. Talin and Joseph were in their rooms, her son's music clearly well beyond the black line on the volume dial Edgar had drawn with a Sharpie. The floors pulsed with bass. Joseph's serpentine jump rope and malodorous boxing gloves were discarded on the laundry-room floor. Hannah didn't have any urge to bother either of them. Even piled into one home, her younger children were as distant as Ani.

Hannah slid the Styrofoam container of breakfast leftovers into the refrigerator by all the other food they could not get rid of. Mold sprouted in the corner of a Tupperware overstuffed with dolma. The grape leaves were near black.

Hannah showered, changed, and cleaned the kitchen. As she puttered around the house, the kids never emerged. In no mood to deal with a face-to-face argument, she texted Joseph and asked him to turn his music down. He did not respond, but the walls stopped shaking a few moments later. Under the protection of their patio umbrella, Hannah wandered out to the back deck and read a literary novel that was soon to be adapted to a television miniseries, wanting to finish the book before the first episode aired. In the middle of reading, she remembered Mari had been the one to recommend the book to her. That had been so much of how they related—a shared love of books, music, podcasts, the type of connection Hannah could never find with her own children. She and Mari always talked about the media they consumed, but never caught up about everything else going on in their lives. Now Hannah wished they had.

August, dry and scorching, the summer unyielding in its reign. Hannah didn't feel like her usual restrained and responsible self. She craved a pitcher of vodka and lemonade, icy margaritas with a rim of sea salt, mojitos overflowing with aromatic mint leaves, anything to cool her down and quash some of her anxiety. She wanted to get drunk. There was certain to be a bottle in Joseph's bedroom or under the basement stairs, leftover liquor from when everyone was last home for the holidays. Ed had always talked about building a bar down there; Karo even drew up some sketches right before Gregor died, but, like so many other projects, the time to complete it never revealed itself, and so the bar never came to fruition. The basement was still unfinished, despite the fact they'd been in that house for more than two decades.

Hannah bent the corner of her page and closed her novel. The garage moaned in the distance. Edgar was home early from the office, which surprised her—he could be off at the casino with that woman he worked with instead. Edgar was smart enough not to charge the hotel room on their joint account, but on two occasions he had paid for the valet with his credit card. A careless mistake. Too confident. He had never had a poker face.

Edgar must have taken a half day to get an early start on the weekend. Summer hours at the accounting firm were lenient. The sliding door cruised open and he walked in front of her. His bulky shadow fell behind him, hands in the pockets of his khakis so that he stood like an enormous sundial. He loomed over her with the sun on his face. The gray hairs in his beard and sideburns sparkled, little peaks of chop on a calm lake. He was in dire need of a haircut, but Hannah remembered why she was attracted to him. His broad shoulders snug in his white dress shirt, a river of blue tie down the valley of his thick chest. A smile that was always soft, like he was embarrassed to show his teeth, his long canines sharper than those of anyone else she'd ever met. The straight triangle of his nose between his high cheekbones. She could map his features so effortlessly. They had been together such a long time.

Edgar sighed. "I see the kids are in hiding. You would think they'd get bored and want to watch television or something."

"They have computers and phones." Hannah laughed.

"Should we order pizza?" Edgar asked. "That's usually a good lure."

"We shouldn't order anything until we're rid of all the leftovers," Hannah declared. The fridge had developed a funk. Every shelf stacked high and deep with plastic containers. She was tired of being a culinary annex for Karo and Hova. Every time Hova ran out of space, she lugged over two canvas bags of food. "Have you heard from Ani?"

Their eldest daughter had been solely texting Edgar, punishment for Hannah's lack of support for the road trip. Even the texts to her husband were terse and infrequent. An unspoken rule decreed that Ani would not be bothered while she was away. The last time Edgar had updated Hannah, Ani was in South Dakota. Two weeks gone, a thousand miles between them.

"Still in the Badlands," Edgar said with a grunt, "looking for the right spot. I sent her some money for a hotel and a shower, but she declined the payment. I should've invented Venmo. We could buy the island and the toll bridge." He laughed at his joke. "Anyway, half of the food in the fridge is on its way out."

"That's my point. There's no need to be wasteful." Hannah was certain her daughter would choose to leave some of Mari's ashes at the Pinnacle Overlook. Whenever Edgar informed her of Ani's new location, Hannah browsed the national park on her laptop and tried to imagine her daughter's whereabouts. She researched the trails and scenic locations. Ani was making slow progress.

Edgar sighed. "I feel like I've had the lamb sweats for weeks."

"Figure it out," Hannah told him, even though he was right. His body odor had been sour from lamb chops and basturma and lahmajoon, abundant garlic in every meal leaking from his pores. Flatulence in the night potent enough that she debated asking him to sleep on the couch. "Tell the kids to make a plate. If we dump everything that's turned, we can probably be rid of it all tonight."

"I don't want to fill up too much," he said. He squatted and placed his hands like two starfish clinging to the rocks of her bare knees. "I'm sure Joseph and Tal will go out tonight. I figured we could spend some time together."

"It's so hot."

"That air conditioner has been running around the clock," Edgar argued. "With how much we're paying the house is practically an igloo."

Hannah could have it out with him right there. He had shown no interest in her in the weeks prior to Mari's memorial. She wanted to tell him, *I see you. I know everything.* Not a confession, not an accusation, simply the matter on the table between them. For the time being, she was convinced she would not let this end her marriage. She didn't want to be alone. They were so close to it being just the two of them again, and they had already waited so many more years than expected for their alone time together.

Hannah was twenty-three when she gave birth to Ani; Edgar, two years older. They were kids. And like an unspoken pact, since Karo and Hova stopped trying after Mari, they too decided their lone daughter brought them more than enough joy and frustration, that Ani and Mari could be sisters to one another. Once Ani left, they were supposed to be empty nesters: vacations of oysters Rockefeller and bananas Foster on luxury cruise ships (screw Karo's environmental scruples), a cabin up north where Hannah could read on the beach and Edgar could fish for pike and small-mouth bass, afternoons of Edgar leaving the office early so they could disappear into their bedroom with a bottle of the same cheap champagne they used to pass in circles around the front lawns of frat houses in East Lansing. The night he pushed her across campus in a shopping cart that she pretended was a race car. The bookcase he built her out of scrapped two-by-fours and discarded sheets of plywood. In those years they had been young and unflinching, certain they would never lose themselves in the dull paces of adulthood, confident they had all the time in the world. Edgar, older, but as electric as ever, carrying Mari and Ani over his shoulders like sacks of potatoes, joking with them, *We bought you off the back of a turnip truck, you were plucked from the ground that very day!* They always planned to have their own time again.

And then, nearly a decade later, a simple month lapse in her birth control. Joseph and Talin, a gift of mis-scheduled appointments and forgetfulness. She would not trade them for anything, even if the consequence was losing her marriage. The truth was, she loved her children more than Edgar now. It had not always been that way, but she didn't have to think about it twice anymore. There was nothing she could do to change that.

His eyes were filled with lustful hope as he clung to her for balance in his crouched pose, back bent, his quads shaking and burning with exhaustion. Looking him in the face, the worst of everything was her realization that she wasn't even upset at him for cheating. She understood his desire for someone else, even if he was an idiot for neglecting her. His physical weaknesses mattered to her so much less than his emotional ones. His family should have been enough for him to not take such a careless risk. And yet, it would be fine. She would make it fine.

"Maybe they'll stay in tonight."

"You're not that naïve." He stood back up. His knees snapped like firecrackers. They had not bought summer fireworks for the kids in years. Not even a pack of sparklers. Karo insisted against it. Now the Fourth would be a sorrowful anniversary.

"Everyone needs a night off now and then."

Edgar slouched and wiped the film of sweat from his forehead. He unknotted his tie as he walked back inside, defeated. Hannah marked her page in her novel again and followed him to the kitchen. She set the book on the table next to a pile of the day's mail: a smatter of glossy restaurant coupons and bills stacked in crisp white envelopes. Edgar opened the fridge and pushed around the containers. The funk of cooked vegetables—browned carrots, translucent onions, blackened bell peppers, mushy zucchini, spinach like wet toilet paper—wafted out.

Her husband reached for a beer and his tie snaked free. Hannah stood behind him and caught the fabric as it slithered toward the floor. She hated to fall right into his trap, but it had been too long for her too. She needed a release from her grief. The gym couldn't always be enough. Joseph's music was once again intolerably loud. He and Talin wouldn't hear them shuffle down the hall to their bedroom.

"Forget the beer for now."

"It's been a long week."

She grabbed him by the hand and closed the fridge. Hannah twisted the tie around his hand like a leash and his posture changed with understanding. She dragged him down the long hallway past the twin bedrooms of their moody children. Joseph and Talin would not hear a sound. If she wasn't going to confront him outright, she wanted to remind him how lucky he was. In some predictable, reactionary way, it might be easier for her to perform outrage or jealousy or vengeance, but there was no right answer in these situations—he had fucked it all to hell for them—and the way forward eluded her. She either forgave him or she didn't; both options were less than ideal, all routes a capitulation. Of course other women had fallen for this man. How could they not? The same as other men fighting for her if she wanted them to. On a basic level, she was more desirable than he was, and attraction for both of them had changed with age, but there was more to it than desire.

She thought back to the sleepless string of nights during her junior year of college, when she sat by his bedside while he recovered in Sparrow Hospital from a nasty bar fight. After he won a hundred dollars playing pool with some bikers who claimed he didn't call bank on the eight ball, they asked him if Hadji was going to do some judo if they didn't pay. Edgar had in fact taken a swing, but, outnumbered and outmuscled, soon wound up on the floor in a barrage of boots. She was so mad at him after that, even when he insisted she didn't understand because no one had ever called her a dune coon or a camel jockey, and for a while she was certain she would break up with him as soon as he could take care of himself again. But she decided to stay through the weeks of physical rehab, spending countless hours listening to Gregor's stories over and over. The old man was insistent on helping, convinced he was the family historian on physical pain. He coached Edgar between his ramblings, her husband never paying close attention, while she absorbed every detail. By the time Edgar was on the up-and-up, Hannah had heard every family secret, and Edgar's parents finally looked at her like she wasn't just a meddling odar. After everything had blown over, she was sure they could get through anything together. They married as soon as she graduated.

Hannah stopped at the end of the hall and flung Edgar by the arm past her into their bedroom. He fell onto the mattress atop the lumped-up comforter, and the maple headboard creaked as the frame absorbed his weight. Hannah remained for a moment outside the door, staring down the hall, waiting for Joseph or Talin to barge out of their room for the kitchen, some sign to shake her from this moment of carelessness. The carpet needed to be vacuumed. The walls needed to be repainted, full of knee-high marks and scratches from when the twins were children. It had been so long since Edgar spent a weekend on housework. There was still time to sell. They could move anywhere and start over. They could buy an RV and roam the country. Ani wasn't the only one who could run away.

Hannah closed the door while Edgar sat on the edge of the bed and untied his shoes. He tossed them in the corner by the wicker laundry hamper and they thudded, the upturned, smooth eroded soles shining like slick tarred tongues. Their matching mid-century pine nightstands with the blue matching lamps, rigid beige shades, stiff hoop skirts covering a harsh womb of light. A thick biography of Truman on Edgar's side, a book he was certain to never finish, heavy and yellowing and, like so many of their possessions, useless. The book on her nightstand was another literary thriller soon to be adapted to a movie. The blinds were closed, but the sun was strong enough to reveal the layers of airborne debris floating around the room. A line of faux-joyful family portraits, her children staring at her from the wall. The ceiling fan was fuzzy with dust.

She sauntered by him toward their bathroom. That small distance like reaching for the opposite shore of a great lake.

"I'll just be a minute," Hannah told her husband.

He smiled like a schoolboy. "I'm not going anywhere."

In the bathroom she sat on the toilet and remained there after she was done peeing. Her stomach grumbled, hollow and hungry. All those damn leftovers and no one had thought to bring a lasagna or taco dip or any of those hearty Midwestern casseroles lined with tater tots and breadcrumbs, not a damn fruit salad to be found, as if comfort food only existed in the ethnicity of the departed. It was no wonder they kept ordering takeout. She flushed and imagined Edgar in the other room, supine across the bed in his black boxer shorts, fiddling around on his phone, his work clothes heaped on the floor. Why were either of them pretending to be young and spontaneous?

Hannah washed her hands and face. She flung her T-shirt off, unclasped her bra, slid out of her dark jean shorts, stood in front of the mirror in her gossamer pair of lime green panties, and felt beautiful. For nearly five decades she had taken meticulous care of her body, and it showed in her muscular shoulders and collarbones, her toned stomach, legs strong enough that she could bicycle clear across the state if she chose.

The counter around the sink was overcrowded with their colorful green and blue toothbrushes, a box of Q-tips, Edgar's electric razor nestled in its charger, her blow-dryer with its black, tortuous cord, a miscellany of lotions and creams. She patted her face dry on her bath towel, which was still damp and wilted from her post-workout shower. She tried to not think about her niece, her daughters, her lonesome, angry son.

She returned to the bedroom, and Edgar smiled again. He was still wearing his white undershirt and she could see the holes forming at the seams in his armpits, a tuft of chest hair rising like smoke above the collar and up the tan chimney of his throat.

"Wow," he gasped.

"I know," Hannah chided with confidence. He brought his eyebrows together in a line. His flattery meant nothing to her. She realized she could do anything. They were bound to one another and not bound at all. He could no longer claim fidelity, and so, she figured, why maintain fidelity to anyone other than herself? But he was more than enough for the moment: pleasant, familiar, a sure thing.

"You don't think the kids will hear?"

She walked to him and put a hand on his side where his gut met his hip. The room darkened, some rebellious cloud masking the sun. "We don't bother them when their doors are closed. They won't bother us."

He was already stiff with anticipation. She guided his hand to her ass and straddled him, dry humping like a teenager in a parked car. Hannah wondered if it was like this for Edgar with the woman from work. Was it slow and routine or fast and unpredictable? Did she suck his cock? She yanked his shirt off and traced the crescent moon scar on his ribs from where the bikers had beaten him to a pulp. It was remarkable and confounding, she thought, the permanent harm we can cause one another.

The following Wednesday, Hannah skipped the gym to walk with Hova. Her sister-in-law spent hours every day wandering in labyrinthine circuits around the island. Ani had walked with her once before she packed up and left. Talin had given up on her morning bike rides and joined Hova the day before, but told her mother she felt like she was intruding, and didn't plan to accompany her aunt again. For some reason, Talin's experience only made Hannah more curious. She had texted Hova later that night and confirmed their departure time for the next morning.

"How do you decide on a route?" Hannah asked. She was in her usual spin outfit of yoga pants and a tank top, but doused herself in sunscreen, a Tigers baseball cap to block her face from the sun. Hova was dressed more sensibly in denim shorts that went to her knees and a blue T-shirt with a maize block M on the chest, a functional straw sun hat that would be cute on the beach but stood out for a casual morning stroll. They were making their way through a series of side streets and cul-de-sacs Hannah had never driven through.

"I try to get myself lost," Hova answered. "The exercise is nice, but it's about seeing if I can find my way back and allowing my mind to stay on one task. Besides, the island is too small to ever really end up somewhere unfamiliar."

At the end of the road, they found themselves looking out over West Shore Country Club's verdant golf course. Edgar played there on the occasional Friday morning with coworkers or clients when they couldn't get a tee time at Grosse Ile Country Club. It was a boring and forgiving course, he complained, all straight fairways and few traps, sparse lines of thin-branched trees that weren't cumbersome to visibility. Karo refused to play golf. *An environmental catastrophe and gross misuse of public land,* he often grumbled.

"It's not actually about the walking," Hova remarked. The road was wide, but Hannah shifted behind Hova in single file to allow a black Mercedes to crawl by.

"I'm sure it's just nice to get out of the house," Hannah offered. "Ed says Karo is still holed up in the basement."

"He's working through it, I guess," Hova said. "I go back and forth between worrying and thinking it's fine. He won't tell me about the project he's working on. Even when he signed secretive contracts with the Department of Defense, he would tell me. He's always told me before. All I know is that for all the hours he's putting in they haven't paid yet. Not that we need it, but Karo's time is not cheap, even if he's in the bottle."

Hannah always wondered how much Karo billed by the hour, but it was none of her business. They cut through the grass onto a golf cart path and snaked around a yellowed putting green until they reached the small cemetery. The Detroit River stretched like a teal strip of fallen sky. The cemetery was surrounded by a black iron gate, and conical ferns were tucked together along the fence to offer privacy. Hannah feared any sign of death could set off her sister-in-law, but it was difficult to catch Hova's expression behind the brim of her sun hat.

They cut across someone's lawn to break out onto the side of the road. There was no sidewalk, so they walked on the shoulder until they could find another entry point to duck back into the island's nexus of residential streets.

"You don't need to look after me. Ed didn't ask you to walk with me, did he?"

"No, of course not," Hannah assured her, but they had talked about Karo and Hova the previous evening. The past few days were the closest she had felt to her husband in months. Somehow discovering his secret made her feel as if she understood him, despite wanting to put on Joseph's boxing gloves and bang some sense into his thick skull. After they had risen from bed and dressed themselves last Friday evening, Hannah assigned Joseph and Talin to eat or dispose of all the leftover food in the fridge. A slate wiped clean. The twins had in fact spent the evening at home, and the four of them sat eating popcorn in front of the television together, watching a bad superhero movie dragged out by excessive commercial breaks and speculating as to Ani's whereabouts.

"I don't even think Ed cares about my walks," Hova said bitterly. "I think he hates that I leave his brother alone in his misery."

Hannah nodded.

"I can't control how Karo grieves," Hova continued. "He's never handled loss well. You remember how it was when their mother died. A week straight of drinking. This time, I don't know if it'll end. He can stew and pickle all he wants, but I need time by myself to work through my memories of my daughter."

Hannah didn't ask Hova to elaborate. They turned inland. A group of kids, Hannah guessed no older than six or seven, played soccer on a wide stretch of immaculate lawn. There were dozens of questions she wanted to ask her sister-in-law about the circumstances of her niece's death, details Hova and Karo had not shared with the rest of the family. Some of the more salacious aspects made the news, but with little background or context. They had found a note in Mari's apartment in a book Hannah couldn't remember the name of. Mari had so many books, shelves upon shelves in her condo. She was always reading. Hannah remembered Mari as a frizzy-haired kid out in the yard with one of her *Goosebumps* books and a box of orange Hi-C, Gushers nested in her lap, one as a reward for finishing each chapter. Hannah had been awed by her niece's patience and restraint.

"It's amazing how some people can be so cruel," Hannah observed. Hova peeked from beneath the brim of her sun hat toward the cloudless sky. They both craned their necks to the wide expanse above. Blue in every direction.

"You mean the video." An airplane spewed two lines of smog.

Their eyes met. Hannah nodded. "You think that's why my daughter ended her life?"

Hannah couldn't think of anything to say.

"It's horrible how much women have to worry about being exposed these days." Hova sighed. "Imagine if we grew up with that. But it was never about the video. Mari was never ashamed of her sex life. We talked about her flings openly when Karo wasn't around, the two of us giggling like schoolgirls. I never wanted my daughter to be embarrassed or ashamed of her choices. I'm not as old school as people seem to think. And Mari didn't care what a bunch of faceless monsters wrote about her online."

Hannah wanted to ask about the note.

"The journalists found the circumstances of her death sensational enough to report and then when they found out about the video, they clung to it like the narrative was obvious," Hova went on. "Everything is a smoking gun to them. They thought, what other cause could there be? And then the online conspiracy theorists got involved, claiming, 'Oh, she was in on it all along and trying to do what Kim Kardashian did, but it backfired,' as if being fetishized is a privilege. Fucking vultures."

"I'm so sorry, Hova."

To Hannah's surprise, Hova laughed. "I remember Mari came home from college for Thanksgiving once and we were gossiping while we made mashed potatoes and pilaf. Karo was outside fussing with the grill. It was too early for the Lions game, so you all hadn't walked over for dinner yet. She was telling me about this guy she was seeing who kept saying she had skin like a caramel macchiato and calling her his Armenian princess. She liked him a lot and didn't know what to do about it."

Hannah's face quirked in a smile—she had never heard this story. "What did you tell her?"

Hova hung her head toward the ground to keep her face hidden beneath the brim of her hat, but Hannah could hear her sniffling. The memory must have weighed her down too much. "I asked her how long she would be comfortable playing that role. I told her men like that don't change. They'll want to slaughter a lamb at their wedding and try to win the egg fight on Easter and always see her in terms of being different without being *too* different. They'll never see her for who she is, only who they want her to be to prove something about themselves."

Hannah thought about her own daughters. They looked more like Edgar's side of the family than her own. She had never considered that boys might see them as exotic.

She knew she shouldn't ask about the note, but she couldn't help herself. "Did Mari explain anything in the note she left?"

Hova paused for a long time. "It was about her job. Some of her students found the video online and a parent caught them watching it. They complained to the superintendent, and the district didn't renew her contract. None of this was made public, of course. The district told her it was a budgetary thing, anything to avoid Mari filing a lawsuit, but there was no denying their true motives. She essentially got blacklisted. She couldn't find another teaching job anywhere. No one would hire her."

Hannah hugged her sister-in-law from the side. They spent the final mile of their walk in silence. Hannah's feet were sore. Their walk was nothing like her routine workouts, the asphalt unforgiving on her arches. She listened to the wash of traffic in the distance as they passed house after house and navigated winding neighborhoods, each lawn and driveway its own unit of measurement, until they arrived at the mouth of their cul-de-sac. On the edge of Hova's driveway, Hannah offered another frail embrace. They parted ways to their separate houses, the sprawl of grass between them so small and yet infinite.

Hannah found Edgar sitting with his laptop and binders sprawled across the dining table. He was working from home. Talin and Joseph were certainly, as expected, somewhere else. Edgar appeared deep in thought, his forehead scrunched so that his eyebrows mashed together. He was usually meticulous about grooming them, his most notable habit of self-care, but with everything going on he had neglected his routine, and the river of skin above his nose looked mossy. He sipped iced coffee from a pint glass and smiled at her.

Hannah's hands shook with sudden anxiety. She shoved them in her pockets. "I think it's time we talk about her."

"Who—Mari?" he asked.

"No," Hannah replied, gathering her resolve. "The woman from work."

His face dropped. He closed his laptop and bent forward to rest his head on its lid, taking several deep breaths before looking back up at her.

"How long have you known?"

"Long enough to be over it, but that means it's over for you too."

His mouth opened and closed a few times, as though sorting through every possible response. He exhaled. "Just like that?"

Hannah brushed a strand of hair behind her ear and smirked at him. It felt like there were no rules anymore, and in some ways that excited her. She was happy to have a certain level of power over her husband. Her whole life, she'd contended with the cultural implication that she was supposed to be supportive and submissive. Now she was taking charge.

"It's just—" She laughed. "Younger and Armenian, Ed? It's very predictable."

He scrunched his brow again.

"You've always been conflicted about marrying an odar."

"Hannah, you are the crux of this family."

"I know," she said. He would be screwed without her. "So act like it."

He sighed. "I'm sorry." It was the stunted apology of a privileged man being let off the hook easy. If Gregor was still alive, he would call Edgar a coward. Gregor would tell Hannah to leave. She could tell he realized how much he'd lucked out, that her reaction could have been so much worse. What he didn't yet realize was that his infidelity would haunt him much more acutely and for much longer than it did her. He would never forgive himself, and she would move on. This was the secret she understood. In many ways, guilt lingered worse than betrayal. She was at fault for nothing. There were more important things to worry about. All of them were in need of a fresh start, and this was her new beginning.

"I don't think we need to tell the kids. We're losing them already."

Edgar looked relieved.

"That said," she continued, "they're not dumb."

Her husband was pale. He looked ill. Weak. She had always been stronger than he was, that in a scenario like this, only she was capable of holding their family together. The last few months were the worst they had faced since before the kids were born. So much of Hannah's life had sped by, the trite pattern of years moving faster and faster until all the milestones jumbled together in her memory. Now each of those big moments felt insignificant in the present, the erosion revealing every layer. All those years ago, when they were still in college, she could have left Edgar when his foolish anger landed him bruised and achy in a hospital bed, but that was irrelevant—it was thirty years too late to undo everything that had passed between them. There was no returning to the beginning. There was only beginning again.

"Will we be okay?" Edgar asked.

"About this or everything else?"

"In general, I guess."

"There's no way of knowing," Hannah told him as she left the kitchen, ready for a shower. When nothing else would do, she could always clear her mind under the downpour of hot water. She could sense Edgar watching her go, hungry for her body, and part of her wanted to invite his desire, but she also would not give him the satisfaction. It was his turn to wait and worry. She could handle herself and let him squirm. She had grown so accustomed to being alone.

INTERLUDE

What Is a Mountain?

Is it possible to imagine a towering peak without the vast nothingness above it? Think of the clear sky, the cutting thin air, the utter absence of surrounding rocks and foliage. Mountains are defined by the loss around them. Mountain ranges. Mountains arranged. Mountains far apart, only visible to one another. Mountains together, meshed at the hip. The mountain of a woman's pregnant belly. The twin peaks of a man's shoulder blades, slumped over in grief. The mountain of dirt beside an empty grave. A mountain of banned books aflame. The mountain of two bodies pressed together in passion. The mountain of a mouth gasping for water. Mountains poking above the waterline, all that is visible, in a biblical flood.

We are defined in peaks and valleys, crests and troughs. There is nothing that cannot be evaluated by its blank spaces, its lacunas, its abyss. The absence is everywhere. There is always something that can't be found. And so the mountain rises from the turmoil of rock and magma, collision and erosion. Earth skyrocketing toward the heavens. Earth driven far below.

Mount Ararat. The mountain we claim, where life was cradled, safe from the torrents below. Musa Dagh. The mountain on which we survived. Where life was fought for tooth and nail. The mountain where a dying people refused extinction. You ask: What is a mountain? What is a foothill? What is a mound of earth? What is a pile of dirt built to hide bodies from the destruction of bullets? What is a pile of dead bodies buried in dirt? What is an anthill in the sand kicked away by a passing child?

We never stop echoing where we came from. We are still the mountain.

And yes, the elements that make up the mountain can be named. Rock. Dirt. Limestone. Basalt. Quartz. Verdant tufts of grass and brush. Tons upon tons of hard ground, unmovable, built by eons of unmanned environmental labor.

Is a mountain unmovable or immovable? A mountain is always still. A mountain is never still. At its base, perhaps it begins at the slight curve uphill, a ladder with no rungs. Ascension of grass and cattails blustering in the wind. No shadow of what's ahead unless you look behind. There are no distinct steps, no guaranteed footholds. The mountain does not know of feet. It does not fret over order or convenience. A mountain can be built like anything else. A grain of sand, a jagged rock, then another and another and another. It climbs and climbs and climbs until there is nowhere else to climb, until there is nothing more than the bulge of the summit at its center.

To defend our people, we believed the mountaintop of Musa Dagh once offered an advantageous position. We remember it well. We never forget that mountain. We never forget being at the top of the world. Would we go back there today if we could? It's hard to say. Home never feels like home once it has stopped being home. Have we not found other places to claim? Have we not found so many other ways to conquer the sky? Have we not learned to stand in the pride of certain defeat? Have we not lost whatever we once clung to at the acme?

Acme. Apex. Apogee. Peak. These words we have learned too. Nothing can stay at its highest point forever. When we left the mountain there were endless places to go. We dispersed across nations, cities, and countrysides, over vast oceans and through undefined forests. We built new lives where we were welcome. We built new lives where we were shunned. We observed other mountains. We saw the clamber of other distant lands—buildings and airplanes and redwoods—reaching for sky. The peaks are everywhere. You can see them if you look. There, there, there.

We built communities. We shared food and music and clothing and spice blends and medical secrets. We recognized our ancestors in one another's hair. Smiled at the faces of our grandparents in a stranger's eyes. Cackled and cackled and cackled at those pesky eyebrows, the bridge of dark stems aligned across our faces, their unruly mountainous edges. We lost languages, but we held on to ways to communicate. We did our best to pass on what we had learned, what we feared, what we dreamt about back home. We kept so much to ourselves, but spared our children from the worst. We spoke to them in English. We warmed them spaghetti from a can. We ordered fried potatoes through car windows. We turned on rock and roll. We stopped going to church.

But we survived. We built businesses. We raised families. We carried our stories with us like they were all we had left to lose. We reminded the world of our existence no matter how many times they tried to erase us. And we rose and rose and rose. We ascended again. We found fresh air at the summit. We breathed in its choking promise. And like clockwork, we again allowed our voices to echo.

We are still the mountain.

Mara Bedrossian

For decades, people asked Mara Bedrossian (for whom her great-granddaughter Mari was named), about the death and suffering she witnessed on her forced deportation through the desert. They told her it was important to share her story, to relive everything she tried so hard to hold inside her. And for most of her life, Mara pointed them to her second husband, Gregor, and the pile of newspaper clippings he had collected from the *New York Times*, *The Nation*, and other major publications. Without fail, every article contained a paragraph like this:

> On April 24, 1915, hundreds of Armenian intellectuals and community leaders in Constantinople (now Istanbul) were arrested and deported—most, later executed—marking the beginning of the Armenian Genocide, the state-sanctioned massacre of as many as 1.5 million Armenians living in the failing Ottoman Empire. By 1922, after Armenian populations

were forcibly displaced, starved, and led on death marches through the Syrian desert, less than 400,000 of the former two million plus Armenians remained there. Today, about three million Armenians live in the country of Armenia, while more than eight million Armenians are scattered elsewhere across the globe.

For Mara, the newspaper version was so much easier to offer up than the image of her younger sister's eviscerated body dusted in sand, the sound of the bullet through her mother's skull. It was only in the last year of Mara's life that she finally told a brief version of her biography to her eldest grandson, who she trusted to keep straight the family history. Sitting next to her bed, Karo wrote furiously, jotting down every last word, which was much less than he hoped for, but resulted in several pages of typed narrative. In summary:

Mara Bedrossian was the sole survivor of her family. Prior to deportation, Mara lived in Harpoot. The men, including her father and her recently-wedded husband, were marched out of town and executed. Later, the women of Mara's family were told to hand over their valuables for safekeeping and that relocation was necessary. In the desert, Mara witnessed the rape and murder of her sister (bayonet), the murder of her mother (pistol), and the theft and sale of her infant niece. Mara was also shot, a nonfatal wound through her shoulder, and left next to the lifeless body of her sister. Before she succumbed to starvation or dehydration, Mara was found by a Kurdish trader searching corpses for hidden valuables sewn into the garments. Upon finding Mara alive, he nursed her back to health and—full of guilt over his thievery—smuggled her to safety in Egypt. In time, a church sponsorship brought Mara to Detroit, where she began volunteering and making a small wage serving food to plant workers. There, she would meet Gregor Kurkjian and marry.

"That's what you need to know," Mara told her grandson. "That's the story of my life." Karo solemnly nodded. Mara refused her grandson's follow-up questions. She would not repeat her past to another soul. There were countless memories she never wrote down. There was so much pain she could not bear to pass on.

Gregor Kurkjian
1994

"What happened next?" Mari asked. Gregor had lost track of where he was for a moment. The lawn had blurred in his vision. He was right back where he was so many years ago, watching his home get smaller and smaller as the ship speared away from Musa Dagh. Until then, he had lived close to the sea his whole life, but he had never seen his home from this far out on the water. He was astounded by its vastness.

"Papa." Karo squatted down next to him. "You okay?"

"Yes." He waved his grandson off again and returned his attention to Mari and Ani. "I was just finding my place. No one ever talks about what happened after we left the mountain. Everyone ends the story there, but I will tell you the rest of what happened to me."

At Port Said, Gregor's family spent weeks recovering and discussed their plans for the future. His father and mother had never lived outside of their village, so they were prepared to wait out the war and return to Musa Dagh once it was safe. Gregor's sisters were half his height and age, too young to venture elsewhere. They would stay behind, too, but, with his parents' blessing, Gregor was ready to see the world. He had fought for his life and now he would go find what other wonders existed elsewhere, in Europe and America. He could find work abroad and dreamed of sending money home. He wanted to believe there was nothing for him but opportunity.

"Musa Dagh was permanently annexed by Turkey a couple decades later," Ed whispered to his wife, who Gregor was certain already knew this fact. Hannah listened when he told stories. Gregor was tired of being interrupted. Why must his grandsons keep adding their commentary?

A month later, after Gregor recovered his strength, he found space on a small French vessel returning to its motherland. He packed his few meager belongings: a dull razor, two changes of clothes, a lambskin journal, the little money his father could spare, and the Mauser, broken down to fit into his rucksack.

Gregor did not stay in France for long. He had witnessed enough of war to loathe the suffering it caused, and he would never feel safe near the Western Front. At the shipyards, he agreed to work as a deckhand on a steamer set for New York City to buy his passage to America. When he was not cleaning to earn his keep, he spent most of the journey holed up in his cabin with seasickness and fever. He never imagined how much ocean stood between him and the United States, and the open seas did not agree with Gregor's stomach. On the journey to Port Said, Gregor had been so malnourished that he attributed his nausea to a lack of strength, but now he understood he was not made for boats, despite the family lore. Still, he worked hard until he arrived at Ellis Island, where his plea for asylum was granted—the Americans knew well the plight of the starving Armenians. His nausea did not fully subside until the day after they had docked and unloaded. New York City, a metropolis he never could have imagined, bustling. No rubble, no soldiers trotting around off duty. More people than he had ever seen, all in transit, mindlessly walking from place to place. He found small enclaves of his country's people as he wandered around the city, homeless, unsure of his next move.

Speaking no English, Gregor struggled for a few days to find a job, but soon an Armenian boy of his age, Tigran, led him back to the shipyards and helped Gregor ask for more work. Gregor spent several weeks breaking his back loading and unloading cargo as fast as he could, nights of sleeping on the docks in abandoned lifeboats or in between pallets of exported goods. Tigran offered him a place to sleep when he could, but his parents and siblings were already piled together in a single room.

"You should go to Michigan," Tigran told Gregor one day as they wheeled cargo onto a freighter. "I have an uncle there. He says it is much cheaper to live."

"And what will I do in Michigan?"

"They build cars there, more every day. You could find work. Easy."

"I am not an engineer," Gregor reminded him, with concern. "I've never even touched an automobile."

"They build them in factories," Tigran assured him. "You

would do one job. It is like this work. Repeating the same thing over and over."

"Where is Michigan?"

"West."

"And where do they build the cars?"

"Detroit."

Gregor could not imagine traveling farther west. He had already come so many miles. He had never heard of Detroit. It sounded French. Gregor told Mari and Ani he had no way of knowing what he would find when he arrived, but he refused to give up. He packed up his belongings yet again and hopped on a train.

In Detroit, by week's end, Gregor found work in Highland Park at the Ford Motor Company. Other workers on the line helped him locate an affordable room for rent in a building that housed a few other young Armenian men. Gregor's apartment was nothing more than a closet with a cot and an uneven dresser, one leg a half inch shorter than the rest. Routinely working extra hours, he saved every scrap of money that wasn't spent on rent and food. In a few years, he reasoned, he could set aside enough of his wages to purchase a house.

It was fate that one day he forgot his lunch tin on his mattress. There was a cart outside the plant the other men raved about, soup and sandwiches better than any diner in town. Gregor followed them to the crowded queue when their midday break arrived, waiting in the rear of the line as masses of hungry workers pushed forward to be fed. Behind the counter stood a woman who was no more American than Gregor. Curly black hair under a bandana, the round glow in her cheeks—he would not have been surprised if she too was a survivor. She immediately reminded him of home.

"Do I even have to tell you what happened next?" he asked the little girls who filled his heart. They shifted in the grass. Ani giggled. Mari put a finger to her chin like she was deep in thought. "You must have figured it out by now."

Gregor had fallen in love.

What Is a Flood?

A flood is an incessant, relentless, unstoppable rush of water, the accumulation of rain and rain and rain, an unwillingness to be controlled, it flows over, it seeps underneath, rises above each brim and dam, expands beyond the walls and hillsides, there is no volume that cannot be filled, no valley that cannot be reimagined as a lake or sea, until the ocean is all one coalescing force, the world aqueous under its weight, waves running endlessly in circles, the surface devoid of islands, and so it is inundation, a drowning, everything wet with sorrow: a flood of potent whiskey, a flood of bathwater as a newborn is rinsed clean, a flood of family and friends cheery at a church baptism, a flood of memories echoing back to a time that younger generations will never bother to learn about, a flood of funereal tears, a flood of fearless protesters, a flood of released bowels at the sight of a gun raised, a flood of men swimming for warships, a flood of men swimming for shore—They are tired! They are hungry!—a flood of people walking into the arid desert to dry up and wither away, a flood that turns everything into an oasis, not a man parched, not a woman thirsty for drink, no one who cannot find water to soak dirty laundry, every dish rinsed clean, every towel and linen soggy all the way through, and the boats rise, the boats rise, the boats rise and waver across the surface until they tumble and sink, the flood so extraordinary that there is not time to comfort the pets, no time to grab passports and social security cards, the flood that sends the birds as high as their wings will carry them until they are exhausted and falter, it is all anyone can do to swim one stroke before the body becomes useless, the flood that is yesterday and today and tomorrow, that has always been, all those years ago, the flood that will come again and again and keep coming, the flood that rises and devours, the water so high as to gobble mountains, the flood that melds water with the blue of sky until there is no discerning where one ends and the other begins, until the surface calms and clouds float above, a flood that never drains away. Water, everywhere, peaceful. It is all that remains.

PART TWO: 2018

Hova Kurkjian (née Nazarian)

These men know nothing of grief, Hova thought, as she dressed for her daily walk. They mourn themselves, the nausea in their guts and the pounding in their heads. They mourn the pain of their personal loss. They mourn the realization of their own mortality. They mourn with work, with alcohol, with violence. They mourn the scandal. They mourn the public spectacle. They mourn the solemnity of their households, the quiet boredom of their days and the restless longing of their nights. But they do not mourn my daughter. They do not mourn Mari's losses and lonesomeness. They do not mourn her unquenchable pain.

Hova laced her new black and yellow cross trainers. She had planned to hit the road nearly two hours ago, but like locusts a tribe of women from the church stopped by bearing baklava and halva and groceries. It took Hova forever to politely shoo them from her living room. Karo did not bother to even make an appearance. He remained hidden in his bunker—unless he was passed out in their bed or in the bathroom.

She removed her water bottle from the freezer, having forgotten about it. Bulging, solid as a rock, numbingly cold in her hand. The sun was higher in the sky than she preferred. It would have to be a short walk today. She was grateful Talin and Hannah had taken the hint to leave her alone after the disparate afternoons they each accompanied her. She felt bad for withholding details from Hannah about Mari's letter, but the walks were not a time for confession. It was not a time to zone out or listen to music or talk about the weather. She never understood why people worked so hard to ignore or run away from what was on their minds. For her, exercise was not a time to escape. It was not meditation. It was a time to face her agony head-on.

Hova exited the cul-de-sac and tried to remember where she had paused in her process of cataloguing her daughter's life. She had nearly made it through fourth grade, but the baklava reminded her of Mari's middle school years. In sixth or seventh grade, her class had been tasked with bringing in a dish for a potluck that represented their nationality. Mari signed up for pilaf, but Mr. Benedict had asked, "Why don't you bring baklava for dessert?" The assignment stipulated purchasing prepared food was discouraged. He clearly had no understanding of what a pain in the ass it was to make baklava from scratch. Hova had spent a frustrated hour supervising Mari as she buttered layer after layer of crumbling phyllo. They burnt their simple syrup and poured it over the dough while it was still steaming. The result was a bitter, mushy fiasco.

A distraction, Hova thought. Chronology was key. On her first walk, Hova had no destination or reason for going, but soon she thought about the day Mari was born. She got lost in that first moment with her daughter, exhausted and drugged in a hospital bed. She decided to remember every moment they shared together. It was not a record that could be completed at rest. When she sat on the couch in her living room and tried to recall Mari, the space was flooded with years of memories. Every picture on the wall or piece of furniture or scratch on the door sent her in a new direction.

She could not prevent Karo from despairing in the basement. He would drink away all his brain cells until their daughter was a blur, but Hova sometimes thought she would never consume alcohol again if it meant she could hold on to her memories of Mari. She already couldn't bear the precious moments that were lost.

Three hours later, Hova loaded the baklava, along with some mediocre torshi and stale lavash, into her canvas *New Yorker* tote to deliver to Hannah. Her food dumps were becoming unwelcome, but weren't Joseph and Talin always in need of more sustenance? Mari would consume anything at that age. Joseph was on the deck with his back to her, smoking in a lawn chair, the familiar funk of marijuana in the air. When she approached, he tried to casually drop the joint to the ground and stomp it beneath his white Chucks.

"Don't worry." Hova smirked. "I won't tell."

"You surprised me, Aunt Hov."

"Your mom's not home, I take it."

"She went to lunch with some friends."

"For the best." Hova couldn't imagine who Hannah was out with. She was almost always at the gym or at home. "Now I can pawn off this food without her trying to stop me."

"She'll be pissed." Joseph smirked. "Last week she made Tal and me try to clean everything out. By the time we finished, Tal looked ready to hurl."

"Better you than me."

Joseph's eyes were red slits. His long hair was a mess. She wanted to brush it back from his brow. He was the perfect mark. He asked, "Anything good?"

"Some baklava."

"You can leave that with me." He laughed. "Tal's inside in her room or somewhere, but no one else is around."

"Why is she holed up on such a beautiful day?"

Joseph shrugged, but she could tell something was the matter. Maybe they were fighting. Teenagers were so moody all the time. She had dealt with it twice: the first time with Mari, and then a second time during the unexpected year Ani stayed in their guest room when the living situation became untenable next door. Mari came home from campus more that year than when she was a freshman. Every weekend Mari either came home or Ani drove to campus. They were inseparable back then. Three years later, Mari moved out of Michigan, so far away.

Hova left Joseph to relax, entered the house, and shook her sandals off on the mat. She dropped off the food in the fridge and wandered toward Talin's bedroom, Ani's old room. How many evenings had she spent in there playing card games—war and go fish and crazy eights—with the girls? The door was cracked open, and the scent of lavender drifted into the hallway. There was a sliver of dresser visible with Talin's jewelry and library card. She knocked.

"Not right now, Joe."

"It's me," Hova said. She could hear Talin's bed squeak.

"Oh! Come in."

Hova pushed the door. The room was cleaner than she expected. Talin was cross-legged on the center of her bed on her phone. A book rested on the edge. Hova recognized the cover and title. The same novel that had been on Mari's desk, holding the note.

Walking through Mari's condo with Karo had been hell. It was evident Mari had cleaned it before she left, but there was so much their daughter had left behind. Food in the fridge, cold cans of beer lined in three precise rows, a full case, unconsumed. Karo drank several of them after they found Mari's typed and printed pages, not even a real signature. The note was what Hova would expect of her daughter: honest, unsentimental, well written. She read it again and again and was certain she could recite the majority of it from memory.

"Oh shit." Talin followed Hova's sight line to the book. "I'm sorry, Aunt Hov. It's just—"

"You wanted to better understand," Hova supplied. She wondered why she never thought to read the novel. The company they paid to clear out the condo listed 732 books as part of the belongings to be sold or donated. Mari's choice of book wasn't an unintentional or inconsequential decision—she was much too detailed for that. The book and note now rested on the desk in Mari's childhood bedroom. The door remained closed and locked.

She had tasked Karo with stowing the few items they held on to from their daughter's condo: the notebooks filled with scribblings and poetry, Mari's laptop full of photos, her first edition of *My Name Is Aram*, a jeweled golden cross Gregor purchased for her the week before she was born, the blue coffee mug with its maize block M they had bought for her after she was accepted to Michigan.

"Yeah. I thought maybe it would make more sense if I read it, but I've only made it through a few pages. I can't focus on it."

"I haven't been able to focus on much at all." Hova was struck by déjà vu. Talin had kept the layout of the bedroom exactly the same as when Ani was there. Mari and Ani had always looked like cousins, related but different, whereas Talin could have been a younger version of Ani to the point it was somewhat ironic to think she was Joseph's twin. Hova felt washed over by the past clashing with the present.

Talin coughed. "I miss her. Ani and her and me always had a group chat going. I felt like I could count on them no matter what. I never realized anything was wrong. I just keep thinking if I'd paid more attention, done more to help, she might still be here."

"I miss her too." She was done crying. Her body had moved past such a reaction. Now, the pain was deep and dull, constant, inescapable. "But you can't think that way or you'll never forgive yourself. She didn't want us to find out. Her letter said as much. She didn't want to bother any of us with her problems. I don't know what she was thinking. This whole thing was so unlike her."

"Maybe we can both read the book," Talin suggested. "We can see if we can figure it out together." She stood to hug her aunt.

"I'd like that." Hova had the urge to go on another walk, no matter that it was late in the afternoon. She wanted to work up such a sweat that she would be forced into a cold shower. Mari's death had awoken something in her that could only be solved by constant movement. She finally understood all the time Hannah spent at the gym. Even with her long walks, so many hours of her days felt mundane and tiresome. She sat around staring at her phone, the television, a magazine, the kitchen table. How much time did she waste away, moving from one room of the house to the next in a state of inertia?

In the kitchen, Joseph leaned on the counter over the last two remaining triangles of baklava.

"Does Tal seem okay?" he asked.

"She's fine," Hova told him. "Processing, like we all are."

"She doesn't tell me anything anymore."

"Maybe she's not ready yet," Hova suggested. If there's one thing she knew about Kurkjian men, it was that they were impatient. They never allowed anyone time and space to work through their feelings. It was either keep emotions buried forever or have them out immediately, no in-between.

"Why can no one in this family ever just say what's on their mind?"

Hova had no answer. He would have to figure it out on his own. She walked over to the opposite side of the counter and placed a hand over Joseph's, patting it affectionately. She slipped out of the sliding door and out into the torrid heat.

The days passed that way until Friday afternoon, when, after spending the morning giving the house a much-needed clean—the stale, sweet odor of brandy had risen upstairs—Hova grew tired of her redundant and circuitous routes and walked across the free bridge and off the island. She was surprised to find Elizabeth Park bustling with people: the usual joggers and dog walkers, but also an early-weekend wedding party taking photos on the riverside path in front of the Chateau, a red brick venue that faced the water. The groomsmen were dressed in dark blue tuxedos with mustard-yellow bowties, a color that matched the bridesmaids' dresses. The bride was nowhere in sight. All of them looked happy. Hova continued along the water until she was in Trenton's downtown. There was a local coffee and ice cream parlor where Hova could stop for a vanilla cone to cool down. She checked the time on her phone to make sure they were open. A text from Talin: *I finished The Awakening. Let me know when you're done* <3.

Hova slid the phone back in her pocket. She could respond later. The book remained unopened in the drawer of her nightstand so Karo would not see it. She wondered what her husband was up to at home, if he had moved at all from his desk since descending that morning. He was drinking less, but she was still worried. Any little thing that reminded him of their daughter sent him back to the bottle. Hova imagined skipping the simple vanilla and instead opting for a waffle cone of melting Moose Tracks to enjoy during the long walk back across the bridge, but as she walked toward the entrance, she recognized her brother-in-law's hunched figure at the nearest patio table.

His back was to her. He sat under a tilted red umbrella, an empty cardboard bowl at his elbow. Edgar held the hand of a woman who was leaning in across the table like they were high school sweethearts. The woman used her other hand to wipe tears from her eyes. Edgar kissed her knuckles. Hova paused for a moment. She wanted to turn around, but she needed to be certain. Yes, the other woman was familiar. Iris, from Edgar's accounting firm. An Armenian girl. Hova had met her during the Memorial Day company picnic earlier that year and realized her parents had been friendly with Karo's parents. But Iris must have been more than a decade younger than her brother-in-law. And why was she crying?

Hova veered down a side street. Edgar and Iris were so engrossed Hova was certain they had not seen her. She wondered if Hannah knew, but no—there was no way. Hannah would have sent him packing. With each step, her confusion transformed into rage. She was angry for her sister-in-law, for her nieces and nephew, for her husband, for herself. How could he be so selfish?

The walk home was long and tortuous. By the time she passed the Chateau again, a few guests had arrived and were loitering around the venue with cocktails in tumblers and highball glasses. The bride had emerged, the pouf of her white dress blinding in the sunlight. A tower of whipped cream surrounded by dabs of mustard. She could imagine Mari in that dress. The shock of unadulterated white climbing until her tan skin bloomed from its hold.

Hova had traveled much farther than she realized and stopped to rest after she crossed back over the bridge. Why had she fled instead of confronting Edgar? She hated to think about her brother-in-law sneaking around, enjoying ice cream with a mistress when he was supposed to be at the office. Ignoring the grief of the people in his life who should mean the most to him. He couldn't get away with it. Hova was covered in sweat. She wondered why she chose to walk at all. This had been her own doing.

When she finally entered the cul-de-sac, she was shocked to find Karo standing with Edgar in the lawn. They were side by side smoking cigars, Edgar still in his shirt and tie and Karo in lumpy dad jeans and a Charles Woodson jersey that had previously not been removed from its hanger in their bedroom closet in more than a decade. Hova could imagine the moldy, unlaundered odor clinging to the fabric. Karo had a beer in hand and a steel spatula dangled from a strip of leather looped around his pinkie finger, the grill smoking behind them. They would be eating dinner together. Karo waved to her. Even though she was parched and soaked in sweat, she passed by her house, removed her sun hat, and walked over to them.

"Your face is beet red," Karo said. She could see the concern in the scrunch of his eyebrows. "Hannah is in the kitchen. You should go in and get some water."

"I'll go in a minute." She held her sun hat in both hands by the brim. Heat radiated off the grill. In truth, she wanted a cold beer. It would be much more refreshing after her trek, and she needed to relax her nerves. Edgar looked at her, clueless. He had no idea she had seen him.

"Long walk today?" Ed asked her. She glanced at the gold wedding band on his hand. Had he worn it all day, even when holding Iris's hand? Did he leave it on when they were together?

"Yes. I regret it, given the heat. I crossed the bridge for ice cream and stumbled past an early wedding. The bride-to-be was taking pictures with her bridesmaids by the river. She was beautiful. A smile on her face like I haven't seen since you and Hannah got hitched."

"*That*," Edgar said—concern flashed across his face for a brief moment, telling Hova everything she needed to know—and raised his beer to her, "was one hell of a party."

Hova remembered it well. A drawn-out, traditional service at Saint Sarkis, but the reception was in a historic hotel ballroom downtown, one of the many landmarks no longer there, torn down and replaced with apartments or offices or some combination of the two. They had shut the ballroom down and danced at a speakeasy until morning. Karo shrank at her side. Shit, she thought, realizing he was thinking the same thing she had an hour earlier: they had begun setting aside money for Mari's college fund and wedding day before she was even born. Hova had taken a shot at her brother-in-law and accidentally hit her husband instead.

"Are there more of those inside?" Hova nodded at the orange can in Edgar's hand.

"Plenty. Help yourself."

Hova left the men to the grill. She found Hannah in the kitchen chopping black olives and red onions for an enormous bowl of salad. There was so much Hova wanted to tell her. A bottle of white wine was uncorked on the counter next to two empty glasses. Her phone was blaring the Cranberries.

Hannah smiled. "The kids are out with friends so it's just us. I figured we could all use the opportunity to get good and drunk tonight."

Hova was surprised. It was unlike Hannah to drink heavily, if at all. She was always eating well, insistent on everything in moderation. Over the years, Hova found Hannah's abstemiousness near prudish at times, but lately, she felt the exact opposite—that Hannah's general attentiveness to her well-being was admirable, clearly doing her body good while the rest of them collapsed with age. Hova was even a little jealous. But now, the one voice of reason at the dinner table was gone.

"I can help you in a moment. Would you mind if I rinse my face in your bathroom first? I just got back from my walk."

"Why don't you stop at home, Hov? This salad will only take a minute and the boys have the grill. We can wait for you."

Hova walked to the fridge and found one of Edgar's beers. It was too hoppy for her liking and the high ABV would leave her tipsy, but the theme of the evening seemed to be excess. Why not? "Thanks, Hannah. I'm taking one of these with me to the shower. I'll be back in a few."

Hannah nodded. Hova cracked the beer and made her way out the back door through the garage to avoid any more chatter with their husbands. At home, she turned the cold spigot on in the shower. She had never drunk alcohol in the bathroom before, but Mari and Ani used to talk about it all the time when they were in college. They insisted there was nothing more relaxing than a glass of wine while they shaved their legs before a night out or a can of beer while rinsing off from a long run. Hova finally understood. The stream of water fell over her hair and body. She felt cooled in two ways at once.

Such a cliché to get emotional in the shower. All that noisy water masking tears. Yet, for the moment, she felt clean and renewed. If she had a reason to hide out from dinner, she wouldn't have to deal with Edgar's adultery, but it was too late to beg off now. She finished rinsing and wrapped herself in a towel, bringing the rest of the beer with her to the bedroom, where she dug out a green sundress for dinner on the patio with her family. This gathering was all part of the post-grief smokescreen: they would drink and joke and laugh to ignore everything that was really bothering them. Even her unreachable husband was putting on a fake-it-till-you-make-it attitude and an ebullient smile, probably to convince Edgar everything was fine so that he would ease off his daily check-ins.

When Hova returned next door, Hannah and Karo were setting the table. Edgar removed some potatoes in tinfoil off the grill. Next to him, massive steaks rested on a cookie sheet in a puddle of melted pink fat. Meat was the one carbon disaster her husband couldn't quit. He'd grown up with lamb chops and kofta and was too old to go vegetarian. In the summertime, they often dined outside together, but they had not eaten like this in weeks, certainly not since Mari's memorial.

Mari had insisted on eating on the deck whenever she was home, even if it was cold. Her condo had a small balcony, but there was only room for two deck chairs. She often ate dinner there after the school day with a plate in her lap and Hova on FaceTime eating a snack at the kitchen table on the other end. It was only after Mari was gone that Hova realized they had not talked on the phone during dinner in more than a month. She had thought it no longer fit into her daughter's altered summer schedule, but she should have seen it as a sign.

Hannah poured Hova a glass of wine that must have been close to half the bottle, then filled her own to match. Edgar carried the cookie sheet around the table and with a set of tongs dropped a T-bone on each plate.

"Medium rare, right?" he asked when he reached Hova. "I can throw it back on for a few minutes if you want it more done."

"That's perfect." She burped, bloated from the beer. Hova was already flush. She wasn't sure her stomach could handle that much meat. She reached for the overflowing bowl of salad.

"Karo won't tell us about his secret project," Hannah joked.

"I told you." Karo laughed. "It's business as usual. Just another big boat."

Edgar pointed his fork at Karo. "Of course it is, that's kind of your job."

"Ed says it looks biblical."

Karo shrugged. "A cruise ship could hold two of every animal and then some."

Hova devoured her salad. She had not seen any of the design work on Karo's latest project. All she knew is he had not even received a retainer for toiling all those hours yet. Their checking account remained the same, a crumb of it disappearing every time she went grocery shopping or bought a tank of gas.

"What do you know, Hova?" Edgar asked. He leaned forward to conspire. "Give us the inside scoop."

Hova sipped her wine. Was he making an ice cream joke to gauge her reaction? She could feel a piece of oily kale caught in her teeth. She shrugged. "Your guess is as good as mine."

Her steak was medium well, tougher than if Edgar had cooked it right. Edgar never did have his father's knack for the grill. Under-salted to boot. She reached for the shaker at the center of the table to hurt his pride. There was no helping a man without good taste.

Edgar glared while she seasoned her steak. A tiny piece of gristle glistened on his upper lip. Hova salted with abandon. She didn't care if she scoured her tongue. As long as it bothered Edgar, the rest of the meal could be tasteless.

"I was telling Hannah we should all make plans for Labor Day," Edgar mentioned. "We can force Joe and Tal to spend some time with family before school starts back up."

"I can dig Dad's old bocce ball set out of the storage room. We could grill some lamb chops."

"I was thinking something bigger. Maybe the beach?"

Hova stared at the table. Edgar could be cruel and unthoughtful. Why would he suggest bringing Karo to the water? None of them were ready for that yet. Hova never thought it was out of mere convenience that Karo had not left the basement over the past weeks. It was easier down there to forget they were on an island.

"Ed," Hannah warned, frowning. He tilted his head at her. "The beach might not be the best thing right now."

He winced and ran a hand through his hair. "We're all still figuring out how to move forward, but what are we going to do? Never look at a lake again?"

Hova was ready to tell him enough. She was in no mood for his bullshit and intentionally scratched her steak knife across the plate. It screeched in agony. Maybe Ed wasn't looking out for Karo at all. Maybe he was trying to actively harm his older brother. This was simply another way to push Karo's buttons, a chance to prove himself somehow superior. Edgar never could get over that Karo was smarter and more successful than he was, their parents' obvious favorite. Edgar was and always would be the second son. Hova swallowed a chewy morsel of overdone steak, ready to put a stop to his foolishness.

"He's right," Karo added, before she could speak. He fluttered his fingers over the candle flame waving in the wind at the table's center. "We can't hide from the water forever. I can't keep hiding from it, even if I want to. Mari wouldn't want us to. Maybe it would be good for all of us."

Edgar craned his arms with his palms out in Karo's direction to show his point had been made. Eyes wide, smug. The matter was settled.

"Even with all this heat, it hasn't felt like summer in weeks." Karo reached for Hova's hand. "We owe it to ourselves to try and spend a day outside together before the weather gets bad."

Hannah sighed. "I'm sure the kids would be happy to go."

"They won't want to spend the weekend with their friends?" Hova asked.

"They spend enough time with their friends," Edgar replied. "They've been doing whatever they please without consequence."

Hova coughed and stared at her food. "No one in this family really thinks about the consequences, do they?"

Karo grabbed her hand. "Hova, please."

Hova knew her husband thought she was talking about Mari, but it was too late to take back what she had said. She had eaten more than she expected. Nothing remained on her plate except the sharp jut of gristly bone in the middle of a pink sea. Her wine glass remained nearly full, but she was lightheaded. And so, it

was decided, another matter she had no say in: all of them pil-
ing in the car to bake under the unforgiving sun with thousands
of other Michiganders stretched across the coastal edges of the
Great Lakes State during a holiday weekend. She gulped her wine
and from the moment it hit her lips it did not sit well. The sun
was low in the sky. They had so much left to discuss, and none of
it would mean anything at all.

Hours later, Hova walked across the lawn with Karo's arm
around her. He was drunk and reeked of cigars and grill smoke,
but it was perhaps the closest she had seen him to normal in
weeks. It was past midnight. They had stayed until Joseph and
Talin returned for curfew. The twins had sat through a grisly horror movie in the theater with friends. One of the many violent
and loud stories about a child possessed. Hova imagined sharp
violins. Dark hallways. Supernatural powers. It wasn't difficult
to picture; she felt so haunted in her own house all the time. Her
imagination could run wild.

At home, Hova undressed and fell into bed. Karo did the same.
He needed a shower, but she didn't say anything. Hova laid on her
back in the dark under a sheet, the duvet pushed to their feet.
Karo mirrored her. He reached over and found her hand.

"Thank you for getting through tonight."

"Me?" she questioned. "What about you?"

"I knew it would make Ed feel better. He keeps stopping by my
office and I can't get anything done."

"You're placating him."

"We're both stubborn."

"And the beach?"

Karo squeezed her hand. "It might actually be a good idea."

Despite finishing her wine hours ago and switching to water, Hova felt like the room was in flux. She stared at the dark ceiling. She had drunk more than intended in momentary abandonment of her good sense. She did not want to forget a moment. Edgar had already ruined her walk that afternoon. Her stomach tightened. She was so tired, she would not sleep well.

"Garabed," she began, using her husband's full name. Hova was ready to break down and tell him everything. That she was scared he would never stop drinking and that she missed their daughter more than anything and that his brother was a selfish cheater. She wanted to have it all out, the misery and sadness and grief between the two of them, but she could picture how that would result in a night of them talking and pacing around the room, Karo going from buzzed to exhausted to hungover, Hova unsure of what to do but cry, and her head was sunk into the right spot of her pillow so that she was comfortable, even if only long enough to drift to sleep.

"Yes?" He sounded hopeful.

"Good night." There would be a better time. She was sure of it.

"Good night."

Karo Kurkjian

They could have visited one of the beaches close to the island without as much trouble, but Edgar insisted the three-hour drive to Port Austin would be more fun. A real road trip. They set out early in the morning, before sunrise, to beat Labor Day weekend traffic and avoid circling the beachfront parking lots along the water. It was a Sunday morning, but better to be on the safe side and arrive early. Without Ani, there were six of them, and they all crammed into Edgar's Ford Explorer. *A gas-guzzler*, Karo thought. *My brother does not think about the damage he is doing to the world.* He pictured his own Ford Focus hatchback electric, only a four-seater, parked next to its charger in the garage, and allowed himself to feel a little smug.

The drive was a straight shot north on M-53 past sprawling cornfields, fenced-off stretches of state land, and a few niche wineries that had recently cropped up along the highway. They stopped early in the drive on the outskirts of Sterling Heights for gas and snacks. Karo eyed the meter as Edgar spent an exorbitant amount of money filling the tank. As the numbers scrolled higher and higher, Karo got tired of waiting and meandered a lap or two around the parking lot to stretch his legs. Hova exited the gas station with a brown bag of pretzels and a ginger ale for him, as he was prone to car sickness. He felt a bit less stiff as they merged back onto the interstate.

"You remember the first time we all went to Chicago?" Hova asked.

"The twins were so small then," Hannah recalled.

Karo remembered. They had taken three cars. Ani followed them on her own, having recently passed her driver's test, until they stopped in Ann Arbor to pick up Mari. The girls brought up the rear for the rest of the trip. His daughter had been overjoyed to get out of the dorms for a couple days. Her freshman roommate was a nightmare: compulsively competitive, sleep deprived, catty, and she left her desk lamp on at all hours of the night. She also didn't tolerate any noise. Mari had complained to them incessantly over the phone about how she had to turn down her music or plug her headphones into her computer. He couldn't remember the roommate's name.

He was so proud of Mari when she decided to go to the University of Michigan. He remembered his own time there fondly, so he was surprised by how frequently his daughter returned home her first two years away. That first fall, he suspected it was as much because she was homesick as it was her dissatisfaction with her living situation. He wanted her to enjoy her college experience the way he had, but he secretly loved taking off half of his Friday afternoons to pick her up after her last lecture was out. If he drove alone, they would grab an early dinner at the food court in the basement of the student union: crispy chicken sandwiches and mushy fries from Wendy's or broccoli beef from Panda Express. If Hova decided to make the drive too, the three of them would pick one of the fancier restaurants on Main Street, then walk down Liberty past the Michigan Theater to State Street for Stucchi's ice cream, which was now closed. That December, the weekend they went to Chicago had been a spontaneous trip, a last-minute decision under the excuse of Christmas shopping.

"Joseph cried when he stood on the glass floor at the top of the Sears Tower." Edgar laughed. Karo watched his brother thoughtfully. He had never noticed that Edgar drove with one hand on the bottom of the steering wheel like their father. "We couldn't get him back in the elevator."

"I was seven!" Joseph yelled. "I thought the glass would break!" A string of licorice dangled limp from between his teeth. They all giggled.

Karo sat quietly as he recollected more details from the weekend. "You remember the girls thought they snuck out of the hotel?" he prompted. He didn't feel like finishing the story.

His wife chuckled to fill the silence and picked up where he left off. "Mari and Ani thought they could get away with anything since they had their own room. They didn't even see us waving at them from the hotel bar when they scampered out of the lobby."

Karo had been so scared when his daughter and niece bundled up to head out into the unknown city on their own after dark, but the others had assured him it would be fine. Mari lived away from home and Ani would be on her own soon enough. "I still can't believe Mari thought a fake ID would work for both of them. The irony was that by the time they got back, we were the loaded ones and they were stone-cold sober. I will never forget the look of terror on their faces."

"See!" Edgar glanced over his shoulder and smiled at Joseph and Talin in the third row of seats. "After all of your sister's hi-jinks, we've loosened up. You guys have it easy."

In Port Austin, they arrived at a calm waterfront. It was early and cool, the sun low in the sky, breezy, but a few other families must have had a similar idea of beating the rush and were already lining coolers and beach chairs and pup tents and pudgy, short-legged charcoal grills helter-skelter across the sand. A group of kids kicked around a soccer ball in no particular direction. The wind came in off the water and Karo could taste the grit in the air. He crunched a fleck of dirt between his teeth, closed his eyes, and listened to the rush of the lake. He hoped his brother had not neglected to fill the cooler with beer. He needed something to calm his nerves. It was so hard for him not to imagine his daughter standing on a faraway shore like this one before sprinting into the cold water and swimming away forever.

"We'll set up down the beach a bit," Edgar suggested. His brother was never satisfied with whatever was right in front of him. There was so much space for them to occupy without a problem, but instead they would trudge their stuff down to a uniform stretch farther away that might be vacant for the time being but would be as crowded as any other spot in an hour. Deep in his basement hideaway, Karo had not spent much time in the sun in the preceding weeks, and he could tell today would leave him grimy and fatigued and itchy with sunburn. His hands were cracked at the arid peaks of his knuckles.

Edgar led the family to a flat patch of sand near the incoming shallow waves, so that once everyone was situated, they were mere feet away from the uneven lines of approaching froth. They had two gigantic beach umbrellas, which despite their size did not provide enough shade for everyone. Joseph anchored his towel against the wind with his smartphone, backpack, and a shoe at each corner, then sprinted to the water. Talin followed not far behind. They had learned this habit from Mari: Get in the water as soon as possible. Shake off the cold. Don't overthink it.

Hova and Hannah dug their canvas chairs into the sand under the shade of one of the umbrellas. Edgar rolled the cooler between them to complete their little makeshift oasis. Karo copied his nephew and used his belongings as anchors to keep his towel from blowing away. He fell across the fabric, his head pounding. He was stiff from the car ride and curled his toes to stretch his legs. In the cooler, Karo found that Edgar had in fact brought plenty of beer, more than they would need if he would cling to an iota of self-control. He could always try to sneak his niece and nephew a bottle or two when their parents and his wife weren't watching. Edgar removed his Michigan State T-shirt, his belly and shoulders paler than usual, and Karo followed suit.

After Hova and Hannah slathered one another in sunscreen, they announced they were going for a walk. They sauntered shoulder to shoulder, surf crawling up the sand to their feet, until they passed a man flying a stunt kite down the blurry edge of the shoreline. The kite was in the shape of a wide V, a canvas sewn together with fabric vibrant shades of blue and red and yellow. The man must have been in his seventies or eighties, certainly much older than Karo, but he was tan and lean with muscled arms, though his skin sagged with age. The man leaned to one side and the kite dove toward the water, but then he deftly shifted his weight so that it glided over the waves and arced back into the sky.

Karo removed a beer from the cooler and tossed one to his younger brother. They were both wearing black sunglasses and black swim trunks. The kite looped one way, then the other. Karo was so thirsty he finished his bottle of beer while his brother still struggled to bend the bottlecap loose against his wedding band. Why Edgar had not purchased cans for once he was uncertain. They were superior to bottles in every way: more sustainable, easier to recycle, less light pollution, a longer shelf life.

"There's a bottle opener on the side of the cooler."

Edgar grunted. "I used to be so good at this when Hannah and I were first married, even before that. My class ring has a perma-nent dent in it from opening so many bottles at parties."

"I remember." Karo uncapped another beer. "But that was a lifetime ago."

Out in the water, all that was visible of Talin and Joseph were their heads, which bobbed up and down in the current. They were farther out than anyone else, conspiring. Joseph ducked be-low the surface and shook his hair like a dog when he reemerged. It was the longest Karo had ever seen it. He wondered how many months it had been since his nephew's last haircut.

"This isn't easy," Edgar confessed. He had pried loose the cap, but his finger was bleeding. Edgar assessed the cut and stuck the wound in his mouth to prevent a mess, always trying to play it cool. Karo didn't see either of their wives down the beach. He felt the sudden urge to join his niece and nephew. He needed to act on it before he talked himself out of facing the water.

"I'm going for a swim," Karo declared. Edgar's reaction was difficult to read. Karo held his open beer in one hand and removed two more from the cooler. Rejuvenated from the drink, he trotted off while Edgar sucked his finger. He picked up his pace into a languorous jog in the shallows, careful not to twist his aged ankles or cut his soles on zebra mussels, and waded up to his knees. The lake was much colder than he expected and when the waves reached his suit, he winced. When was the last time he swam? He glugged from the bottle. By the time his chest was covered, Karo felt frigidly complacent, the beer making its due course through his body.

"Hey," Joseph greeted him.

"I'm not interrupting, am I?"

"No," Talin replied. "We were talking about going back to school on Tuesday."

"I hope everything is okay." Karo was concerned for them. He remembered the monstrous ways adolescents gossiped, how their anguish could become cafeteria small talk, a spectacle or point of weakness. Adults were no better. They knocked one another down to nothing and thrived off of harming others. It was one of the reasons he hated trying to be productive in an office full of coworkers. As far as Karo was concerned, professionalism was a myth. Working for himself was one of the smartest decisions he ever made. He continued, "I imagine school will be difficult right now with everything that's going on."

"It'll pass," Talin said. So kind and compassionate, his niece. She was so unlike the rest of their angry and unforgiving family.

"Our family has survived a lot," Karo assured them. The open beer he'd carried out with him was gone and he used the neck of the empty to open the other two. He felt good and buzzed now. He pocketed the bottle caps. No matter the inevitable, he could not convince himself to litter. He peeked back at the shore. Edgar was at their camp alone, belly down on his towel in the sun, either asleep or oblivious. Karo passed the beer to his niece. "You're right, of course, we will survive this too."

"Dad never really talks about all that." Joseph splashed his own face. "Ani told us he used to bring it up more before we were born."

His niece faked a sip from the bottle and handed it to her brother. Too honest to even take a slug of beer from her uncle, he thought. He remembered finding Mari and Ani drunk in the basement when they were younger than Talin was now. Mari must have been sixteen and Ani fourteen. His daughter had only just passed her driver's test. They had tried to play it off like they were having a movie marathon in the basement, but the room reeked with the sweet scent of peach vodka and Sprite. He went along with their act, but later found the plastic filth buried beneath the sofa across from his workshop. His daughter was such a clandestine troublemaker during her high school years; his niece a much more transparent one.

He missed Mari so much in that moment, knowing that if she were out in the water with them, she would be encouraging her cousin to drink up. His daughter was fearless. What had changed? Maybe it made sense that Talin would not even risk a nip of lite beer. Joseph, on the other hand, drank greedily.

"When your great-grandparents died, many years apart, it was difficult for both of us. It can be complicated, bringing up those memories. It's our history, but it feels like it doesn't belong to us."

Joseph nodded toward the beach and pushed the bottle, half submerged, across the water to his uncle. Hova and Hannah had made their way back to their chairs.

"I don't know anything about our history other than what we learned in school," Talin complained.

Karo smiled sadly. He had framed the newspaper from the day Michigan passed a law making it mandatory for public schools to teach on the topics of the Armenian Genocide and Holocaust. "I'm sure your father will tell you if you ask him."

"Will you tell us?" Talin asked. Her eyes were bloodshot and shiny. She dunked her head below the water, but Karo was certain she had been about to cry. Soaked, she pushed the wet black hair back from her face and waited for his reply.

"It's not the right time," Karo hedged, deflecting. "It's too much to try and explain out here." The kite flew above them to the west. It dove down again, but this time the operator miscalculated, and it crashed in a burst of froth.

"I wonder if any of them will get in the water." Joseph nodded in the direction of their beach camp, shaking his wet hair.

"Your aunt might at some point."

"I'm surprised Mom isn't already out here," Talin said. "She would probably tread water just for the exercise. Dad never will, though."

Karo drank more beer. "He's always been a poor swimmer."

Joseph surreptitiously took the bottle from his hand. He splashed Talin to get her attention. "Remember when we were little, Dad told us he wouldn't get in because it would wash off his birthmark?"

"Birthmark?" Karo didn't remember this story. Edgar had no visible or memorable birthmarks.

"The one on his ribs?"

Shit, Karo thought. He forgot that Edgar used to call it that. Edgar had buried the stories of his rough and wild days in college. Hannah never liked him encouraging violence around the kids.

"That's a scar, not a birthmark," Karo revealed. He felt loose lipped. "Don't tell them I told you though."

"A scar?" Talin gawked. "From what?"

Karo glanced toward the shore. Hova and Hannah had disappeared again, maybe off to find a bathroom. Edgar had moved from his towel to one of the canvas chairs and was pretending to read a book. "A bar fight," Karo whispered. The twins' eyes widened in disbelief.

"It's not as bad as it sounds," Karo continued. The beer was coursing through him now and he could not stop talking. "A couple guys at a pool hall called him a camel jockey after he won some money. They ganged up on him. He spent a couple nights in the hospital, mostly bruises and cuts, but he broke an ankle, and one of his ribs was cracked through. He was on crutches for a while."

"No fucking way," the twins scoffed. Joseph took the last beer from Karo and chugged. When he had finished it, he coughed. "Oh, shit."

Karo followed Joseph's eyes to the beach. Hova and Hannah were glaring at them, arms crossed, unamused. He could feel the death stare from behind their sunglasses. "I should go back." Karo sighed. "I'm certain there's an earful waiting for me on the beach. Keep what I told you between us."

His niece and nephew gave him knowing expressions. He stuck the empty beer bottles over his middle and ring fingers and thumb and waded away from them. He slowly emerged from the water, and as more of his body rose out of the lake, he felt as if a monumental weight had been lifted from his frame. The water dripped off his shoulders and legs. He clicked the bottles together like talons, a scene from an old movie. Heat from the sun caressed his neck. He thought about turning around and diving right back in.

"Why are you encouraging that kind of behavior?" Hova asked, recrossing her arms.

"It's fine," Hannah assured them. "They're getting into much worse than splitting a warm beer. I'm pretty sure both of them were sick with hangovers last weekend. We'll drop the hammer on them once summer is over."

Hova pointed at Karo. "It's not your decision to make."

"You're right," Karo sighed. "I'm sorry. Please, let's not let it ruin the day."

The morning turned to midday turned to a hotter afternoon than expected, and the six of them rotated between lounging in the shade, lying in direct sunlight, and wading into the lake. Edgar was the only one not to dampen his swimsuit, refusing to march out past his shins. The beach was overcrowded and noisy. Joseph walked into a game of ultimate Frisbee with some locals. Talin read the summer novel assigned for her upcoming English class and blocked out the world.

By three o'clock, they were all lethargic and sunbaked. Karo could feel the burn on his shoulders and nose and shins, the beer overtaking his body. Even lying supine in the sand, he felt as if he was drifting through the thick of the lake. Every hour, he ran back out and paddled up to his neck to discreetly relieve himself. After their snacks were gone and the cooler was empty, Edgar suggested they call it a day and find a drive-through meal before the dinner crowd swarmed every restaurant near the highway. Hova and Hannah immediately started packing. Karo wondered how long they had been ready to go.

Edgar whistled to capture Talin's attention. Once it was clear they were leaving soon, she had left her book on her towel and swum out by herself for one last cool down. She didn't appear to hear him.

"I'll go get her. I need to rinse off anyway."

Karo trotted back to the water. The waves were tall and truculent compared to the morning. By now, he had made so many trips back and forth that the water neither felt cold nor warm. It was tepid and welcoming, familiar. Karo felt the serenity of its embrace and it filled him with a strange sadness. He understood why Mari had chosen to end her life this way. The lake was uncompromising, a force more powerful than anything else Karo could imagine outside of the Atlantic or Pacific. They would all be submerged in time.

Talin had her back to him. She was peering out over the endless sightline of blue. He called out to her, but she remained still. He could hear her sniffling as he approached.

"What's wrong?" he asked.

"Nothing." Talin wiped tears from her eyes. "This summer . . . it's just all been a lot."

"It's been a lot for me too," he admitted, sharing with his niece what he could not bring himself to say to anyone else. "I miss her so much."

They stood in the water staring at one another for a moment. Karo didn't want either of them to have to leave their hiding place. Out there, they didn't have to worry about keeping their emotions at bay. There was no need to explain their pain. Karo knew it couldn't last. He stuck his thumb over his shoulder like a hitchhiker. "We're heading home."

"I know. I heard him." She dunked her head again to rinse away the redness of her face and swam back toward the shore. Karo let his niece go ahead without him.

In the distance, a seagull struggled to lift a beige plastic grocery bag as if it was a big fish to carry off and devour. He remembered when Mari was in middle school and he helped her with a science project on the buildup of plastic in the ocean. *Captain Planet* had been their favorite show to watch together when she came home from school. When she got older, she was so interested in his work, fascinated by the environmentally friendly boats he toiled over for years at a time in his workshop.

For the sixth-grade science fair, he called in a favor from an old professor so they could access academic articles through the University of Michigan library, and they spent hours researching what types of plastic caused oceanic pollution, where the currents bunched it together into floating islands, and how such negligence and indifference was harmful to sea creatures and the planet at large. Karo compiled all of the statistics, of course, but seeing his daughter's growing outrage as she acquired new information filled him with an amalgamation of pride and fear. How bleak, Karo thought, for Mari to learn so young that humans were rapidly destroying life on Earth. What a terrible legacy his generation had passed on. A catastrophic inheritance. He had worried his daughter's climate anxiety would consume her. Maybe he was right. Maybe it had done just that. They were running out of time.

Karo pushed his feet free from the sand and leaned into a clumsy front crawl. As his face dipped below the surface, his senses were immersed in the rush of the lake, its sounds and movements all around him. His paddling was labored, but also soothing. He soon realized the bag was farther out than he had originally guessed. With each stroke, the detritus appeared to drift toward the horizon. Yet, every time he began to tire, it bloomed back into focus. The plastic glistened in the sunlight in front of him. As his breathing became strained, his left hand came down atop the bag and he dragged it to his side.

He was disoriented and his muscles ached, so he treaded water to get a sense of his surroundings. On the distant edge of beach, he could make out the puny figures of sunbathers and children running in the surf. Talin and Joseph were closer, standing in water up to their waists, waving for him to come back. They shouted but he couldn't make out their words.

His arms were gassed and his energy flagged; he allowed his body to sink. He didn't feel any ground beneath his toes. The whoosh of the water all around him was tranquil. Loud and silent at once. There was no reason to panic. He wondered what it was like for his grandfather to swim into deep water toward the salvation of rowboats all those years ago, if that part of the story was even true. He thought also about his daughter. Had she swam toward the same thing? He relaxed for a moment, then bobbed back to the surface and paddled with measured strokes until he was certain he could touch the bottom. Joseph and Talin met him in deep water. Talin must have been bouncing on her tiptoes. Karo held the bag high above his head.

"You had us scared," Joseph told him, his brow furrowed with worry. "We thought you caught a riptide. All that for a bag?"

The three of them arrived on the shore to concerned looks from beachgoers in every direction. A park ranger pulled up on a golf cart. Edgar and Hannah were huddled around Hova, who convulsed with sobs. Karo approached her and she softly punched him in the chest.

"All that for a bag?" she wailed.

"That's what I said!" Joseph yelped.

"For Mari," Karo tried to kiss Hova on the forehead, but she dodged his lips.

"I thought you were following her," Hova whispered. He could barely hear her.

"I would never do that to you."

She glared at him, unconvinced.

He walked by the onlookers until he found a recycling bin at the edge of the beach, where the sand met the parking lot. He smashed the bag through the circular hole meant for bottles and cans. When he glanced behind him, his family was lugging their belongings in his direction, ready to get as far away from the water as possible.

Joseph Kurkjian

Joseph waited longer than usual for the bathroom while Talin showered and readied for the first day of junior year. Her makeup was done and her hair was straightened and she wore school colors like she was excited to be back, even though he knew that wasn't true. Boys leered in every direction that first day back—and yes, he was among them—like they had spent the summer in isolation and were suddenly faced with all the girls their age at once. His sister was a shade darker than he was from afternoons on the pontoon with Gwen while he had sat at home playing games on his phone and hitting the heavy bag in the basement.

Talin drove them to school in silence. The first year with no busses or bike rides. Joseph even let her choose the music in hopes of cheering her up.

The car was spotless. They had cleaned it together on Labor Day morning. Joseph could tell something had been on her mind.

She spent most of the past month ignoring him after their fight in the garage, and one day when he had reached to remove her backpack from the backseat, she snatched it from him like it was full of dynamite.

"What's the plan today?" Talin asked him.

"Goddamn it, Tal." He was so tired of everyone treating him like he couldn't hold his temper. "This shit again, for real?"

"It's the first day back," she insisted, turning into the parking lot. It was already nearly full. "You think it won't come up?"

Joseph coasted his palm over the prickle of his buzzed hair while he let his other arm hang out the window. The haircut was an impulsive decision he made yesterday after their car was washed and drying in the sun. The barbers were closed for the holiday, so Joseph convinced his mother to dig their father's clippers from beneath their bathroom sink and shave his long hair away in the driveway. His mother hadn't cut his hair since he was a kid. His head felt lighter from the weight removed, down to a one-guard's worth of stubble. His only regret was waking up early that morning to realize there was a pale ridge along his forehead and the back of his neck. He should have gotten rid of his mane a few days ago so it looked more natural.

Talin pulled into a spot at the rear of the parking lot. His window pushed to a close and he shrugged his arm back into the car.

"You could warn me," Joseph said. Talin was provoking him, but he refused to get mad. She yanked her backpack out of the backseat and exited the car without responding. They wove through the maze of cars without speaking. It was the first year they weren't in any of the same classes.

Through the front doors, past a security guard and hall monitor talking over tall cardboard cups of coffee, Joseph felt naked with his bare head. He hated that at school he was always on display. Grosse Ile High School enrolled well under a thousand students and it was on an island he could bike around in less than an hour. He was a known quantity, even by the teachers whose classes he was yet to take. His haircut was a distraction. Ani had graduated a decade ago, his cousin nearly twelve years, but a few of the faculty remembered their last name, and everyone was familiar with it now anyway. There was an unshakable feeling of small-town awareness. He could sense people gossiping and judging his family.

Talin split away from him to meet Gwen and some other friends in front of a row of lockers. Gwen always looked good, put together, but Joseph had accepted he didn't stand a chance. He continued to the end of the hall to the corner spot where he'd met up with Cal and Eric every morning since freshman year. They leaned against the wall with their backpacks at their feet. He felt out of place in his plain black T-shirt with fuzz pilled in random spots, the damn bits he could never get off from the dryer.

"Dude," Cal exclaimed when he realized it was Joseph approaching them. "Nice. Looks tough. Can I touch it?"

Joseph leaned his head forward and Cal affectionately grazed a hand across his skull. Eric followed suit. Their caresses felt soothing. He never thought much about being taller than they were, but bowing over made it hard to ignore.

"Taking that boxing seriously," Eric observed. "You look ready for the ring."

"It's just too fucking hot." He lined up on the wall next to Cal with his backpack still hanging over his shoulders. There wasn't much time until the bell. His textbooks bulged thick and clunky against his shoulder blades. For some reason, he had packed *Musa Dagh* even though it weighed as much as a brick. He would have no time for leisure reading now. The summer had escaped from him and he was only three hundred pages in. Karo's notes were slowing him down. He tried to read past his uncle's musings and questions, but he couldn't help but stop to consider them. Karo's annotations were better than any cursory fact-checking he could do on his smartphone.

The halls echoed with chatter. A group of hockey players entered through the front entrance. Zack, flanked by a couple other seniors who would never make it on the ice past high school. Joseph felt an ache in his gut. He had been wondering for weeks if Zack was the reason his sister was acting so moody, ever since he peered out the back window of Gwen's house and saw Talin enveloped in his sweatshirt out on the pontoon. He didn't remember much from that night, but that image was clear in his head. The first bell rang. No one motioned to go to class. It was syllabus day after all. A joke.

Talin made eye contact with Zack as he passed. He could sense the pain in his twin sister's expression. No sixth-sense bullshit, he just knew her too well to doubt himself.

"She's a babe, dude," the kid on Zack's right said. Joseph didn't know him.

"As hot as her cousin." Zack laughed, not recognizing Joseph, even though he was in hearing distance. "Those Armenian girls are freaks."

Joseph lurched off the wall, finding his balance as his

backpack shifted around. He felt Cal's hand firm on his arm before it slipped away. Zack caught Joseph's eye and reacted to what was coming two steps before they met. Joseph flung his body forward, hands at Zack's chest, and attempted to push his opponent to the ground. Zack stumbled backward and the goons flanking him freed up some space. Joseph nearly fell forward before he found his balance. Bodies circled toward them and Joseph was surrounded immediately, at the center of a spectacle. He couldn't retreat now. He was hands down the underdog. Perhaps equal in terms of height and reach, but his opponent had at least forty pounds more muscle.

Zack carelessly shook his backpack loose from his shoulders. Joseph felt the weight of his own bag and wished he had not made such a rookie mistake. Hockey had taught Zack to shrug off any impediment right away. He was trained to fling his gloves and helmet to the ice to have a clear shot, knuckles to face, skin to skin, nothing interfering. Joseph tried to mimic him and clumsily slid the backpack off one strap at a time. He felt a fleeting surge of thankfulness that Zack waited for him; a moment of good sportsmanship. Joseph kicked the bag toward the wall. Zack didn't bother to raise his fists. He stood patiently waiting, palms forward as if ready for an embrace, provoking Joseph with his indifference.

Joseph approached cautiously, light on his toes, textbook boxing stance with the hope he could land a couple quick jabs and circle the perimeter, using the audience like a ring. He had trained all summer. He bounced on the balls of his feet. When he threw the first jab, fast and confident, his muscles fresh, he was confounded by how easily Zack slapped it away. He poked two more at Zack's jaw in quick succession, but landed nothing other than a passing glance on the shoulder. Joseph had to change tact. His mental clock was attuned to three-minute circuits. He was accustomed to exerting his energy until the bell dinged. A lifetime had passed in what he guessed was maybe twenty seconds. Desperate, Joseph tried a right hook, an unruly haymaker that shifted him out of position and brought his guard down. Zack evaded, found his center, and before Joseph could snap back Zack's fist was coming square at his mouth.

Joseph could feel where his upper lip tore against his top row of teeth. He balked, chin up, off-kilter, but before he could right his balance, Zack dug another fist into his solar plexus. Joseph felt deflated and fell to a knee. It was over as fast as it began. Zack picked up his backpack and shuffled away, surrounded by a shield of his teammates. The rest of the kids scattered like confetti and briskly walked to their classes. Joseph went from being at the center of the ring to being utterly abandoned. The bell rang again. He suppressed the urge to vomit. Talin was next to him. He couldn't remember how she got there. She helped him up. Derek the security guard jogged in their direction. Blood pooled under Joseph's tongue. He wiped his mouth with the back of his hand and thin streaks of pink spit glistened across his skin. He swallowed and couldn't breathe. Talin handed him a Kleenex from her backpack.

"You want to tell me what happened?" Derek asked. Years ago, Derek was a linebacker on the Grosse Ile High football team. He reminded Joseph of one of the superheroes from the Marvel movies, but he never remembered the actor's name. The one who played Captain America. Joseph remembered Mari and Ani talking about how hot he was when one of the movies was re-playing on television over the holidays.

"I slipped and fell on my face." Joseph dabbed at the mix of fluids dribbling down his chin. When he glanced at the white tissue there was a blotch the color of strawberry lemonade.

"Malarkey." Derek made a point never to swear around students, but Joseph couldn't help but laugh. This hardly seemed the time to fret over politeness.

"Doesn't matter." Joseph yanked his backpack from Talin's hand and limped down the hall, holding his gut. They were late to class. His first day attendance didn't matter.

"Mr. Kurkjian!" Derek shouted behind him. Joseph chuckled at the atrocious pronunciation of his last name. The fourth Kurkjian on Derek's watch and he still couldn't say it right. Everyone loved using that long *I*, like a country singer. "Where are you going?"

"Chemistry!" Joseph shouted. He realized Talin would be late for class too, stuck making excuses for him. If he wasn't so wounded, perhaps he would stay and take responsibility. Talin would be fine though. Derek was certain to have heard the whole tragic story of their family, and he would take sympathy and release Talin with a yellow hall pass and no questions. He couldn't imagine where he would go from here.

⁓

Talin had the car keys, so Joseph decided to walk home. He dug a spliff from a peppermint Altoids tin in his bag. He tucked the paper in his mouth as far away as he could from the fresh cut on his lip, but the first inhalation made him wince. He smoked while he wandered. He was in no rush to go home. His mom would be at the gym for a while, but then she would come back to shower and eat and change before running errands or whatever she did with her afternoons. He needed to wait it out until after lunch and hope she left again.

Heat radiated off the sidewalk. Joseph was thirsty and tired. He thought about their outing to the beach and how relaxed his uncle seemed before he swam out for that stupid plastic bag. For that brief time in the water, the two of them drinking beer and laughing, it felt like things were returning to normal. At least, the new normal. The ride home had been horrible. Long and uncomfortable, his father's classic rock on the radio cutting through their shared silence. Everyone tense. Starting back at square one.

The last time he saw Mari was also the first time he ever had a drink. Talin and him had driven to Milwaukee to visit their cousin for three days, since their spring break lined up with Mari's in mid-March. They technically didn't have their licenses yet, but their parents okayed the trip because they were picking up Ani in Chicago, who took the weekend off work and could serve as the adult in the vehicle for the final leg of the trip. The three of them continued together for the last hour and a half north through heavy metropolitan traffic into Wisconsin. They arrived early enough in the evening that a dull gray light hung in the air.

Mari was waiting for them with breakfast for dinner like their parents used to make when they were all home and no one wanted to put in the effort to cook a real meal. On the kitchen island, Mari had plated a mountain of scrambled eggs topped with melted cheddar cheese, pancakes the size of dinner plates, bacon and sausage leaking grease onto a bed of paper towels, fresh-grated hash browns they could drown in runny hot sauce, and orange juice and champagne for mimosas.

"I made a meal that would prepare your stomachs," she had said, winking at her younger cousins and giving Ani a conspiratorial nudge. "You'll be off to college soon enough, so we need to teach you how to chug a beer."

They ate the humongous meal and Mari gave them each a Tupperware container to build a leftover serving for the next morning. Mari's condo was nicer than Joseph imagined. It was the first time they had been there since she'd bought a place. Until the year before, she had rented a studio apartment near the school where she taught, and anytime they visited they'd have to build a nest of blankets on the floor because there was no bedroom or room for a couch.

The four of them played beer pong across the island. His cousin and older sister insisted on being teammates and chanted "pros versus schmoes" after they won the first two games by a six-cup margin. Joseph found he didn't mind the taste of the cheap beer—a thirty pack of Rolling Rock, which he was informed was a step up from the Busch Light that was apparently the norm for Michigan college parties—but was surprised by how quickly it filled his stomach and made him feel top heavy. By the time they were racking the cups for the third game, he thought he could sink into the couch and stay there for the rest of the night. He had smoked weed before and the occasional cigarettes when they were offered to him, but this was different. The feeling filled his body, uncontrollable.

"Isn't this weird for you?" Talin asked Mari. "Like you're partying with your students?"

"You're family, Tal," Mari cooed. "Besides, some of my students show up to class high or drunk most days, so I get to party with them all the time." She tossed the Ping-Pong ball directly into the front cup. "But instead of playing beer pong we talk about Shakespeare and Edith Wharton."

"I hated *Ethan Frome*." Joseph took the ball out of the cup and drank its contents. He threw the ball back, but without much arc, and it bounced off the rim of the front cup.

"Boys tend to," Mari lectured. "They can't handle that Wharton shows how weak and pathetic men can be."

The back-and-forth went on like that through the night until Joseph and Talin were both too tipsy and uncoordinated to put on a good showing. They didn't win a single game. Mari turned on a James Bond movie for them, one of the new ones with Daniel Craig, while they waited for an order of pizza and Crazy Bread to arrive. She asked about where they planned to apply for college and if they were dating anyone and what their parents were up to on the island. Ani was hooking up with a coworker at the restaurant where she bartended in the city and Joseph wasn't sure what to do while the girls talked about it. He tried to focus on the poker game unfolding in the movie, but it was difficult to tune them out.

The farthest he had gone was when a girl from his biology class rubbed her hand over his pants while they were prepping for a midterm exam at her house after school before her parents returned from work. It had been pleasant and exciting, but his jeans were gritty and coarse against his soft skin. She didn't keep her hand there for very long. They continued making out until the garage door rumbled open. Her father had looked at him like he knew what had occurred and Joseph spent the rest of their study session with the heavy textbook in his lap until he calmed down. The girl had not invited him back over.

When Mari and Ani forced Talin to field questions about boys in their grade, he lurched off the couch and went to the bathroom. He didn't want to hear any details about his twin sister's experience with the guys from their school. Assessing his reflection in the mirror, the depth of his intoxication finally sunk in. He could see it in his face and feel it in his body while he washed his hands. The girls stopped talking when he wandered back to the couch.

"The moral of the story is stay away from men, Tal." The doorbell buzzed and Mari met the pizza delivery boy at the threshold. Joseph checked his phone. It was only eight thirty and already he was exhausted and couldn't concentrate. He thought they had played beer pong for hours, but they hadn't even arrived that long ago. He felt light and dizzy.

"Don't worry, JoJo." Mari smirked, seeming to read his mind as she returned with plates and napkins and packets of Parmesan cheese. She was the only one who called him JoJo. "A little pizza will perk you right up."

His cousin was right, of course. The pizza fortified him, and they spent well until after midnight joking and catching up. The case of beer dwindled until it was gone and Joseph scarfed slice after slice of lukewarm pizza. When James Bond ended, they turned on *Planet Earth* until Joseph couldn't fathom how he was so tired earlier in the evening. In the nascent hours of morning, the four of them had fallen asleep piled across the couch and floor.

Joseph's spliff burned down to a nub and he squashed the roach under his foot. He absentmindedly wondered how many leaves were on the trees in his view, soon trying to multiply by how many trees he guessed were on the island. He thought about the whole state of Michigan, and couldn't keep track of the rounded zeros in his head. The number might as well have been infinite. Funny to think about, considering so many of them had been cleared and cut down. There could be so much of something without it changing the world's inevitable destruction. Imagine, all the leaves that would exist if trees weren't incessantly being killed—and Joseph puzzled over whether the total number of dead trees was larger than the number of those living. He continued trying to solve this made-up equation to pass the time until he realized he had walked straight back to his neighborhood. His mom's car stood guard in the driveway.

To avoid being seen, Joseph ducked into his aunt and uncle's garage. He wasn't sure whether Hova would be home or out. His throat was scratchy, and he needed a glass of water. A row of dusty model sailboats lined the shelving on the garage wall. As a kid, Joseph helped his uncle assemble one with wood glue. The process was meticulous and boring. In the end, the boat's mast wound up crooked from Joseph's impatience. His uncle ordered a second identical model and built it himself. The one Joseph worked on was now in his bedroom closet, gathering dust next to board games and the old clothes he had outgrown.

Joseph tried the back door. It was unlocked. Inside, the house was quiet.

"Aunt Hova?" he grumbled. Her walking shoes weren't in the laundry room. Joseph knew what they looked like because they weren't her usual style, more something his mom would wear. He lumbered into the kitchen and turned on the cold tap and dunked his head beneath the faucet. He wasn't feeling as high anymore, but his mouth throbbed where Zack had made contact. Every time he thought about the pain, his whole face tensed up. The water cooled him down and he let it douse his short hair and cascade over his torrid scalp. He shook himself dry like a dog.

His uncle was certain to be in the basement at his desk. Joseph was pretty sure Karo never left his office anymore. He came heavy down the basement steps so Karo wouldn't be alarmed.

"Joe." Karo peeked up from his computer monitor. "I thought maybe Hova was back from her walk early. Shouldn't you be in school?"

"It's the first day. It'll be okay."

"What happened to your face?"

Joseph shrugged. "Just some overeager sparring."

Karo chortled. "Come on."

An open bottle of brandy on the desk. Ararat. The infamous mountain. His uncle's tall Detroit Red Wings coffee mug rested next to it.

"Have a little." Karo gestured to the brandy. "I don't doubt you'll hate it. It's an acquired taste."

Joseph uncorked the Ararat and took a swig. He wanted to spit it out the moment it hit his tongue, but he forced it down. The cuts on his lips burned as though on fire. He shook from his head down to his waist and coughed. It was awful.

Karo laughed. "That's about right. I remember the first time my father let me have a taste. We were having a neighborhood barbecue out in the backyard. I was maybe fifteen or sixteen.

About your age. My dad accepted that Edgar and I drank beer when we were out, but he figured I'd probably never had the strong stuff. He was standing at the grill, smoking a cigar with your great-grandfather. Even in his old age, Papa was an imposing guy. My dad said, 'Go ahead, at your age your grandfather was preparing for war.' They smiled and pointed at the mountains on the bottle. After taking a shot, I threw up a hot dog and potato salad in the bushes."

"But the bottle has a picture of Mount Ararat. Not Musa Dagh."

Karo smiled. "Two different mountains with equally important symbolic value."

"Different and the same, I guess." Joseph picked up the bottle and inspected the label. His uncle wrinkled his eyebrows and waited for further explanation. "In the end, they're both places where people survived."

"That's true," Karo conceded. "I've never thought about it that way."

"I've been reading Werfel. Your notes are helpful."

Karo's face scrunched again. "That old book," he sighed. "It's a mess, isn't it?"

"It's definitely a slog."

"I don't only mean the length."

Joseph raised his eyebrows.

"Just don't let it tell you who to be," Karo warned. He drank from his mug and puckered his lips as he lowered it again. "That was a mistake of my generation. It's okay to learn from the past, to believe it is important to remember the past, to never forget the past, to let the past help you interpret the present, et cetera, without it solely defining you. There are many ways to fight."

"I'm not sure I get what you mean."

"Good!" Karo laughed. "You'll figure it out for yourself."

"I guess." Joseph massaged his hand over his swollen mouth.

"That whole side of your face will probably bruise. Did the other guy have it coming?"

"Fuck yeah, he insulted Tal."

Karo nodded.

"And Mari."

Joseph waited for the anger to blossom across his uncle's face, but Karo only grimaced. Joseph wanted to keep going, but Karo raised his hand and motioned him to stop.

"Please don't tell me. It will bother me for months if I know what the boy said."

Joseph thought about the video. He would never watch it, but a lot of people he knew had. Sometimes he worried Cal and Eric might. He wondered if his uncle ever thought about revenge. That guy was out there somewhere. They could find him. They could make sure he paid for what he had done.

"It sounds like he deserved it." Karo laughed again. "I'm sorry you got hurt in the process."

"I'm sorry I didn't do a better job standing up for her," Joseph sulked. "I thought I could be a fighter."

"Your context is different," Karo told him. "This is what I was talking about. Your circumstances are nothing like the past. You can't compare. Your great-grandfather was fighting for his life. Everyone was. Sure, he always put on a big show for others about his bravery, but he never forgave himself for the men he killed. He never knew peace."

"I can't imagine."

"And it's good you don't have to." Karo placed a hand over Joseph's purpled knuckles. "My grandfather was tough as nails. It's a tragedy you never met him. He was so proud to have lived to see what his family became, knowing they would never be in harm's way like him, but he was haunted until his final days. He never could escape what he did. Here, let me show you something."

Karo arose from his chair and slunk out from behind his desk. Joseph followed him to the storage room at the other end of the basement. Inside was a dusty mess: tattered beach chairs, threadbare kites, a full shelf of Mari's field hockey and track trophies, old boat sketches, a miscellany of car parts. Joseph peered over the decades of family junk the house had accumulated. His uncle bent over a plastic shelf in the corner and turned around with a canvas rifle case in his hands. Joseph let Karo pass and followed him back to the desk. His uncle slung the rifle case atop his drafting board.

"This was your great-grandfather's Mauser." Karo unzipped the case and butterflied it open. Joseph was surprised to see that the rifle remained in good condition, marred by nothing more than a spatter of rust on the outside of the barrel. It was like something out of a video game. A few rounds of ammunition were lined in a small pocket of the case. "Your great-grandfather refused to part with this rifle for what it symbolized, but he also never wanted to see it. It's been buried down here since long before he died. Your grandfather promised to hold on to it. Now it's another family heirloom stored along with all of our crap." Karo lifted the rifle to feel its weight. He handed it to Joseph to hold.

His uncle continued, "Even though Ottoman soldiers were trying to kill his family, Gregor was traumatized for a lifetime because he witnessed so much violence and suffering. The mountain doesn't offer happy memories. Your dad has probably never told you about our grandfather's night terrors or depression, even if they didn't call it that back then. When we stayed at his house in Dearborn as kids our parents would lock us in the guest bedroom so we wouldn't run out when he screamed in his sleep. He drank too much, ate to excess, smoked cigars in remorse. This is all to say that whoever the guy is who did this to your face said something that hurt you, but hurting him back probably won't bother him as much as it bothers you. It will stick with you and haunt you. Even if you're on the right side, it doesn't mean you don't live with the pain."

"Why . . . why show me the gun then?"

"Have you ever held a gun, nephew?"

"No."

"Does it make you nervous, the weapon right in front of you, in your grasp if you wanted, one that has in fact killed people?"

"Yes."

"Imagine then what it means to use it. Imagine what it means to hurt someone, whether with your fist or your words or worse. We don't need this rifle anymore. No one should need guns. There's already so much violence in a world, a world closer to the brink of destruction every day. We're already all going down with the ship. Why add to it?"

"I think I see what you're saying." Joseph nodded. He was ready to go home and sleep. His mother must be gone by now. He wanted to ask his uncle one last question. "Does it bother you when you work on warships?"

"I've always been torn about it," Karo admitted. "They'll be made either way, I just help them run more sustainably. My hope is that in some small way my work will help them kill less."

"But they can save people too, right? Look at our family legacy. Those French ships."

Karo grunted. "Don't confuse this. Weapons are never designed to help people. Their singular purpose is harm. Violence is what they are meant to do. Any other use—self-defense, heroism, protection—is coincidental."

Joseph rubbed his neck. He turned to go back upstairs.

"Nephew," Karo slurred. Joseph paused and looked over his shoulder. "Don't tell your father I said this, but I would've taken a swing at him too."

Joseph smiled. His anger would return in waves, but for the moment he was floating.

At home, Joseph showered, roamed the empty house in a towel, and turned the television on SportsCenter. He dressed in comfy clothes, loaded a sandwich bag with ice cubes, and plopped down on the couch. He nursed his swollen face. After emerging from the basement, he had stood at his aunt and uncle's kitchen door and confirmed his mom's car was gone. He decided it was a safe bet she would remain away from the house long enough to never find out he skipped school. He hoped his father was too distracted at work and would miss the email from the front office alerting him of Joseph's absences for the day.

Joseph fell in and out of a stiff nap. A little after three, Talin barged in without bothering to take off her shoes.

"How was school?" he asked.

"Unbelievable." She ducked back into the laundry room to hang her backpack on a coat hook. "Where'd you go?"

"I walked home. It's not a big island, sis."

"Your phone is off."

He scowled. "Would you want to see videos of someone beating the shit out of you from every angle on Instagram?"

"No one is telling you to look at it. I've been texting you all day. I drove around at lunchtime trying to find you."

Joseph flipped the channel while Talin loomed over him. He hit the button again and again as if it would change the situation. Talin tromped off toward her room. Joseph did not know what to say to her. All of them, he thought, were like little boats floating off in tumultuous currents, no sense of direction. He flipped the station again and landed on *Law & Order*. He hated that Ani had gotten him hooked on it during her short time home. They couldn't even sit down in silence without the constant reminders of tragedy: people lost, bloodied bodies, sirens shrieking, police lights aglow.

His sister returned and sat on the opposite side of the sofa.

"All you had to do was walk away."

"So what? That hockey asshole can keep thinking he's hot shit?" Joseph asked. "I hope one of the puck fucks gives him chlamydia."

"Stop! Don't talk about women like that."

"I didn't mean it like that."

Talin rolled her eyes and plopped her hands across her chest. "Then how did you mean it?"

"It was just a joke."

"Not a very funny one," Talin fumed. "If you talk like that, you're no better."

"Better than who?" Joseph glowered at her. He couldn't believe she was comparing him to them. He rose to his feet. He felt menacing, towering over her. He remained that way, eyes locked with her, for a few passing breaths. The television flipped to commercials. "Who, Talin?"

She stared at the coffee table. The same red ceramic bowl overflowing with candy at its center since the day they were born.

She sighed, defeated. "Have you *read* any of the things men said about Mari?"

Joseph hurled the remote control across the room and it dented the drywall. Talin flinched. The batteries flew out and ricocheted to the floor behind the television stand. He stomped off to his bedroom and closed the door. There was still vodka under the bed. He excavated it and downed the last couple slugs. He texted Cal and asked if his older brother would buy him another fifth.

It felt impossible for him to do anything right. All his life he tried to stand up for his sisters and cousin when friends said disparaging shit about them, but if he turned violent or angry, he was the bad guy. He was only trying to make a point and Tal had turned it into an argument. He didn't know what to do with his anger.

Joseph cranked his music to the max volume. The first warm waves of alcohol drifted through his body. He turned his phone back on, but ignored the string of messages from Talin and Cal and Eric. The subwoofer felt like an earthquake. Hip-hop was his inheritance from Mari and Ani. Sure, he listened to the new stuff on the radio, the up-and-comers his friends on the track team insisted were better than anything on the charts, and dug into the vault with Spotify playlists focused on the golden age, but it was the passed down Eminem tracks he kept blaring on repeat. Slim

Shady had grown up down the road. Off the island, but nearby, nonetheless.

There was something about being geographically close to the music, feeling the full fury of the Midwest in Slim's unrelenting lyricism. Mari and Ani cycled through old Eminem albums until the CDs skipped more than they played, scratched to the point of being unreadable. It made sense to him that Eminem was mad at everyone. There was too much bullshit in the world to not be pissed off. The calming buzz made him feel like he was sleep-walking. He flopped across the bed and let the music wash over him. No one would assign homework on the first day. He could easily catch up tomorrow. His phone buzzed—a text from Talin. *I fixed the fucking remote.*

I'm sorry, he wrote before deleting it and tossing his phone out of reach. He wished Ani were home. She would know what to do. He dozed off with the music so loud he couldn't tell whether or not his ears were ringing.

A pounding at the door shook him awake. "Joseph," his father yelled, "come out for dinner. We need to talk. Now!" Joseph shot up, his throat scratchy. He appraised himself in the mirror to make sure his eyes weren't too red. He unwrapped a stick of spearmint gum in case there was any alcohol on his breath. His short hair looked more natural now, as if it had filled in over the course of the day, and his tan lines were faded. Skin flakes fell from his scalp and he realized he might have a slight sunburn from the walk home. Half his upper lip was puffed up like a discolored slug and his cheek was dark purple.

"Shit," he whispered. His father banged on the door again. Joseph turned off his speakers. "I'll be right there!"

At the dinner table, he sat down next to Talin, across from his mother and father. His mom had baked chicken breasts and sweet potatoes. There was an arugula salad with walnuts and pumpkin seeds and feta cheese. A dripping glass of milk was already set next to his empty plate.

"Your face," his mother sighed. She glanced back and forth between Joseph and his sister, as if trying to decide who was more likely to provide an explanation.

"What the hell happened?" Edgar asked. "This is why you were out of school all day?"

"It's nothing."

"I didn't say anything about that dumbass paintball welt," Edgar grumbled. Joseph could tell he was doing his best not to shout. "But it's not the summer anymore. Use your head for once!"

"It's not that bad," Joseph insisted.

"You're grounded," his mother added. "And we're taking the punching bags out of the basement for a while."

"Fuck that." Joseph swallowed his gum.

"Language!" Hannah whispered hotly.

"Look at your face. All that conditioning clearly hasn't been paying off," his father sneered. "And you do not speak to your mother that way. We're tightening up around here. Tal, did you see what happened?"

Joseph turned to his sister, who was cutting up her chicken breast as if they were having a normal dinner conversation. She stared at her meat and shook her head. He wanted to hug her and apologize. Why was he being such a prick to the only person looking out for him?

His mother stood from her chair and walked over the freezer.

She found a bag of frozen peas. "Ice your bruise at least. It'll go away faster."

Joseph smushed the cold bag above his mouth next to his nose.

"You could have been suspended," Edgar growled. He wanted to tell his father he was one to talk, now that he knew about the scar, but didn't want to out his uncle. Talin kept her head down. Her food had nearly vanished from her plate. Why wouldn't she say something?

"I was trying to stand up for what's right," Joseph argued. It sounded cryptic. Only Talin would know what he was getting at. His head was foggy from the booze and he was hungry. He just wanted to eat and return to his room.

"What do you mean?" Hannah asked. Her expression had softened. Joseph could always see her emotions in her eyes, whether his mother was angry or scared or concerned. She wore everything on her sleeve.

"Nothing."

"Talin is in charge of the car until we say otherwise," Edgar decreed. "No driving. No nights out. When your face has healed, we can talk."

Joseph nodded his assent and stabbed his fork into the meat. They spent the rest of the meal silent under the din of forks and knives. Talin asked to be excused early and fled back to her room. Joseph ate three full chicken breasts, two sweet potatoes, and drank two glasses of milk. He skipped the salad.

Edgar ordered him to do the dishes. When Joseph finished, his parents were on the couch facing away from him in front of the television.

He lumbered down the hall and to his bedroom and texted

back and forth in a group chat with Cal and Eric. Joseph was not surprised to find everyone was talking about how he got his ass kicked. The following day at school would be hell. He wanted to cocoon into his comforter and emerge around Halloween, transformed. Maybe the heat would have finally died down. He spent the night sweating through his sheets.

The next morning Talin was sick with the stomach flu. Joseph waited with his mother, who was convinced she had undercooked yesterday's chicken and caused this whole fiasco, for Tal to finish throwing up so he could shower and shave. They sat with their backs against the wall next to the door. His mother nestled a sleeve of Saltines and a glass of water in her lap. Joseph had demolished half of the crackers by the time his sister came out. Joseph wanted to accuse her of faking, but she looked too awful for that to be the case. While Hannah tended to her, Joseph took over the bathroom and closed the door, locked it, undressed, and hopped in the shower, swishing the curtain back behind him, all before he exhaled. He hoped to avoid the odor of vomit, but it was pungent and monopolized the room. He ran the water cold, coaxing the smell to dissipate faster. He still wasn't used to how much the temperature of the water falling over his short hair could cause his scalp to shiver or burn. He tried to shave in a rush and his gummy razor caught the swollen skin beneath his mustache, leaving a cut like a little bloody frown. He covered it with a dab of toilet paper and gathered his books for the day.

It felt nice to drive without anyone else in the car, his grounding already compromised by his sister's illness. Hannah did not want to bother chauffeuring him. He opened all the windows and the sunroof and thought about speeding around the island, but instead scrolled to an old Kanye West album on his Spotify and drove slow. He craved a cigarette. Everyone at school had vape pens, but he thought they were silly. He didn't want his smoke to taste like bubble gum or cotton candy and figured that's how you could actually get addicted. He liked known quantities. He parked in one of the back spots in the school lot and waited until the bell was about to ring. The fewer people he bumped into the better.

He spent the morning with his head down reading over the syllabi he missed the day before while trying to keep up with the lectures. People asked him about his face throughout the day, wanting to view the swirl of purple and sickly yellow for themselves. Some were kind and others were cruel, but he knew better than to cause any more trouble. For once Joseph decided to stay cool, even if it felt like a defeat. He embraced what he was walking into.

Lunch with Cal and Eric was uneventful. They asked about how Joseph's parents had reacted, and Joseph deflected as much as possible. Cal's brother had purchased Joseph a fifth of green-apple vodka. They moved the bottle from one backpack to another under the lunch table. Joseph slid Cal a twenty.

In fifth period, Joseph asked for a pass to use the restroom. He always drank too much water at lunch. The halls were empty and quiet except for the clop and echo of his sneakers. He walked into the boy's bathroom and found Zack at one of the sinks meticulously washing his hands, lathered with soap down past the wrist like he was a surgeon.

"Hey."

Joseph ignored him and unlatched his belt in front of the urinal. Someone had spit a white wad of used gum out and landed it right on the pink deodorizer at the center. He hated using the bathroom at school.

"I wanted to apologize for yesterday," Zack continued as he rinsed the soap from his hands. Joseph didn't like having his back to him. He felt vulnerable, exposed. "I didn't mean for shit to escalate like that."

Joseph pulled the lever to flush and adjusted his shorts. "Maybe don't talk about my sister then."

"I was just shooting the shit, man." Joseph turned around and Zack faced him, leaning against the wet counter. "You know how it is when you're joking around with other guys."

Joseph scoffed, "Locker room talk."

"Ooph." Zack looked offended. "I didn't mean it like that. That guy is a prick."

"Tell me the difference then."

"I'm sorry." Zack brought his hands up in surrender. Joseph veered past him to the other sink. "Look, I like your sister a lot."

Joseph felt fire blaze behind his eyes. "You stay the fuck away from my sister."

"That's not really your choice, is it?"

"Whatever, man." Joseph shrugged derisively. "An asshole like you? You have no shot anyway."

"Okay, Joe, sure." Zack walked to the door while Joseph shook the excess water from his hands. "If that's what you think."

By the time Joseph dried his hands and exited the bathroom, there was no sign of Zack in the hallway. He returned to class frustrated and confused. Why would Talin ever fall for a guy like that? It felt like a betrayal. He couldn't ask her about it. He didn't want to know.

After school, when Joseph pulled into the cul-de-sac, Mari's dirt-spattered Subaru was in their driveway.

Ani was home.

He sped into his parking spot. Inside, he lugged his backpack to his bedroom and slid the booze under his bed, then went to look for his sisters. Laughter echoed across the hall from Talin's room. Neither of his parents were around.

Talin and Ani were sitting next to one another on the bed. He could tell Talin had been crying. She tried to hide the wad of tissues in her fist.

"You're back."

"Joe." Ani smiled, visibly taking in his battered face. "Nice haircut." She stood and he walked over to embrace her. He squeezed her tight. She was tan and wayworn.

Joseph let her go and looked over at Talin. "Everything okay?"

"Just not feeling well," Ani told him. She reached up and rubbed a hand through his hair. "I like it, makes you look even taller somehow."

"Tal," he started. He itched at his head, retracing the spectral lines of Ani's fingers. "I'm sorry about yesterday. I was out of line."

"It's fine." Talin wiped her eyes. "To be honest, it wasn't really about you."

Joseph turned back to his older sister. She looked different. He couldn't pinpoint the change. Not older, but aged. "I didn't think you'd be back this fast."

Ani glanced at Talin. "It seemed like I'd spent enough time away. Talin's been texting me, keeping me updated. I thought it would be good to come home for a little while."

Joseph nodded. She had to be home because of his fighting

or Uncle Karo's stunt at the beach, but he didn't see why it mattered now. Ani punched him on the shoulder. "Did you finish Werfel yet?"

"Are you kidding?" Joseph groaned. "I'm not even halfway through it."

"How are we supposed to talk about it then? I'm rereading."

Joseph's stomach growled and he rubbed a hand over his abdominal muscles out of habit, but his hunger had dissipated. "I'll get to it." He walked over to Talin and sat on the edge of the bed to give her a hug. Talin swung her arms around him, but he could tell she wanted him to leave them alone. As soon as he walked out of the room, Ani shut the door behind him.

He wanted to know what his sisters were discussing across the hall, but was unwelcome for the time being. *Musa Dagh* sat heavy on his dresser. He grabbed the book and plopped down. He thought about turning on some music, but the quiet was comforting for once. Every burst of laughter from his sister's room made him grin. He would read until dinner was ready, then Ani's stories from her road trip would provide a much-needed distraction from his darkening bruise that only grew more hideous by the hour. It had been a few days since he picked up the book, and it felt like reading it for the first time.

Ani Kurkjian

When Ani was preparing for seventh grade and Mari was about to enter high school, their family took their first big backpacking trip. The girls weren't sure what had gotten into their parents, because none of them had experience beyond car camping. Karo checked out two guides from the public library and learned all the essentials. Then their dads spent a rushed afternoon in REI purchasing enormous backpacks, hiking boots, food storage cannisters, basic first aid, and a red can of spray to fend off black bears. They bought matching headlamps and wool socks, plastic sporks and neon water bottles. The twins were too young, so they were left with an old family friend of their grandparents.

"Where do we poop?" Mari asked moments after they parked Edgar's brand-new minivan in a makeshift lot on the shoulder of a dirt road and set off down a thin, branch-laden trail toward their site.

"In a hole," Edgar replied, his black mustache contrasting the grin of his teeth. "Dig and bury. We brought everything you'll need."

"What about toilet paper?"

"We found some that's biodegradable," Karo shouted back. "You bury that too."

Near the shoreline, steep dunes plummeted all the way to the blue shallows below. There were no trees along the shore, only endless hilltops of sand that hurt Ani's eyes when she stared out over them for too long. The wavy, beige expanse stretched along Lake Superior as far as she could see.

They continued their trek on the far side of the dunes for half an hour without chatter, but after a mile or two Mari exclaimed, "Jesus, it's like you're marching us into the desert."

All of the adults stopped dead in their tracks and looked at her in horror.

Ani couldn't believe it. She had no idea what had gotten into her cousin.

"We don't joke about that," Karo growled. Her uncle could be stern, but it was rare to see him visibly angry. "Never joke like that. Never. Your younger cousins haven't even learned about all that yet."

"I didn't mean anything by it," Mari protested.

"Damn it, Mari, it doesn't matter how you meant it. If you joke about something that most people don't even remember, how can you expect them to take it seriously?" Ani's uncle raised his voice. She was used to him being more patient and laidback than her father, but his anger consumed him now. "Mari, do you understand?"

"Yes, I understand." She nodded, her lip quivering. "Sorry, Dad."

For the rest of the four-mile hike they walked in silence, a single file line with Mari and Ani whispering as they languorously brought up the rear. Mari pouted and stomped extra loud at the sticks on the ground. The twigs cracked and snapped, as brittle as bones.

Ani wondered what her younger siblings were doing. A boy in her class had smirked that, given the large age gap between them, the twins were probably an accident. Later, when she told Mari what the boy said, Mari told the boy's older brother, another freshman who had a crush on her. The boy, bruises up his arms, sheepishly apologized to Ani the next day.

That evening, after pitching their tents, they boiled a pot of water over a teeny kerosene burner, and it took over an hour to warm everyone's meals—bland, individual portions of grains and vegetables stashed away in clear plastic pouches. At sundown, Karo doled out globs of toothpaste for everyone before sealing all of their food and toiletries away in a drawstring bag. He hooked it with a long pole—much like the one her father used to hang Christmas lights across the pine trees in front of their house after Thanksgiving—and placed the bag atop another metal pole near their campsite. Around a small bonfire, Karo told a ghost story about a man with yellow eyes, but no one thought it was scary, because he kept messing up the suspenseful portions and added revisions as he talked his way through it. By the climax, there were so many amendments and asides that no one could follow what was happening.

The part Ani remembered most fondly was later that night. Long after everyone went to bed, Mari elbowed Ani's sleeping bag. They were given their own tent while their mothers slept in another. Their fathers had hung canvas hammocks between the trees and slept cocooned beneath mosquito nets, Rambo knives and bear spray across their chests, holding on to some sort of masculine ideal of guarding the site.

"Wake up," Mari whispered. "I have to pee."

"So go pee then," Ani mumbled, turning back over in her sleeping bag.

"How am I supposed to see? It's pitch-dark out there."

"Use your headlamp."

"But what happens if a bear comes up behind me?"

Ani sighed, exasperated. "Listen, why did you say that dumb shit about the desert earlier? You knew they'd get mad."

"Don't worry about it."

"You can tell me."

"I'll tell you if you come with me to pee," Mari wheedled.

Ani rolled her eyes in defeat. "Ugh. Fine."

Mari unzipped the tent flap between her thumb and index finger to muffle the noise. Ani exited behind Mari on the far side of the tent. They shined their headlamps out into the darkness, making sure not to turn toward their dads' hammocks. The men were snoring, and Ani doubted they would've noticed anyway. They were heavy sleepers, brothers alike in a million ways, down to their thick eyebrows and prematurely graying sideburns. Other than the beams shooting out from Ani and Mari's fore-heads, everything was too dark to distinguish. A black bear could be standing right next to them and they wouldn't know it. Ani couldn't even make out the sky above the canopy of trees. It was the darkest place she had ever been. They walked a few dozen paces and Mari started to speed up.

"Don't you think we're far enough away from camp for you to piss?" Ani asked. She was relieved to use such language after a day of minding her mouth in front of their parents. She and Mari cursed all the time when adults weren't around. Ani didn't want Mari to think she was afraid, but the darkness was astounding, like the scenes from *The Blair Witch Project*, which they had watched during a sleepover. She felt lost in an abyss.

"C'mon." Mari turned toward her, but not enough to blind her with the headlamp. "I don't have to pee. We're going to the top of the dune."

"What?" Ani asked, her voice louder than intended. She didn't want her voice to carry. "What about bears?"

"Black bear sightings are rare, and we can scare one if we need to. We just need to shout and look big. I read the pamphlet at the ranger station while you were in the bathroom. We're fine. Trust me on this."

"What if we get caught?"

"Trust me."

Ani, not wanting to wimp out in front of her cousin, obediently followed Mari down a narrow path that soon led up a steep hill to the top of a secluded sand dune overlooking Lake Superior. When they emerged from the forest, it felt as if the sun was rising. The water was black as oil, but Ani could see the peaks of waves flicker in moonlight. There were more stars than she'd ever seen. The Milky Way was glowing and immense, enough so that Ani could see the light shadow of her body across the ground.

"So why the joke?"

Mari sighed. "A guy asked me out this weekend. A junior with a car. It would have been a real date, not the weird shit where my dad drops me off and talks to his parents. But they made me cancel to do this."

"Isn't this better though?" Ani asked, worried Mari was bored of her.

"Now it is." Mari laughed. "It's always more fun when it's just you and me."

"I don't know why they got so mad. I can't figure out what you were talking about."

"Do you remember the story we were told when we were little?"

Ani tried to recall their great-grandfather. She could barely remember his face, but could visualize where they once sat on the lawn in front of him. "All I remember is that he lived next to the sea. I wonder if it looked like this."

"Let's go there someday," Mari said. "We'll see the whole world together."

"Deal."

They counted shooting stars for hours and gabbed on and on about whatever came to mind after that, boys and music videos and summer camp, until they tried to sneak back into their tent when the morning was too dark to be considered morning at all, and where their fathers, having waited patiently for their daughters for nearly an hour, hidden behind gargantuan oak trees, pretended to be black bears and snarled and pawed at the tent, scaring the shit out of Mari and Ani so that their shouts woke everyone at the nearby campsites before dawn.

Ani had deposited her first spoonful of Mari's ashes on that same dune in the first light of sunrise. Lake Superior was as beautiful as she remembered: serene, vast, clear, endless, somehow hidden from the pollution tearing away at the rest of the world. It amazed her to find an area so unchanged. Her campsite was exactly as her family had left it fifteen years ago. She spent four nights reading books under a lantern in her tent, wishing she had asked Hova to save some of Mari's library for her. As far as she knew, and to her great irritation, everything had been sold. She had packed the dozen books her cousin lent her over the years that she never got around to reading.

During the day she rented a kayak and paddled along the cliffs, which were layered with shelves of multicolored rocks a hundred feet high. She ate overpriced sandwiches soggy with mayonnaise in Munising, the town down the road, and wrote copious notes in a fresh Moleskine journal. Mourning, she thought, is thinking through everything, and so she willed herself to think through it. She also wanted to have a record of her travels whenever she got off the road.

On her last night in Michigan, Ani wrote down the earliest memory she had of her cousin. The two of them nuzzled up on their great-grandfather's lap, rocking in the chair where he snoozed while they played with dolls. The family was celebrating an anniversary or birthday or new job, some vague milestone. All the parents drinking and celebrating while Gregor rested with the children. That was years before her family moved to the island. Her parents had joked around in the front seat as they drove home in the pouring rain, happy as they had ever been.

Ani made several more stops on her way west, spending a week's stretch in the Badlands, but she didn't stay anywhere else for too long until she reached a small village on the edge of Glacier National Park. Polebridge, Montana, was peaceful. A town of no more than three dozen in the winter, maybe a hundred during camping season. Ani parked her car in a dirt lot, then set up her tent at a distance from a tiny bar, the Northern Lights Saloon, and the Mercantile, a local bakery and general store that had serviced the region for more than a century.

She wasn't sure how long she planned to stay. The cold wet ground could suck the warmth out of anything, and she was sore from nights on her thin sleeping pad or curling up under a blanket in the back of Mari's Outback.

The national park tour was not going exactly as she'd expected. Only having stopped at a couple state parks in Wisconsin and Minnesota, the Badlands, and Mount Rushmore, it was clear her funds would dry up faster than she'd hoped, and she fantasized about the hot shower and freshly laundered bed of a hotel room. The nomadic lifestyle was more mundane and exhausting than Instagram had led her to believe. Once she settled her camp, it was difficult not to get overwhelmed by the vastness of each distinct place—Glacier alone was nearly sixteen hundred square miles—but she would find herself tired from unpacking the tent, putting together a warm meal, and cleaning up afterward, so that some nights all she had the energy to do was gather enough firewood for the evening or sit around reading Mari's books and writing in her journal. If she wanted to change locations, the process began all over again.

But she liked Polebridge and the locals seemed to tolerate her, so she had kept her site for the past five days with no intention of heading out right away. Most mornings, the urge to pee awoke her before anyone opened up the Mercantile. The store unlocked its doors at seven a.m. sharp from Memorial Day to Labor Day, and usually whoever was behind the counter was there much earlier. Her camp was not close to the storefront, but the area was so quiet that the creak and slam of the screen echoed a quarter mile away.

The sun hadn't yet risen, but it was a matter of minutes, drawn out as the darkness slid away from its blues and grays to a burst of oranges and reds. Ani checked her body for ticks and picked the miscellany of detritus from her hair that had collected in the night: sleeping bag fuzz, dead bugs, grains of sand. Her mouth was dry, and she needed to brush her teeth, but she decided to hike around for a while before the day was too hot, even without her boots. In South Dakota, she met a septuagenarian in moccasins who swore by them, claimed he wore them for long hikes and running marathons and lounging around alike. She thought his arches must be made of steel.

Her favorite spot to walk was through a patch of forest that had burned a few years earlier, row after row of bare blackened stumps climbing high like gigantic, charred toothpicks stuck into the ground. All the branches reduced to ash. She thought it was a fitting place to part with another spoonful of Mari's remains. The ground was already full of charred carbon waiting to reemerge into something new and beautiful. Ani imagined her cousin's ashes amongst the wreckage in the soil, muddling together with the snow and rain until a lush forest bloomed and her cousin was part of its green birth.

The mason jar went with her nearly everywhere. If not, she kept it wrapped in a beach towel in the trunk of Mari's car. Before leaving Michigan, she had purchased a pack of two plastic camping sporks, a blue one for her food and a green one to apportion out the jar's contents. She didn't want to risk spilling too much by tilting the brim. When she finished, she wrote a description of the surroundings in her journal, enough detail to remember the location if she ever returned.

It amazed her how far she could see. She thought about driving past boundless acres of cornfields in Michigan and how, for a split second, each row revealed a narrow hallway with no end in sight. Distance broken down in natural increments, the necessary measure for life to grow and thrive. The sun was visible now, low and beaming at the horizon. Ani wandered back toward town.

It had been a couple days since she had checked her cell phone, which was buried in the glove compartment of Mari's Outback. The temperature would have long since drained the battery, and it had been nearly a week since she charged it. Even when it was powered, she had limited the device to its bare essentials, deleted every app that wasn't necessary. She plugged the phone into the dashboard and waited a few minutes for the juice to return.

There were several missed calls. Hannah called every night in hopes that she would answer. It was an unspoken agreement that whenever she did turn her phone on, the first thing she did was send her father a text message, a few rushed words informing them she was fine. Most of her friends and co-workers in the city had stopped contacting her. They could only be supportive for so long and had forgotten about her now that she was out on the road. But there was a pair of texts from Talin.

I need you. Please come.

Soon.

Ani knew her little sister. Talin was more collected and level headed than anyone else in their family, even at sixteen. She wouldn't send a message so brief and desperate unless something terrible was happening at home. She had used the phone so little it felt as if her thumbs had forgotten how to type out a response.

When her words did come, they were plain and unoriginal. *What's wrong?*

She sat in the driver's seat and ate a granola bar, drank water from a bottle she'd left in the cupholder. Was Talin back in school yet? Ani could not remember if they started before or after Labor Day. Either way, Ani was sure that would not prevent her sister from replying. When Ani was in high school, teachers took away the cell phones of students who used them in class, but now smartphones were so ubiquitous that she couldn't imagine many teachers bothered. More trouble than it was worth. Her phone dinged.

It's a lot to explain by text. Where are you?

Montana. Talin, how bad is it?

Just come home.

Ani called twice but Talin didn't pick up. The sun leaked over the mountains and dew glistened everywhere, everything wet with the new day, slick and wilted. Ani needed a shower. She had not shaved her legs and armpits in weeks.

No one would blame her if she turned around and went home before finishing her trek around the country. Her parents would be ecstatic. Ani had already seen so much more than she imagined, left her cousin's ashes in six states, mourned in some ways that were unhealthy and unsustainable and other ways that were so fantastic and indescribably beneficial she could never properly explain their value to anyone. It was hard to give up. Hard to admit the trip wasn't everything she needed it to be. And it might have been harder still, perhaps, if she kept going, but that too felt impossible.

Ani would go home to her sister. She could not help Mari anymore, but she could help Talin.

I'll come, but you have to give me a few days.

Talin sent a string of emojis: hands in prayer thanking her sister, noisemakers, a slew of red hearts. Ani texted her father and returned the phone to the glove compartment.

She was already in the process of mentally rerouting the remainder of her travels. South through the Tetons and Yellowstone, a night in each, to give the rest of what she had of her cousin's ashes back to the wilderness, to the trees and rivers and mountains that they had never wandered together. From there, Ani could drive through the endless cornfields of Nebraska and Iowa, the countryside doldrums of uniform highway that were straight and unending, hundreds of unchanging miles back to Michigan. How good it felt to be needed. How good it felt to feel the impending relief of returning somewhere familiar.

The sign had flipped on the door of the Mercantile, so Ani lumbered in. Her slippers clopped on the hardwood. The aroma of fresh baked goods and meat pies filled the shop. The store had everything she could ever need. Her route was circuitous and nonsensical, but it didn't matter—she had no timeline, no job to return to.

Ani grabbed a bag of licorice from a shelf at her chest and carried it to the counter. She needed to stop hemorrhaging money—September rent on her studio back in Chicago would automatically leave her checking account in a few days—but she couldn't help craving sweets while she was traveling.

"A healthy breakfast," Francis remarked. He was home for the summer from the University of Wyoming. His family lived in Whitefish, but he worked at the Merc and stayed in a tiny cabin for a few days at a time until his weekend arrived. Francis was a rock climber, tall and lanky, but veiny with muscle, if not appearing a bit undernourished. He had a long, messy bowl of blond hair and a thick ruddy beard trimmed so no hair covered the skin of his cheekbones. He opened the store on most mornings when Ani came in for food and coffee.

"I'm carbo-loading for when I make a break for Canada." Ani winked. This was an inside joke between the two of them. The first day Ani came into the shop, Francis had asked if she was running from the law, since they were only a few miles away from the Canadian border. Ani played along without missing a beat. The backstory became more and more elaborate each day.

"Remind me what you did again," Francis prompted. "Held up a bank?"

"At least a dozen."

"Well, do you want to purchase anything else with your ill-gotten gains, Bonnie?"

"A beef pasty and a cup of coffee, please."

His smile wavered a little as he rang up her items. "Are you ever going to tell me what you're actually running from?"

Ani ripped open the bag of licorice. Francis knew nothing about her. His insistence that she was on the run was an assumption. She told him she was just passing through. She kept her troubles quiet.

Everywhere she'd traveled, people asked these types of questions, all curious as to what a pretty girl was doing driving across the country all alone. In eastern Montana, an elderly couple that owned a mom-and-pop diner offered her a job waiting tables while she leaned over the chrome-lined counter in front of them and gobbled down meat loaf and over-whipped mashed potatoes drowned in thin gravy. They had an extra bedroom where she could stay since their daughter had married and moved to California. Ani considered the offer for some time. She spent a whole afternoon mulling it over and writing in her Moleskine journal while the couple took turns freshening her mug of bitter coffee. By dinnertime, she was wired and there was a thick enough layer of grounds at the bottom of her mug to pot a small plant. When both of them were occupied with customers, Ani left more than enough bills to cover her check and snuck out the door without having to provide an answer.

She sighed at Francis. "I don't think you've earned it yet."

"Well how about I start by buying you a drink tonight?"

Ani smirked. "Are you even old enough to drink?" she asked. She handed Francis her thermos to fill with coffee from behind the counter. He slid the beef pasty on a paper towel in the microwave, then snagged a rope of licorice and bit down so that Ani could see it dangle between his perfect teeth. If she were feeling flirty, she would have yanked it from his mouth and eaten it herself. Instead, she sipped her coffee, which burnt the roof of her mouth. She was never patient enough to let it cool. The same mistake, morning after morning. Her gums felt leathery from the scorch of the liquid.

"Actually," Ani started, "I'm going to need a few more things. It's my last night here."

Francis's disappointment was clear, but he faked a smile. "Well then I definitely need to take you out tonight."

"Where are we going?"

"I know a place."

An hour before sundown, Ani met Francis outside the Mercantile. He had a schoolbag sagging over his shoulders, weighed down with what Ani guessed were loose cans of beer. She'd been to enough backyard bonfires on Grosse Ile to recognize how the cans gathered and sunk into the hollow of a boy's lower back. She imagined the constant chill Francis must be feeling along his spine. It was as if every fit young man had a cradle there, a natural divot for whatever contraband materials were at the bottom of the biggest pocket of their backpacks.

Ani had a near-empty nylon drawstring. All it held was a water bottle, some granola bars, and her driver's license in case they were attacked by grizzlies or slipped off a steep rock face. She figured it was a good idea to have identification in case of the worst. No more bodies identified by tattoos. No more hours of her family waiting in terror for news. She would not withhold that certainty from them.

"I brought an extra hat and gloves," Francis bragged, patting his backpack. "It gets colder than you think once the sun goes down."

"I'm from Michigan," Ani replied. "I know cold."

"Sure you do, but not at this altitude."

Ani couldn't argue. The truth was it was getting more difficult for her to sleep through the night without shivering. September was hot, but the temperature could be erratic. When she left home, she hadn't packed many clothes for the seasons beyond summer. She wasn't sure whether it was more surprising that she had lasted this long without checking into a hotel or that she had mentally prepared for a few more months of meandering around the country, making her way through Utah, California, Nevada, Arizona, New Mexico, wherever else she decided to go. But that wouldn't matter now that she was going home. By now, Ani had realized she didn't have enough ashes to leave some everywhere, and Talin needed her. That was enough reason.

Francis nodded toward the mountains and they set off. At first, Ani walked beside him, but once they broke free of town, she filed in behind him and they hiked an unmarked trail in silence. It was a risky path to take without much light, lots of roots and rocks jutting out to snag an ankle. Maybe a half hour in, Francis shuffled behind a massive pine trunk and signaled for Ani to do the same. She stood facing him, tucked against his chest, overcome by the grassy scent of his deodorant.

"Bear?" Ani mouthed.

"Worse," Francis whispered. "Moose."

Ani could hear the animal clopping along. She hugged Francis so that their bodies were less conspicuous. They might resemble a lumpy tree trunk, she thought. She hadn't realized how much taller Francis was. They stood huddled for a few minutes, breath muted, listening to the fading thrash of branches and leaves and the occasional hoof against a rock. The sound dissolved in the distance.

Ani craned up at Francis. She knew the answer, but asked anyway. "Are moose that bad?"

"It's mating season," he explained. "And there's not much food this year. Those fuckers can get pretty ornery. More dangerous than any bear when you piss them off."

The sun was low enough that the forest accelerated into nighttime. Ani had to tilt her head straight up to see the pink light of day. They wouldn't be able to make out what was in front of them for much longer. Francis removed two headlamps from his backpack. Ani adjusted hers and they continued at a brisker pace, the path entering a slight climb. Ani was hot from walking but she would need the hat and gloves the moment they came to rest.

They arrived at a clearing atop a ridge of limestone with an abandoned fire pit and a few scattered cairns. Francis turned off his headlamp and Ani followed suit.

"Best spot to see the stars," Francis declared. "No light pollution from town."

"Lights?" Ani laughed. "Polebridge isn't exactly Chicago."

"Is that where you live?"

"I told you I'm from Michigan."

"Doesn't really answer the question, does it?"

Ani wasn't sure how much she wanted Francis to learn about her. She had no idea how up to date he was on the news, but her full name and a little backstory might be enough for him to figure out what she was fleeing. At first, Mari's death only made a brief mention anywhere outside the Midwest, but internet opinions and misinformation flourished. The revenge porn angle attracted real journalists and lengthy think pieces, not just those looking for something sensational to broadcast on TV. She worried about him connecting the dots if he noticed the flag tattoos on her ankles before she realized that train of thought suggested he would have a reason to see her ankles at some point in the first place.

The same tattoos as her cousin. They'd gotten them together at a parlor in Ann Arbor right after Ani bought a fake ID at sixteen. Wearing pants and long socks every day, she intentionally avoided giving away this detail about herself around Francis.

"I was living in Chicago," Ani offered, hoping it was enough for him to stop prodding, "before I decided to take some time on the road."

"I've always wanted to visit the city."

"It's nothing like this."

"That's why I want to visit."

Ani could see her breath. It was less than an hour after sundown and the sky was so clear that more stars were visible than she had seen since sitting on the dune with Mari all those years ago. The forest around her was black and indistinguishable, the bases of the trees surrounding them climbing upward forebodingly until they disappeared, and she could hear insects buzzing and screeching, enough noise to nearly match the sirens and traffic that lulled her to sleep in the city. The environments were disparate, but filled her with the same sense of overwhelming calm, like she couldn't hear herself think, which was exactly what she wanted.

"What are you studying at Wyoming?" she asked Francis.

"Finance."

Ani rolled her eyes. She thought of her father. "How fun."

"I wanted something stable. It will be easier for me to not get tied down here if I have transferrable skills."

"You really want to get out of here, huh?"

Francis turned his headlamp back on without answering and rifled through his backpack. He dug out four cans of beer and handed two to Ani. "You're going to want to knock back the first one quick just to stay warm."

They drank their first beers without returning to the subject. More and more of the dark sky came to life by the minute. A bat flapped in the clearing overhead. Ani fell back onto the limestone and Francis leaned back next to her, like they were in a goddamn romance novel, Ani thought, but the rocks beneath them were jagged and freezing, sending a shock of cold through her body. Ani drank her second beer, hoping the alcohol would warm her up, but instead she started to shiver. Francis kept clapping his hands together to circulate his blood.

Within a few minutes it was clear neither of them was any longer enjoying the view, so Francis turned his headlamp back on and they hiked back to town, both a little wobbly and out of sorts in the darkened wilderness. Ani had never felt so vulnerable in her life. She wondered if Mari felt vulnerable or empowered in the minutes she swam out so far past where she could touch the bottom. Was it taking control or giving it up? When they arrived back in town, Ani could hear music and chatter coming from the one local bar, the Northern Lights. Francis leapt to grab a tree branch and did a few quick pull-ups.

"A bit obvious, isn't it?" Ani asked.

"It's not always easy getting exercise out here." He flexed his biceps. "You don't think this body comes without maintenance, do you?"

Ani smirked. "I haven't seen enough of your body to make that distinction."

"Ooph," Francis groaned, his hand over his heart. "Now who's the cliché? That's straight out of a rom-com. Flirting 101." He frowned. "Are you really ready to leave?"

"My sister needs me. I have to go home."

"And you're ready to go home?"

"Why wouldn't I be?"

"I'd tell you if I had any idea what you were running from."

The bar for men was so low, she thought, but she was grateful he had not tried to make a move. Francis removed his water bottle from his bag and loudly downed the better half of it. Ani dug around in her backpack and found the mason jar of ashes. When she got a hand on it, she held it up for Francis to inspect. He took the jar from her and turned it around in his hand.

"A jar of dirt?" he asked.

"My cousin died," Ani explained.

"Oh." He carefully handed the jar back to her and gently brushed his hands on his pants.

"We were very close. She was only a couple years older than me. I've been leaving her ashes everywhere I go."

"I'm sorry, not many left."

"I didn't have many to begin with. Her parents wouldn't part with most of them."

"And you don't get along with them?" Francis asked.

"We get along swell," Ani joked. "They live right next door actually, in my grandparents' old house. But my cousin was their only child. They want to have her ashes buried with them, but they also understood I would know what she would have wanted done with her remains, so they gave me an equal share."

"And so this is what you're doing?"

Ani nodded. "We used to always talk about driving around the country. I've been saving for years. So yes, I believe I'm honoring her by leaving her ashes in all the places we always dreamed of traveling."

Francis cracked his knuckles and removed a meager apple from his backpack. "I have a brother somewhere. Eight years older. Left home at eighteen and none of us have seen him since."

"I'm sorry."

"You shouldn't apologize. Here I am comparing the fact that someone I barely knew abandoned my family and is probably just fine with the fact of you losing someone who meant the world to you. I should be saying sorry."

"Why bring it up to begin with then?"

"Human nature, I guess. We're always comparing traumas."

Francis was getting a little philosophical for Ani's liking. Tomorrow she would be gone, and she didn't want him to feel left behind. She tried to stick to the basics of her story. Not too much detail, no names. "My cousin was like a second sister. She was the oldest. We were always together. Me and my baby sister looked up to her, I guess."

Francis chomped at his apple, no bigger than a plum. Half of it disappeared in one bite. Men can devour so much, Ani thought. Being out in the middle of nowhere with Francis, a man twice her size, was reckless, a brash example of the fleeting trust people placed in one another, nothing more than bad judgment. She grazed her hand over the Swiss Army knife in her pocket.

"When will you go?" he asked.

"First thing in the morning," Ani replied. Why did she offer information up so freely? "I've got an alarm set and everything."

"Can I stay with you tonight?"

Ani snorted. "That's a bit forward."

"I don't exactly have a lot of time for courtship. And I'm not expecting anything. I just want to be by your side every moment I can be until you leave."

"You don't even know me."

"I know you enough to mean it."

Francis hucked his pale apple core out into the darkness.

She wished she didn't want to say yes. There was something presumptuous and boring about the whole thing. Men always pretended to be patient until things got physical and then they never slowed down. He was feeding her a line like any other guy. She leaned in and kissed him, and Francis drove his lips back at her with too much eagerness, desperate and lonely. His unruly kissing did not help his cause.

Ani pulled away from him. "I don't think it's a good idea," she said firmly. "I expect you to respect that."

"I will."

"I don't need anyone trying to hold me back when I go."

Francis nodded. He zipped his backpack. He was ready to head back now. Maybe he would lose interest, forget about her the instant he left Polebridge and headed back to Wyoming. Ani was half certain he had a girlfriend or hookup back on campus, someone he was always texting.

Francis marched toward the Northern Lights and his mood seemed to improve after they sat down at the bar. Surprisingly, neither of them was carded. They drank a round of Moose Drool and continued to talk about where they came from and where they ultimately wanted to go. They ordered sandwiches for dinner, and when Francis didn't finish his french fries, Ani scarfed them down. He asked Ani for her phone number and texted her as soon as she finished listing the string of digits. They were tipsy and in good spirits, so Francis ordered them each a shot of whiskey before they settled up. She shouldn't drink anymore but knocked back the dark liquor anyway.

Outside, in the hazy periphery of the bar, Ani thought it looked like nothing existed outside of the little patch of land that marked Polebridge, that if she ran into the unrecognizable dark forest or shadowy mountains the world would end, no different than the space between the stars in the sky or the earth and the moon. Francis swooped a hand around her waist and pulled her to him.

"Let me stay with you," he pined.

"I already told you no."

"C'mon. No expectations. I'm not ready to say goodbye yet."

"You boys all use the same lines," Ani spat. The men she met in Chicago weren't so different from this country kid. She shook free of his grasp. "And it sucks because by being impatient, you fuck up any chance at getting anywhere in the future."

"It's not your fault, what happened to your cousin."

Ani stepped back, shaking her head. "You don't know anything about her."

"Ani, c'mon." He dropped his hands in his pockets and smirked. "It's isolated out here, but we're not exiled. I saw her picture all over. You look just like her."

Tears sprang to her eyes. "Fuck you." She was nauseated and dizzy, the darkness of the night no longer magical; instead, the lack of clarity disoriented her. She wondered if he was serious about seeing Mari in passing, it seemed so unlikely. Was he just another monster who'd slavered over her cousin online? Had he googled Mari after he met her?

Before she could think about it too much, she threw up on Francis's boots. She should not have ignored bar axioms. *Liquor then beer, you're in the clear. Beer then liquor, never been sicker.* He jumped backward, and Ani charged forward while he was off balance and pushed him to the ground.

"So what? You read what happened to my cousin and thought you'd have a shot with me? Your very own Kim K?"

Francis said nothing. Ani left him in the dirt trying to catch his breath.

She tromped back to her campsite and frantically packed. She was in no shape to drive, but it didn't matter. There was no one out there to stop her, not another soul on the road at night. It would take her more than an hour to get out of the curving, un-paved roads of Glacier and, if needed, she could stop in Whitefish for coffee and breakfast, take a parking-lot nap, and drive full steam ahead to the Tetons. If nothing was open, she would drive straight through the night or sleep outside of a grocery store, somewhere at least well lit with cameras, pocketknife in hand. Ani had made sure never to settle into a place with less than three-quarters of a tank of gas. She tossed her tent and sleeping bag and clothes into the backseat and slammed the door shut.

The car's interior was cold against her body. She locked the doors, ran the engine, cranked up the heat on the defroster, and punched the button on the side of her seat so that it would warm. She was nervous Francis would try and stop her from leaving, but she didn't see him or anyone else out around town. When she was satisfied everything was loaded in the car, even if haphazardly, Ani downed a bottle of water, then composed herself for the ride ahead in case she was pulled over. She was grateful Francis had not tried to follow her and talk her into staying again.

On the dirt road, Ani could see nothing outside of the beams of her headlights. The GPS on her phone told her to veer one way or another. The drive was exhausting and slow going. She crawled along so that she could react in time to avoid gigantic potholes and fallen branches and critters scampering in the night, especially since she was still sobering up. She soon had to stop so a herd of deer could trot in front of her, indifferent to the headlights as they took their time crossing the road. Out of the corner of her eye, she swore a grizzly bear was scratching against the jagged bark of a pine tree.

When Ani hit the main road, paved and even, she relished in hitting the accelerator. The Tetons were another seven hours away. Forget Whitefish, she thought; if she made no stops except for gas, she would get there around daybreak.

Ani was amazed again to find how small and insignificant she felt driving through the middle of nowhere. Every time she was certain she could feel no more alone, the world around her grew until it was more barren and terrifying. After an hour of mindless driving, singing along to the radio at the top of her lungs to stay awake and sober up, an orange flicker poked at the horizon in the distance, which confused Ani because sunrise wouldn't be for hours. As she sped along, a construction sign holding a grid of round orange lights came into focus, blinking on the shoulder of the road. *PLANNED BURN. NO STOPS FOR 20 MILES.*

Ani kept driving until she passed an entire prairie engulfed in flames. A cloud of black smoke rose off and blended with the night sky, and Ani could feel the heat through her car. There had been no gas stations or rest stops for miles.

After another hour, Ani pulled into a twenty-four-hour Shell station off of a short exit. The yellow logo was a herculean beacon so far from the seashore. Shell-ter, Ani thought, hungover and delirious. She giggled to herself.

A few men slept in parked cars out front. They were in neon construction vests, faces marred with dirt and ash. Ani figured they must have been part of the burn team. Locking the car, she went inside to pee and buy Gatorade and coffee before refueling the Subaru. While the gas chugged into the tank, she shook out her legs and scrolled through the map on her phone. The service was spotty and the GPS wouldn't load, but she could zoom in on the map to browse the route. There was so much more ground to cover—Nebraska, Iowa, Illinois. She doubted she'd make it home for another week.

Early in the morning, Ani crossed through the national park gate, bantered with the park rangers for a bit, paid her camping fee, and found a secluded spot in a gift shop parking lot near a public bathroom. She brushed her teeth, washed her face, and took a nap in the car. Her alarm rang after forty-five minutes, enough time so that she had recharged and could drive the remaining few miles to her campsite and get some true rest. After pitching her tent, she tossed her sleeping bag inside and changed into basketball shorts.

When Ani awoke, her tent was so humid she couldn't breathe. Her mouth felt filled with cotton. The sun must have risen right above her. She drank from her water bottle and slunk out from under the rain fly to assess her surroundings. Her site was at the far end of a figure eight loop of car campsites, and it was by far the most meager setup. The other clearings around her were occupied by extravagant tents, grills, coolers, and even some trailers hooked up to water and electricity.

Ani changed back into her hiking clothes and gathered a few belongings—her water bottle, the ashes, a book, and some assorted snacks—and dressed for a short hike to a nearby lake. On the shore, there were a few cars with canoes or kayak rigs strapped to the roof. Small vessels, slivers of hunter green and papaya and ketchup red, were out on the water. She removed her book from her bag and found a vacant spot to read on the beach. A few yards away, two women, maybe in their forties, drank tallboys and peered out over the water. The lake was deep blue and Ani couldn't make out the far side. It was enormous. She didn't realize there were lakes this size other than the Great Lakes. She wondered if they taught the HOMES acronym outside of the Midwest.

"What are you reading?" the closer woman asked Ani. Ani couldn't make out much of her face behind her black baseball cap and sleek sunglasses, but what she could see was reddened from the sun. "That's a hefty tome."

"*The Forty Days of Musa Dagh,*" Ani replied. By chance, she'd found a used copy on the shelf of a bookish bar in Madison being used as decor. It was a reprint and in mediocre condition. She snuck it in her backpack without anyone the wiser. "I read it years ago, but thought it warranted revisiting."

"Hope it's a page-turner," the other said, making a movement like she was lifting weights. She was wearing a straw cowboy hat that shaded her head and neck.

"It moves quickly once you get into it." Ani flipped through some of the pages. She missed having her uncle's notes to guide her reading. "What lake is this?"

"Ha." The woman faked a laugh. "Yellowstone Lake. You would think they could come up with a more creative name."

Ani laughed. "Thank you. I just got here. Haven't really found my bearings yet."

"Want a beer?"

Ani hesitated. She was sleep deprived and dehydrated. Her headache had been so constant for the passing hours she had forgotten about it. This, she thought, may very well be the last trip she took like this in her life. She wanted to take advantage of every moment.

"Sure." Ani walked toward the women. The one in the baseball cap dug around in their cooler.

"I'm Cindy." She smiled, handing Ani the beer. "That's Eileen."

"Ani," she said, accepting the wet can. "Thank you."

They shot the shit for a while. Ani found out they were about as local as you could get, living in a town thirty miles east on the other side of the park. Ani told them she was from Michigan, but left the details vague. The women asked more about her travels and when Ani placed her finished can next to their empties, they passed her another without a word. Ani's hangover faded into a calming buzz. Talking to the women felt liberating, the first time in weeks she'd relaxed. The women held no expectations. They asked her nothing about men or her job or politics, and soon Ani found she was comfortable sharing the real reason for her road trip with them, more so than she ever was with Francis.

"Have you left any here yet?" Eileen questioned. "I haven't been too many places, but this lake is the most beautiful spot around here."

"I haven't, but I've only been here for the morning. I haven't had a chance to explore the park yet. It's likely to be my last stop, so I'm trying to find a place here that's meaningful."

"You should take the kayak out," Cindy offered. "You could head straight out on the lake."

Ani had been wondering if the two yellow kayaks resting on the beach were theirs. Mari had always loved the water when they were kids. Whenever they went to the beach, she was the first to run straight in without worrying about the temperature. Mari could spend the whole day out there without bothering to join the rest of them in the sand. After spending weeks thinking about it, Ani realized there was no other way for Mari to go. Maybe she was wrong about Mari knowing she would drift back toward shore. Maybe she wanted to be lost in the lake forever.

Ani stuttered, "You wouldn't mind?"

"We're not going anywhere." Eileen cracked open a new beer to emphasize that they were stationary. The water was smooth. Ani could see the reflection of the sky in the surface.

"But you have to take a life vest," Cindy added, "especially since you've been drinking. There's one in each of the seats."

"Thank you." Ani chugged the rest of her beer and found the mason jar in her backpack. It was eerie to look at the ashes through the translucent glass, the last few in the bottom like gray sugar at the back of the pantry in need of a refill. Ani didn't

232

have a swimsuit, so she rolled her jeans above her knees so she could walk the kayak out into the calm water without the denim getting wet. The other side of the lake must have been miles away, but Ani thought she could maybe see the blur of land somewhere on the horizon. Ani knew no matter how hard she paddled there was no way she would reach the far shore. She clipped the life jacket over her tank top.

The water was cold on her feet and caused the hair on her forearms to prick up. She imagined the lake was too big to ever warm. Given the elevation, the surface probably froze over in the winter. She hadn't kayaked in years—not that it was difficult to maneuver, but she felt a bit off-kilter when she sat down in the seat. Rather than scrape the oar against the submerged earth, she plunged her hand to the shallow rocks and pushed herself out until she could no longer find a handhold. Ani turned the craft adjacent to the beach and yelled to her new friends back on shore, "You sure you don't mind?"

"Why aren't you gone yet?" Cindy chided. "Get moving."

Ani nodded and fell into the rhythm. She lost track of time that way, cruising toward the opposite shore with no real destination, until her back ached with fatigue. When she looked over her shoulder, she couldn't make out any landmarks around the area from where she'd set off. The haze of land was undefined in both directions, water surrounding her, and Ani was alone again. A predictable moment to cry, but she just couldn't help herself, and she stopped paddling to grieve in peace and quiet. All she had wanted to do this whole trip was find a spot where she could mourn Mari without being bothered, and there was no better spot than out on the water. It was just the two of them again.

Ahead, a teal patch of sandbar came into view. Ani could imagine parting with the jar there. After paddling languorously to its center, Ani could see the sand rising from the depths like a little underwater mountain. She floated above the submerged peak. Everything was clear. The water and sky and space in between were serene and unfettered and so damn perfect that she thought Mari would make fun of her for doing something so sentimental, but that was the way things went sometimes, those moments of perfection were few and far, and this one had aligned to help her complete the difficult task at hand.

If she dumped the ashes they would float across the lake. Instead, she opened the mason jar and filled it to the brim so that its contents were gray and murky, like the Dixie cups of water they'd dipped their paintbrushes in during elementary school art class. She tightened the two-part metal cap so the whole thing would sink. It left her hand and drifted below until it came to rest in the flushed sand, making a crater in the mountain's peak. Someday the glass would break, and Mari would be united with the lake. Mari's journey, and Ani's journey, too, was coming to a close.

Distracted, Ani had to recalibrate her path several times as she paddled back to find Cindy and Eileen. As she neared, their car and picnic table came into focus and the two women waved at her. Ani sped up her stroke to make it back, not wanting them to be stuck waiting for her if they planned to leave soon. The sun was low and her shoulders were chilled. She had no idea how long she'd been out on the water.

"We were worried you decided to run off with our boat!" Eileen exclaimed. They were in the same seats as when Ani left them, drinking what must have been the last of their beers, because the cooler was open and tilted on its side to drain and dry out. Cindy had her phone to her ear, but waved to signal that she was glad Ani had returned safely. Ani stepped out of the kayak and dragged it up the beach. The sand scratched at the skin between her toes.

Cindy hung up the phone. "Had us scared for a second. We lost sight of you."

"I didn't realize how far I was going," Ani offered, apologetic.

"We rarely do in life."

Eileen groaned. "Don't give her your parlor-room wisdom."

Cindy ignored her friend's derision with a smile. "Can you help us load it up?" she asked.

The three of them worked together to lift the kayak over their SUV and attempted to strap it in place. Wet, Ani's bare feet slipped on the back bumper and she fell hard on her shin, but luckily her jeans were still rolled up and the bumper caught the thick roll of denim. Still, it would certainly bruise. The women drove off with a wave.

Ani's shin pulsed with pain, but she began to laugh and couldn't stop. It felt unnatural given how little she had laughed lately, especially after coming back in from the sandbar, but it was impossible to stay somber forever. There was so much for her to be happy about in the moment.

Ani decided to return to her tent for the remainder of the evening. After the short walk back, she hooked her lantern by a carabiner to a loop in the dome of the canopy of her tent and dug back into *Musa Dagh*. It felt somehow more meaningful to be reading the novel in the mountains. Werfel's writing was much more melodramatic than she remembered. She tried to recall how her great-grandfather told his version, but the two had bled together in her mind, legend upon legend.

Ani was supposed to be exploring and experiencing the great outdoors, but when she wasn't dog tired, she enjoyed nothing more than holing up in her tent with a good book and a sprawl of snacks surrounded by the sounds of the wilderness. Yes, it filled her with fear, the threats of hungry animals and violent strangers and unlivable weather, floods and tornadoes and vicious strokes of lightning, but there was also beauty in the multitude of sounds, the thrill of a personal hideaway, reading for hours on end without interruption. Her sleeping bag was cozy and mitigated some of her anxiety. After all the weeks on the road, she recognized how vulnerable any person was at any given moment. Safety was a myth, she thought. Some have luck and some have more of it, but she caught herself in the middle of this line of reasoning and decided that it, too, was bullshit. The truth was it was a matter of privilege. She had so many advantages that had allowed her to take this trip, that had ensured she'd reached its end.

Ani read for hours, lost in the cramped lines of Werfel's massive book, wishing again for her uncle's notes in the margins, but still seeing all of its unsubtle flaws as if for the first time. There were so many things she wished she could change.

In the morning, Ani packed her camp and loaded the car. The Labor Day weekend crowd was already mounting, a matter of time before traffic jams clogged the nation's circulatory system from coast to coast.

Meanwhile, Ani had sent several more texts to Talin trying to poke free information, but her younger sister wouldn't offer any clues. Every text was some version of the same simple message: *Come home*.

After Ani heated an instant oatmeal packet and scarfed down a green, soapy banana, she set out knowing the remainder of her drive would be dull and tedious. She first needed to cross the flats of Wyoming. Interstate 80 would take her through the cornfields of Nebraska and Iowa and Illinois. According to her phone, if she made no stops, it would be a day's worth of driving to get home. Twenty-four hours. With stops and food and rest, that could add up to two or three more days.

She wondered again if she was failing herself. She had planned to be on the road for months, certain she would visit every state outside of Hawaii and Alaska. A part of her had hoped she would never go back to her old life at all. She had read books about people casting aside all of their belongings and starting over, seen social media stars living out of vans and backpacking from place to place, but only a few weeks had passed, and she was exhausted.

While she had finished what she set out to do, a lingering sense of defeat remained, reminding her that her grief would take more time to subside. Her whole life she felt she had intrinsically understood grief, had learned what it meant to bear it on her sleeve. Thinking of the mason jar sinking into the sand, she felt it had been lifted, if only for the day ahead of her, and that seemed a good enough reason to return to her family. Ani called

Talin again, and when her younger sister sent the call straight to voicemail, she replayed Talin's texts in her head like a mantra. *Come home come home come home.*

The following evening, desperate for a shower, Ani decided to check into a Super 8 near the Iowa-Nebraska border, having driven for most of the day.

A few pickup trucks littered the parking lot, but otherwise Ani was surrounded by verdant walls of cornfields. After she parked, she cleaned out her car: peeled trash and debris from the floor, recycled her empty cans and bottles, consolidated her loose change in an old ibuprofen bottle, repacked her miscellany of belongings, and compiled the items she would need for the evening in her drawstring bag.

Ani took the elevator to her floor and found her room, dead bolted the door behind her, locked the chain, found a laundry bag in the closet, and jammed her clothes until the translucent plastic stretched. She carried the pocketknife with her into the shower, set it on the caddy next to the petite complimentary bottles of shampoo and conditioner, and reached for the taps. Once she could see the steam, she jumped in and let the temperature go beyond her comfort, layers of dirt dribbling off her in tiny brown rivulets. The tiny bottle of soap barely offered enough for her to scrub herself clean. She drained the bottles of shampoo and conditioner. By the time she'd finished shaving her legs, Ani had spent more than half an hour in the shower, and the bathroom was so foggy she couldn't make out her reflection in the mirror.

Feeling rejuvenated in fresh gas station clothes she'd purchased on the road that day, Ani turned on the television and dug her laptop and charger from her bag. She had not used the computer since leaving home and was out of the loop on news, social media, all the happenings of the internet. She hoped the time away might have been long enough that all the mentions of her cousin, the comments and condolences flooding every feed, may have finally disappeared.

It was bizarre sitting in a room alone with the television, stentorian compared to the sounds of nature she had lived with for weeks. Ani turned on something inconsequential. No news, no real engagement with the outside world. She found a Quentin Tarantino flick on one of the premium stations. Onscreen, Brad Pitt was marching down a line of soldiers in World War II regalia. The men stood firm and answered his questions in unison. It was only a matter of time before there were dead Nazis falling left and right.

How nice it must be to have the privilege to rewrite history. She wondered if Tarantino would make a similar film about the Armenian Genocide. He could turn Musa Dagh into a bloodbath that ignites an Armenian resistance of biblical proportions. Maybe they could even find an actor to play a sharpshooter like her great-grandfather. The three pashas forced to wander into the desert with no food or water.

Why bother, though? The Genocide was the historical truth. To reimagine the violence any other way would only muddle the past—a past too many people had forgotten or simply never known of. It would play into Turkey's hand. There was enough propaganda already, so many atrocities brushed under the rug.

On her computer, the flood of technology was overwhelming. Facebook, Instagram, Twitter: her social circle was abundant with exotic vacations, new dog dads, rosy-cheeked babies, raises and promotions, unintelligible political ranting. *Wow*, she thought, *have I really missed this all that much?* An hour later the movie was nearly over, but she continued scrolling through the endless stream of updates and opinions. She fell asleep with the computer warm against her legs, the television blaring into the night.

The next morning, after three cups of coffee and two full plates from the continental breakfast, Ani gathered her belongings and loaded up her car. She planned to make it back to her studio in Chicago by the end of the day. She was worried the place would be rank with laundry and spoiled food. None of that had mattered to her in the wake of Mari's death. She had not thought about housekeeping when her father was on his way to pick her up. She simply packed her bags and was ready to go.

When the skyline came into view, with its silhouettes of the Sears Tower and the Hancock Building and even that fucking glass monstrosity she despised peeking somewhere between the other two, she was overcome with joy. As soon as she could make out the cityscape, the traffic came to a near halt, and she began the sluggish stop-and-go crawl home.

There was a sticky note on her mailbox in the lobby when she entered her apartment complex. Too many items had piled up; a basket awaited her behind the front desk. Ani brought her ID to the security guard and he dug around until he found a plastic bin from the postal service, overflowing with a hodgepodge of letters and parcels. Most of it was useless recycling, but a few were pleasant surprises. There were letters from friends and family, a novel she had forgotten she ordered, wedding invitations, a check from when she accidentally paid an electric bill twice.

Her studio was as bad as she expected. The trash can below her sink was half full, the acrid bite of rotting food wafting around the room. Unwashed bowls and cups filled the dishwasher. Her laundry was everywhere, hanging from her desk chair and across the bed, bunched in the open basket in her walk-in closet. Everything was stale, even though she had accidentally left her lone window cracked. She yanked it all the way open.

There was little in the refrigerator except for moldy fruit and bottles of condiments. It was time to get her shit back together. Tomorrow, she would return home and help her sister. Despite Talin's urgent texts, she was sure it was nothing that couldn't be resolved in a few days. Then it was back to her apartment, finding a new job, back to trying to live an independent, fulfilling existence. There was only so much grief she could bear.

The next morning, Ani drove the final five hours home. By the time she crossed the toll bridge onto Grosse Ile, she felt nauseated from the long ride. Ani had not told anyone she was coming home except for Talin. It was the middle of the day, and there were no cars in the driveway. Ani punched in the code to open the garage and decided she would worry about unpacking later.

To Ani's surprise, her sister was lying on the couch watching television. Talin jumped to her feet. Ani couldn't figure out which emotions were moving across her face.

"You came," Talin croaked.

"I told you I would." Ani braced herself as Talin gripped her in a tight hug.

"I just wasn't sure how long it would take." Ani sighed, wishing she'd spent less time on the road in those final few days. "Why are you home?" she asked. School was back in session. Her brother must be there now.

"I sort of faked sick."

"Sort of?" Ani realized Talin was crying. She could feel the warmth against her shoulder.

"I'm pregnant," Talin whispered.

Ani squeezed her sister closer. "Pour us a couple glasses of water and let me go to the bathroom. You can tell me everything."

After talking with Talin, Ani dug through Joseph's room until she found his stash of weed. She rolled a loose joint and sat on the back deck while Talin lay in bed. Joseph's weed was weak, but Ani was grateful for the light high.

"You're home," her father gasped as he exited the house. He knelt and hugged her before she could get up from her chair. He was back early. Edgar sighed with relief. "I was worried you would be gone so much longer."

"I thought I would be too."

"Did you do what you set out to?" Edgar asked. "Hova and Karo will want to hear all about it."

"I did," Ani confirmed. She puffed on the joint.

"Can I have some of that?" Her father took it from her before she could say no. "This smells like Joe's weed."

"I stole it from him."

They both laughed.

"I didn't know you smoked, Dad."

"This stuff"—Edgar held the joint out like he could assess its quality—"not since you were born."

"What about Mom?"

"In college, yes." He passed the joint back to her. "Tell me about the road."

In need of this distraction, Ani efficiently recounted her travels, omitting many of the details that would make her father cringe. She told Edgar where she had stopped in each state, even if he had already gleaned this information from her infrequent text messages. Her father's expression veered in a million different directions. Ani had never seen him so animated. He was clearly high.

When she finished, he lamented, "I thought you would at least spend a few nights in hotels or hostels."

"Couldn't afford that, Dad. I didn't want to spend your money."

"There are too many crazies out there to be off in the woods for weeks on end. I tried to help but you kept declining! I thought you were being too proud."

"I know."

Edgar sighed. "I need to shower and change before your mother gets home. She will be overjoyed to see you and I don't want to sour her mood by smelling like a skunk. Go next door when you have a chance."

He fled back inside, and Ani was left alone. She slouched into the canvas chair and let all of her weight fall away. Her muscles relaxed. The trees looked pancake flat. Her depth perception always went to hell when she smoked. She wanted to give Talin some time to herself, but soon they would need to talk more. They were both exhausted. For a few more minutes, Ani would enjoy the comfort of relaxing outside without having to worry about setting up camp or finding a bathroom or whether or not she left any trace in the wilderness.

Ani returned to Talin's room so they could discuss options. Ani thought it best they tell their parents, but wondered if they could easily keep it from Joe. Talin thought it best for everything to stay between the two of them.

"Why tell Mom and Dad?" Talin asked.

"The usual," Ani replied. "Money, assurance, adult perspective."

"Ugh, I didn't think about money."

With Ani's bank account drained, money was the first thing that had come to her mind. She needed to leave soon, go back to Chicago, beg for her old job back or find something new, any bar with a decent crowd, so that she could pay rent. Ani's buzz was wearing off, and a glass of ice water sounded terrific. Edgar clunked around in his bedroom down the hall.

"You remember when I moved next door?" Ani asked. "Senior year. The idea was then you finally got your own room."

"Yeah. I thought it was strange but didn't care because I wanted my own space."

"Mom and Dad were so tired of all my bullshit. Sneaking out, drinking, boys. You and Joe really have it easy." Ani laughed. "We made up right before I graduated. I think Mom and Dad couldn't imagine me going off to college and still being mad. They saw how hard it was when Mari left even though she was just an hour away. The whole balance of everything was off. Anyway, we were all good, then sophomore year I had a pregnancy scare."

"Shit, Ani," Talin started.

Ani waved her off. "It's fine. It actually brought us closer together. I waited a while, longer than I should have, but I told them everything. I came home and thought I was going to have to get an abortion, but then I had a miscarriage before the appointment."

Talin sniffled. "You never told me."

"I never really talk about it. People are so judgy and awkward about this stuff. The point is Mom and Dad were way more supportive than I expected. They wanted me to be safe and cared for and let me make my own decision. I've never been able to figure out what they'll get mad about and what they'll let slide, but I know with this kind of thing they'll have your back."

The back door slammed to a close and Ani wondered whether it was her mother or brother returning home, but the rapid thump of shoes through the house gave her the answer. Joseph emerged at the door and she nearly didn't recognize him. Talin had not mentioned his haircut. All his long beautiful hair was shaved away, his head round and lumpy. The buzzcut made him appear even leaner and taller. There was a bruise across his upper lip. His cheek, the color of sickly lemonade. He was menacing. Had it not been early September she would wonder if he was dressed for Halloween, some zombie version of his former self.

"You're back," he said. He approached her with open arms, and there was nothing to do but accept his embrace.

Joseph Kurkjian

As the days passed and Joseph waited for his face to heal, he tried to tamp down his lingering anger, but his mind would unexpectedly snap to the memory of the moment Zack walloped him in the stomach, or the terrible things he'd said to his friends about Armenian girls. He couldn't stop replaying the whole scene in his head. Talin was out sick for two more days, resting under the care of Ani and Hannah, while Joseph went through the repeat motions of the school day alone.

In the evenings, his family gathered at the table for dinner whenever Talin was feeling best, but otherwise his sisters sequestered themselves to their room, Ani's passed-down domain to her younger sister, now shared by the two of them until Ani returned to Chicago.

Saturday night, Cal texted when he was on his way to pick up Joseph so they could go to his older brother's apartment and blow off some steam. Cal's brother, Jack, was out of town for a company retreat with his team at Quicken Loans. He always left Cal a key. Joseph's car privileges remained on hold, except when he was driving to and from school. He couldn't figure out how to pack his vodka without getting caught.

"Tal," Joseph called. He knocked on the door.

"Come in."

Joseph entered and found his sisters laying on their stomachs on the bed, watching *Mad Men* on Ani's MacBook. He closed the door. "Cal is going to pick me up."

Ani assessed his appearance. He had put on tight black jeans and a black T-shirt, a splash of body spray. It was more hipster than his usual clothes. Ani smiled with concern. "Mom and Dad are letting you go out?"

He laughed. "Yeah. They have one less thing to be anxious about now that you're back, so I guess I'm off the hook."

"Maybe for another week or so," Ani warned. She stood and approached him, picked some laundry fuzz off his shoulder. "I need to go back and start making money again soon. My apartment is gross." She pinched another pill of fuzz and a snap of static passed between them. "Ouch. Do you use dryer sheets?"

"No, I don't like the scent."

"It might help your shirts look less wrinkly."

"Have you told Mom and Dad you're going back?" he deflected.

"I think Uncle Karo is going to sell Mari's car, so it's either Dad drives me, or I'll take the train, but I have a bunch of stuff."

"Okay." Joseph tried to flatten his shirt over his body. "Let's do something fun before you leave."

Ani nodded in assent. Joseph's phone dinged. Cal was in the driveway. He rambled into the hall. The television blared and he imagined his parents stretched out on opposite sides of the couch, their feet tangled in the middle of the L. He was glad he'd worn his shoes to his room, so he didn't have to retrieve them by the back door. If he was quiet, he could duck out the front without an interrogation.

"Joe!" his father called. Shit, he thought. He walked out through the kitchen and to the living room. His father was sitting with his mother's feet sprawled atop his lap. A bunch of people were baking in an enormous tent.

"Joe," his father said again. "I can't control what you do outside of this house, but remember that I can take away the privilege for you to leave any time I choose. No more fights, no problems, no driving, no drinking, and be back by curfew, or there will be consequences. Clear?"

"Yeah, Dad." For the first time in weeks, Joseph didn't feel like drinking to abandon anyway. A casual buzz would do. He was tired. He poked his tongue against the rough patch on the inside of his lip. It felt dry and scabby, but was nearly healed. His jaw had stopped clicking when he ate. He wanted nothing more than to enjoy a beer or two with Cal and play video games, maybe order a pizza. "Cal's outside, I should go."

"I'll be here at midnight waiting."

Outside, the headlights of Cal's old silver station wagon burned Joseph's eyes. The crickets were chirping up an apocalypse. The hair on Joseph's forearms prickled; it was chillier than he anticipated, the summer heat flagging to the longer nights. He opened the passenger door, ducked his head, and fell into the car. The aroma of cheap pizza overwhelmed him.

"I picked up a couple hot and readies on the way. One sausage, one pepperoni," Cal said. His stomach gurgled. "Sitting out here has been torture."

"You should've dug in."

"Too messy dumping ranch in the box."

"Damn it. I momentarily forgot you're a monster."

"You're welcome." Cal chuckled as he pulled out of the driveway. His brother's apartment was off the island in Allen Park. It would take them a half hour to get there if they didn't hit traffic, but it was already past eight. Joseph leaned his seat back and stretched out his legs. The station wagon was much roomier than his car. Cal's cassette adapter had long since busted, stuck in the slot, so they listened to the radio, the same classic rock station his father played. Cal was big on the sixties.

The Hendrix cover of "All Along the Watchtower" came on as they crossed the toll bridge. Joseph realized he had not been off the island in days; strange to think that their trip to Port Austin was only a week ago. It felt like he lived in the shadow of Detroit, the line of skyscrapers across the river, the casinos, the sports arenas, the restaurants. He had grown up next door and rarely gone into the city.

He couldn't picture where exactly Allen Park was in relation to the rest of the area. Mari used to tell him and Talin never to say they were from Detroit or Metro Detroit, because that was a lie. They all had friends who told out-of-towners they lived in the city under the excuse of convenience. Mari insisted claiming they lived in Detroit was some bullshit white and wealthy suburban kids fell back on for street cred, even if their parents or grandparents had bailed during white flight and economically gutted the downtown. Joseph never understood what she was talking about when he was a kid, but he thought he understood it now. When he told people he lived on Grosse Ile, it resulted in blank stares, even some Michiganders pointing to their hand like show me where, but it was the truth, not a dishonest approximation.

Joseph had gotten used to the absent expressions he received when he talked about growing up on an island. There were all sorts of invisible barriers in his life. He was privileged in so many ways. The river might as well have been a great wall. When he thought too hard about it, he was filled with an erratic sense of guilt.

In Jack's apartment, Joseph and Cal devoured the pizzas directly out of the boxes. Jack had left them a twelve-pack of Molson Canadian with a magenta sticky note that read *one of you idiots stay sober enough to drive*. Jack had a collection of old vinyl and Cal slid *Strange Days* by The Doors out of its sleeve and flipped to the B-side. They nipped at the brown bottles and played Mario Kart on Jack's old Nintendo 64. It was exactly the kind of evening Joseph needed.

"Hey, I have to talk to you about something, but don't get mad." Cal kept his eyes on the screen as they drifted through the mayhem of Bowser's castle. Joseph hopped over a pit of lava.

"Damn it," Joseph swore. He ran into a green shell and fell from first to fifth place. He hated losing. "I'm good, you can tell me."

"Zack was in the hall bragging to a couple of the other hockey guys that he hooked up with your sister."

Joseph thought back to when Talin was talking to him out on Gwen's boat, the bike rides, and their fight. He thought he knew her so well. "Nah man. There's no way."

"I'm just telling you what I heard."

Joseph could feel the truth of it in his gut. If Cal had heard about it, other people around school probably had too. On the drive over he thought about how the island blocked people out, but now he realized it also kept them trapped. A rich little bubble. There was only so much to talk about at school. He paused the game, chugged the rest of his beer, and shook himself off the futon. "You want another?"

"I'm good for now."

"You know Tal," Joseph said. "There's no way."

"Yeah, it's stupid." Cal shrugged. "Just thought you should hear it from a friend."

Joseph was angry, but also grateful. He could feel the adrenaline rush of alcohol and frustration. Now he wanted to fight Zack all over again. Tonight, none of it mattered though. He was at peace with his sisters relaxing at home together. He deserved a night to enjoy himself.

At eleven, they turned off the Nintendo 64 and cleaned the kitchen. Cal had only drunk two beers and switched to water more than an hour earlier. Joseph was grateful for the designated driver. Cal offered him a piece of spearmint gum. They walked the pizza boxes and empty bottles to the recycling bin in the parking lot and headed home.

Cal dropped Joseph off in the driveway with plenty of time before midnight curfew. Joseph punched in the code on the side of the garage, kicked off his shoes in the laundry room. The house was quiet except for the whisper of voices on the television. His father sat in yellow lamplight, another crime procedural on the TV while he fiddled with his phone.

"You're on time," Edgar noted. Joseph realized his father was a mess too. Edgar's hair was getting long and his beard was a disaster. They looked more alike than Joseph wanted to admit.

"You sound surprised."

"Should I be?"

Joseph had to piss, but he didn't want his father to think he drank enough that he needed to rush to the bathroom after the ride home. "I was just hanging out with Cal."

Edgar set his phone upside down on his thigh. "Cal's a good kid."

"Well," Joseph sighed. His parents always told him Cal was a good kid. They acted shocked that he had nice friends. "I'm going to call it a night."

"Good night." He picked his phone back up and started typing again. Joseph wondered who he could be talking to at this hour. The rest of the house was dark. Everyone must have been asleep. His father, a lone guard, keeping watch and waiting. Joseph pissed, brushed his teeth, washed his face, undressed, and fell into bed trying not to think about Zack and his sister.

On Monday, Talin finally appeared well enough to make it through the day. Ani left for the gym with their mom, their dad was off to work, and Joseph drove them to school. Talin seemed energetic and nervous, but in much better spirits since Ani had returned home, nearly normal. She even offered to let him select the music.

"You pick." Joseph knew it would make her happy.

She grinned and found an old J Dilla album, *The Shining*. Mari used to play it all the time when she babysat. "So Far to Go." The song always made Joseph think about clear, endless blue skies and green lawns stretched forever, like there was no horizon. It was a beautiful beat.

He was happy cruising around with Talin. If she hadn't already been absent most of last week, he would have tried to convince her to skip the first half of the school day. They could drive off the island to the beach and stare off into the water.

Then again, looking out over the lake didn't hold the same comforting appeal it once had, especially not after their uncle almost drowned. It was difficult for him to admit that sometimes the way Mari had ended her life made him angry. She hadn't only marred Lake Michigan, but every waterfront, each stretch of beach and glistening water. For the rest of his life, every time he stood on the shore and tried to guess how far out the line was where the water met the sky, he would think about her swimming toward it.

Once they exited the car, Talin peeled away from him, bumping into Gwen in the parking lot. Joseph probably wouldn't see her for the rest of the day.

After school, it was back to Eminem. Joseph soaked up the anger in every nasally line. He clung to the gloomy beats and violent hooks. His parents bothered him less when they could hear the music coming from his room. They left him alone, and he wanted to be left alone. In the weeks leading up to the fight, Talin hadn't even bothered to cross the hall to talk to him anymore. She'd holed up in her room texting her friends and watching Netflix until they hopped in the car to drive out to eat or fell into the lullaby of the movie theater.

They had lost something that summer. He wasn't sure how to put a name to it, but they were growing further apart, even if Ani temporarily bridged the distance. In less than two years, they would leave for different schools. Her grades were much better than his. In another week or two, she would go back to student government and tutoring freshmen in math after school. She had the GPA to skip to the East Coast or follow in Mari's footsteps to Ann Arbor if she wanted. He would wind up like Ani at State. Even that might be a stretch, leaving him with other in-state options like Central or Western. Somewhere close by. A party school. A place Talin would come to mock, the way the U of M fans chanted, *If you can't get into college go to State.*

Joseph wanted to get back on his sister's good side. He planned to take her to Coney Island after school and buy her a root beer float with the money their dad had given him for mowing the lawn that weekend, but she was insistent on heading home right away. Something was going on with her and Ani and their mom. Damn it, Joseph thought. His face was sore. The bruise, faded, near gone. All the remaining damage was beneath the surface. He was glad he could at least take a punch.

Maybe it was time for them to start following their own roads. He didn't understand what her deal was lately anyway. She was acting funny, quiet, moody. They were all miserable, but his twin wasn't one to show it as much as the rest of them. It had been more than two months since Mari had died, but Talin was closing herself off more and more instead of less and less.

The fifth of green-apple vodka under his bed beckoned him like a siren at sea. Joseph figured maybe he could convince Ani to buy him one more bottle before she went back to Chicago. He was not a fan of the green apple. It was disgusting on its own and wasn't that much better when he mixed it with Sprite or Vernor's. He took a swig from the fifth and chased it with his water bottle, but the medicinal taste lingered in his throat and sat heavy in his stomach. A couple pulls helped numb the buried tissue damage around his cheek and nose. More for him, since Talin couldn't hold it down right now.

Joseph didn't want to think about school or Mari or what was going on with his sisters anymore. He was exhausted by everyone in his life. No one understood he was on his own island. That first afternoon back, he'd been so excited to see Ani, but now his sisters had forgotten all about him, so he dialed his speakers up a quarter turn and stared at the ceiling in the isolation of his bedroom.

Joseph had a paper to write for English class, a personal essay, so that his teacher could get to know them better as the semester started, and it wouldn't hurt to loosen up a bit. He realized he talked more openly when he was drinking, so he figured the same idea could apply to his writing. He hadn't completed his chemistry or math homework since the year began. There were plenty of people to copy from at lunch.

He and Talin were both supposed to be slowly compiling materials for their college applications for the following year, but he had not even considered what schools he wanted to apply to, never mind what documents were required in the admissions process. He had time. There was nothing in particular he wanted to study. Maybe he could go out of state, move far away even if it wasn't to some fancy university, to New England or California or Florida, anywhere to give him some space from all the grief smothering him at home.

The alcohol was going right through him. He hopped off the bed, turned off his music, and cracked the door to see out into the hallway. No one was there. He slid from his room, but paused, hearing voices from behind his sister's door. His mom was in there with Ani and Talin, talking. Joseph stepped around the squeaky floorboards and stood at the threshold to listen.

"You don't have to jump to any rash decisions," his mother said. "We can sit down and talk this out together."

"See?" Ani sounded relieved. "I told you Mom would be cool."

Joseph could hear Talin sniffling.

"Tal," Hannah continued. "I don't want to make any assumptions, and it is entirely your business, but is the father someone we've met?"

Talin bawled, uncontrolled breathing raspy with spit. He anticipated what she was going to say. "No. It's this boy from school, Zack."

Joseph wanted to believe he had misheard, but he had suspected that's who his sister was visiting on her bike rides. He stood silent in the hallway, afraid to move, listening to more of the conversation. Fucking unbelievable. He couldn't fathom why Tal would sleep with that asshole. Zack was a piece of shit. And here was Talin, his sister, smart and funny with the world in front of her, buying into his bullshit, his false sympathy, his sob story about his mother, like he could have any understanding of their situation.

Joseph quietly made his way down the hall until he was certain they wouldn't hear his steps. His father and uncle were shouting at one another on the back deck, his aunt spectating from the sidelines. He stood for a moment and stared at them through the kitchen window, like a television on mute. Uncle Karo was in the middle of berating his father. He couldn't imagine why. Everyone was fighting and sharing secrets and leaving him out of the loop. He needed to get out of there.

Seeing his opportunity, Joseph exited through the front and jogged next door across the lawn. He snuck into his aunt and uncle's garage. When he entered, the house felt haunted. The air conditioning eerily hummed through the vents into the empty rooms. The kitchen was a mess of dirty dishes and discarded Tupperware, malodorous with old food but also sterile like a nursing home. Outside, storm clouds loomed in the distance.

Joseph flipped the light switch to the basement, heading downstairs in hopes of finding brandy on his uncle's drafting board, but the only thing across its expanse were plans for one of his boats. Joseph couldn't tell if his uncle was designing something ancient or modern. He flipped through the drafts, read a few of the measurements, and wondered if Karo had lost it. They were the meticulous drawings of someone possessed and delusional. They shared a romantic sense of scale. Like no one else in Joseph's life, Karo understood what it meant to be capsized by the enormous consequences of small actions. The boat was a brilliant monstrosity, one that couldn't be designed by anyone else.

For a moment, he pitied his uncle. There were more practical ways to survive the worst. There were more efficient ways of exacting revenge. Everyone in his family just quietly went about their boring routines and never bothered to take action. He thought of his great-grandfather, Gregor, at a younger age than he was now, already having no choice but to defend his family, then uprooting himself from everything he'd ever known to make a new life. He understood their circumstances were different, but he felt an intense connection he could not fully explain.

In the storage room, Joseph found a few dusty liquor bottles in a limp cardboard box. He uncorked the Ararat and drank without hesitation. It was worse than he remembered. He nearly threw up at the taste, bitter and smoky with a deep volcanic burn. His head spun. A YouTube video he'd watched claimed the earth was spinning faster every year. The aftertaste of the brandy clung to his throat. Even the apple vodka was better, but not as potent.

The canvas gun case was hanging in the same corner where his uncle had excavated it from earlier. Joseph slung the strap over his shoulder and the contents felt lighter, less substantial, than he imagined. He understood that whatever he chose to do next would change his life forever, and that there was no turning back, but also that everything would occur as it was supposed to. He would do what needed to be done.

Karo Kurkjian

Each new storm felt stronger than the last. They would only get worse. Karo laughed when people marveled that he lived on an island. Didn't they realize everyone lived on islands? There was nowhere you could go that did not end in a shoreline, not one land mass on the planet that could not be drowned. But it would not matter—in the end, everything sinks. The world was subject to water. Plants were subject to water. The body was subject to water. They were all islands, each one an isolated gift until they were submerged.

But that was the problem, he thought, nervously entering his own home. He had not been paying attention. He had not saved his daughter. The house, now three generations old, would likely leave the family with him and Hova. He had already failed. Mari was dead. He could not stop thinking about her, and after the moments that his mind uncontrollably drifted elsewhere, he returned to Mari's memory feeling a heavier sense of guilt. His forgetfulness dishonored her. It nauseated him to imagine that for even a second he could move on.

The truth was, long before his daughter died, Karo had dreaded the world drowning in sorrow. A platitude, but he had been happy for too long. His past life had been full of bliss and ease. A cushy job, a kind and loving spouse, a successful and charismatic child. Family and friends always close by. Sometimes he swelled with so much happiness it was difficult to imagine harm could come his way. Sometimes his happiness swelled so much that he believed the inevitable nadir would break him.

Even when his mother got sick again and he felt the descent begin, there was joy in her company. There was joy in their conversations and her advice. After she realized she wasn't going to recover, she tried to leave Karo with every memory and family recipe and tidbit of untold gossip, all of it pouring out of her, vibrant with love and energy for her family, until it became too difficult. Edgar was a bonehead for thinking their mother loved him less, but he was afraid of the hospital, incapable of wading through all the discomfiting, brutal hours at their mother's bedside. Their mother told Karo everything because he was the one who showed up. And yet, her death was the first stage of his unraveling. The first crack in the dam. With Mari gone, he would never recover.

There's something I have to tell you, Hova had whispered over his shoulder only a few minutes ago. At first, he had not even glanced up from his drafting board, but once she had said what she needed to say, he raced out of the basement and across the lawn to where his brother lounged on the back deck. Now, he had to deal with his idiot brother's problems, too, the realities of Edgar's infidelities no longer submerged. The change in Edgar occurred months ago, but Karo had been so distracted, convinced that everything bad that was happening was already right in front of him.

Edgar stood as Karo approached.

"How long?" Karo shouted. He pushed his brother. "Hova saw you! Out for ice cream. Something sweet for Ed!"

Edgar glared at Hova. "She must have misunderstood the situation. I was in the middle of ending things."

"And that's supposed to justify your stupidity?"

"Hannah already knows." Edgar sighed. "We're working on it. It's not your business."

Karo could not believe his brother's casual tone. He was so tired of no one in his family taking things seriously. For so long, they had ignored all the signs. He had failed. He and his brother were both failures.

"It's predictable."

"That's what Hannah said too."

"And pathetic."

"And why is that?" Edgar asked defensively. Karo could hurt his little brother. All he had to do was push hard enough. Edgar was angry at the world, angry at them, angry at anyone who could see his flaws. There was nowhere for him to hide. Hova stood between them.

"Do you realize how difficult it must be for Hannah to feel at home in this family?"

"Ugh." Edgar tossed his hands skyward and dropped them toward his thighs. "Don't make this an Armenian thing."

"The woman? I remember her. That gaudy bouquet of flowers she sent. She's Armenian, isn't she?"

"What does that matter?" Edgar countered. "Just a coincidence."

Karo felt his rage expand. This was untrue. Nothing was a co-incidence. Their lives had been planned for generations in one way or another, and so much of the past remained unknown, the circumstances of how they ended up in that moment familiar to Karo in an ephemeral sense, but so far out of his control if he took everything into account: the slow evolution of creatures emerg-ing from sea to land until they were sentient and hungry and driven toward violent progress, his ancestors fleeing the desert to cross oceans too big to fully comprehend in mileage and depth and total volume, the vast majority of which were unexplored, only for them to assimilate into a country that was always trying to decide for his grandparents and parents and even him what box to check on the census; then for himself and Edgar to be on the receiving end of xenophobic jokes in those last falsely labeled golden years before most of the world was finally crumbling, the environment and economy collapsing just in time to echo his personal despair—and if his mother was dead and his daughter was dead, how could he connect to the past or the future, where was there to go but toward his own drawn-out end? So much would be gone in an instant.

As his anger mounted and the fight unfolded between himself and his younger brother, Karo noticed from the corner of his eye his nephew, who was lumbering toward his house, of all places—and with the clouds darkening in the distance, this could not be a good sign. Joseph could wait, but not for long.

"Are you trying to please Mom and Dad after all these years? They were never like that, like the old women at the church. It's all in your head." Karo poked at his own temple and felt Hova's hand on his arm. He worried Hannah might find them outside airing out the dirty laundry she was already privy to anyway.

"You can't pretend Mom and Dad never had a favorite."

"Maybe that's because I never fucked up!" Karo shrugged his wife's grip away. He wanted to punch his little brother. He was tired of all his pain. He was tired of being expected to be the old and measured and wise one. He had nothing else to give. "You're so selfish. You'll never get it!"

"Please stop."

Karo had been too preoccupied to realize Talin, Ani, and Hannah had walked outside. It was Ani who had spoken. Karo's expression softened. Everyone was there except for Joseph.

"Edgar," Hannah sighed. "We need to talk. Inside. All of us."

Edgar nodded. Then Karo heard it, the distinct pop of a gunshot. Though no one else reacted, he thought immediately of Joseph's absence, of their conversation the other day in the basement. He lunged and shoved Edgar with all his weight. His brother stumbled backward, but avoided falling to the splintered deck. Karo ran across the lawn before anyone could argue. He did not know what he would find, but he knew he could not let anyone else get there before him.

"Garabed!" Hova called to him, her voice strangled.

He waved a hand over his head and felt the first disparate drops of rain. A gust of cool wind gripped at his body. They would follow him, but he must get to Joseph first.

The house was cool and dark. The door to the basement was open and the stairwell light aglow. He could hear Joseph rifling through his papers and was flooded with relief. His nephew was okay. Maybe the gunshot was a figment of his imagination, his worst fears breaking free. He never really believed in the naval refuge he was drawing. He realized that now.

He descended the stairs and the tiny windows at the basement ceiling snapped in a split second of illumination, like flashbulbs on a vintage camera. Lightning, too quick to capture. The thunder followed a few seconds later, a runner eternally in second place. His fight with Edgar had not ended. He hated that everyone had been told except him, unaware of the goings-on in his own family. He could smell gunpowder. Joseph stood over the drafting board with the rifle tucked under his arm. The rain arrived, so heavy that the windows were immersed, they were sunk in a glass bubble at the bottom of an aquarium.

"Joseph."

"Shit," Joseph mumbled to himself.

"Whatever it is," Karo said gently, stepping toward him, "that's not the answer."

"I loaded the rifle and it misfired," Joseph confessed, tears in his eyes. He turned and Karo shuffled in front of him. How could Joseph be so foolish? His nephew's voice cracked. "You don't understand. It's Talin. There's . . . something has happened."

Karo was shorter than Joseph, but held his position firm. Neither of them moved. Joseph's eyes were glassed over, brandy strong on his breath. A clatter of shoes banged upstairs. They would only be alone for a moment.

Finally breaking, Joseph wheezed and began to sob. Karo grabbed the rifle and placed the heirloom atop the papers on his desk. The stray bullet had poked a hole through the middle of his plans. A fatal blow to the hull. It felt like so much of their family history was with them, weighing everything down. Karo pulled

Joseph to him and they fell into an embrace, heavy and drunk and exhausted. They kept one another afloat until the basement filled with his family.

"What happened?" Edgar demanded.

"I left the rifle out. Loaded," Karo lied. "Joseph was looking for some drafting paper for school and when he moved the gun it fired."

"Karo," Hova scolded.

"I know," Karo said. "I'll get help. I need help."

His nephew's warm tears hit Karo's shoulder, but his feet were suddenly frigid and drenched. A puddle of water had soaked his socks through. Karo looked down. An inch of standing water rippled over the toes of Joseph's scuffed basketball shoes. Water spread across the cold basement floor. There was no stopping its brutal, steady flow, as if it would rise forever, until everything was ruined and there was nothing left to salvage. His family. The flood.

"Damn sump pump," Edgar mumbled.

When Karo was a boy, Gregor had told him that the earliest records of their ancestry dated back to boatbuilders in the thirteenth century. Karo had taken that legacy to heart. How beautiful it must have been to sail well before the industrial revolution, to fish without worrying about microplastic and mass extinction, to see the world lush and plentiful with life.

He could get them back there, he thought. He could help rebuild the family vessel, keep them all from sinking. He was already sketching out the plans in his head: replanting his mother's forgotten garden, accompanying Hova on her walks, checking in more on his nieces and nephew, dumping the sea of old brandy.

He would donate the rifle to the museum, where it would be properly restored and cared for, a part of his family history that symbolized so much but served no purpose now. He would try to forgive his brother. He would love his daughter, remember her, speak her name. He would let the memories wash over him, without fear.

"Oh shit, it's getting worse." Joseph shook free from his uncle's embrace, the water splashing as he scrambled backward.

"It's fine." Karo laughed. He would drain the basement in the morning. "It's just a bit of water."

Gregor Kurkjian

A member of the nursing home staff called to the children gathered around that the egg hunt was about to begin. Gregor shooed Mari and Ani away, wishing them luck in their search for the hollow plastic shells filled with chocolate and other goodies. They ran from him and he was filled with awe knowing he had survived so much to see them start to grow up. He was stiff in his wheelchair. It had been a long morning. His eldest grandson quietly stood by him.

"You tell that story differently than you used to," Karo said.

"You've had more time to receive it."

"I meant all the embellishments. The last man standing on Musa Dagh?"

"I am an old man. Memory changes when you get to be my age."

Karo dragged a wicker chair across the patio and sat down facing his grandfather. Children shrieked all around them, searching everywhere for hidden eggs.

Gregor knew he would die soon. His family would be left to figure out so much on their own.

"And why, I wonder," Karo began, "did you leave out the rest of the story? The death marches and statistics and the disputed Hitler quote, the numerous times you were nearly mauled on the assembly line, that you were beaten up for taking jobs, the houses you couldn't purchase with your last name, that you lost all contact with your family?"

"Your grandmother went through so much worse."

"That's not really my point."

"They are just babies, Karo."

Karo smashed his hand over his face in exhaustion. "Yet you told them about starving on Musa Dagh."

"I told them about fighting back."

"What about the rest of it?"

"They have their whole lives to learn the rest, but I won't be around then. I need them to know the truth." Gregor grunted. He caught his breath. Anger was too extreme an emotion for him to physically handle at his age. "But I'm not ready to give them the full burden. They are still young enough to believe in happy endings."

Karo laughed. "You're getting sentimental, old man." He stood and gripped his grandfather's shoulder. "Mari has your spirit though." They watched together as Mari plopped down on the grass with her basket in front of her. She had stopped her hunt and was now patiently opening her pile of eggs one by one. Karo smiled. "She told me when she found five eggs she would stop. We did the math together. Ten kids and fifty eggs, she didn't want to take more than her share."

Karo walked across the lawn toward Mari to help her sort through her haul. The spring sun was warm, heartening. Gregor could have fallen asleep right there. He could never figure out how to tell his family that while he had never really left the mountain, he did not want them to feel obligated to stay there. He was a spectator to the world now, too old to do more than sit in his chair and watch his family having fun. Soon, they would leave, and he would be alone again. In his lifetime, the world had changed so much and not at all. What had happened to his family was happening all the time. It was happening today.

Gregor drifted off. He was not sure for how long, but when Karo squeezed his shoulder he opened his eyes to find all of his family gathered around him. It was time for them to say goodbye. Mari and Ani each gave Gregor a bashful hug, unsure of how to wrap their tiny arms around his wheelchair.

"I'll stop by soon," Karo promised. "Maybe next week."

Gregor nodded. Something in his heart told him this was the last time he would see them. It was out of his control. There was nothing more for him to say. His family was thriving. Everything would ebb and flow as it always had, and even if he was not there to witness it, he was certain they would be fine.

Mari Kurkjian

On what I've decided will be the final morning of my life, I wake the same as any other day, the nascent caffeine headache nudging me out of bed. I had stayed up late cleaning, finishing *The Awakening*, and writing. I promised myself when I arose I would not take one glance at my computer, no awful screens at all, and so I hold to that promise, even though my brain eggs me to cave so I can see the new comments and videos, the tragic headlines, the never-ending tweets. It is the first morning in months I will not complete my daily crossword puzzle. It is the first morning in months I have a sense of clarity.

Looking around, I'm not exactly sure why I bought this condo. It's lovely, but it's not a home. Standard capitalist wisdom told me owning anything was better than renting an apartment, that millennials like me would never really have the finances for a down payment to purchase a gigantic carbon nightmare in the suburbs—not on a public-school teacher's salary anyway. A condo seemed so practical, but even after only a year of payments it's yet another thing weighing me down. I never have people over anymore. No dates or friends or family. I was fed up with teaching before I was fired, but there were also many days I adored my work. I thought I would leave the profession on my own terms. When I peruse the books on my shelves and consider how many of the authors I admire chose to end their lives despite their successes and legendary friendships, no matter the spouses and children at home, no matter the books left unwritten, I am reminded that everyone has a choice. Every beginning has an end, whether or not we're ready for it.

Chopin's novel sits on my desk. I open it and unfold the pages of printed text addressed to my parents for a final review, knowing well they will be the ones to find the last thing I'll ever write.

After rereading, I must admit, I don't think any of them will forgive me. What an inadequate, self-involved note. A shitty first draft. It'll have to do. I'll lose my resolve if I have to rewrite it. My parents always wanted me to live closer to home. I wonder if maybe things would have been different if I moved back near the island. I could have taught in Detroit or Ann Arbor. I hate how much of life is full of what-ifs and missed opportunities. There's so much I could have done that I didn't.

My walk to the water is about a mile. I lock the condo even though there's no reason to do so. Force of habit, I guess. I pass the noisy coffeeshops and closed breweries. Cities are never quiet, but there's something special about the early morning hours when they feel nearly abandoned, when a few early risers are taking out the trash or smoking cigarettes on back steps or jogging over sidewalk cracks, the funk of the tossed food and drink from the night before heavy over everything like a fog, and the sun just peeking through the buildings. It's the air that gets me, how the streets can smell fresh and putrid at the same time.

I remember working on a science fair project with my father about plastic in the oceans, the hours we spent poring over research together. His career never made sense to me until I was forced to confront all the harm we caused the planet. When I was young, I thought he designed fancy boats and that was it. Everyone in the Midwest says the landscape has changed, but it's true that the Great Lakes look so different to me now than they did when I was small. The destruction we're causing has been too much to bear, and it's gone by so fast, but I'm at peace. I'm too tired of life's immense disappointments and anticipatory grief.

Out on the calm water, some kind of industrial tanker blurs in the distance. My family supposedly once sailed merchant ships, and my great-grandfather once told me a story about arriving in the United States on a ship, and my father has spent more than half of his life designing them. We have developed so many brilliant advancements to compensate for the vast limitations of our bodies. I will never be able to swim across the great lake, the most direct route to the state where I was born and raised. It is my earliest memory. On Easter morning, my great-grandfather telling me the story of his life, that he was born on a mountain by the sea, the details of his youth still fantastical, but also undeniable, and how the water burned when he swam toward the French navy, that the cold plunge was shocking enough to fill him with warmth. That warmth runs through me too. I will swim until I find my way home.

Acknowledgments

This novel would not exist without the immense support of many mentors, friends, and family members. There are more people who have contributed to this book than I have room to thank, and to those I have thanked, my gratitude is far beyond what can be expressed in these few pages.

To my parents: Thank you for your unwavering support and belief in me. Neither this novel nor any of my other writing would have come to fruition without your lifelong encouragement and trust. I hope this book makes you proud. I hope someday I can find a better way to show you how thankful I am. I love you guys. And to my younger brother, Nick, thank you for always being there and keeping me grounded. I love you, bro.

To my wife, Kelsey: You have supported my efforts to be a writer more than anyone. You've stood by me through multiple moves across the country, career changes, many failures, buying and selling hundreds of books, and rescuing the best dog in the world. You'll always be my most trusted reader. I am so grateful for the life we've built together. I love you.

Thank you to Ryan Amato and Rakesh Satyal for seeing the vision and giving this book the perfect home. Ryan, your thoughtful edits and enthusiasm for this novel have made it immeasurably better. I'm so grateful for how everything has come together. I hope you know how much of a rockstar you are. Huge shout-outs to Stephanie Shafer for creating this gorgeous cover and to Yvonne Chan for the stunning interior. It's more than I could ever imagine. I feel so lucky to have my work look this good. Thank you!

To Nat Edwards: You are so much more than the perfect agent. You are a friend, a collaborator, and a much-needed voice of reason. I never would have made it this far without you. I'll always be in your corner. Thank you too to everyone else at Trellis who supported this book—I'm honored to be part of the family.

Finishing this novel would not have been possible without the support of Creative Armenia, the Armenian Professional Society, and the International Armenian Literary Alliance. I have been overwhelmed with gratitude by the kindness and generosity of these communities. Thank you!

Thank you to Ravi Howard for seeing this novel from early pages to finished draft and for chairing my dissertation committee. Our weekly prelims meetings, talking about books and writing, remains one of my fondest memories of graduate school. Thank you also to the rest of my committee—Skip Horack, Dr. Diane Roberts, and Dr. Lisa Ryoko Wakamiya—for their thoughtful insights and recommendations. Thank you to Mark Winegardner for leading the brilliant workshop that allowed this novel to grow and develop, bringing me to Florida State, and the continuing career advice. Thank you also to everyone in that novel workshop who made it such a special community right before the beginning of the pandemic.

Acknowledgments

To the Northwestern University School of Professional Studies MFA: Thank you for believing in my potential when no one else (including me) did. Thank you to Reginald Gibbons for bringing me into the program and trusting me at the helm of *TriQuarterly*. Thank you to Stuart Dybek for teaching me how to navigate a writing workshop, Juan Martinez for tireless mentorship and teaching me how to revise, Naeem Murr for teaching me how to close read, Rebecca Makkai for teaching me how to be a considerate educator and build literary community, Susan Harris for mentoring me as I learned how to be an editor, and Christine Sneed for always treating me like a professional and helping me find my way, even long after I graduated. To the friends I made in that program—especially Joshua Bohnsack, Jonathan Winston Jones, Allison Epstein, and Tara Stringfellow—thank you for making me better and pushing me to stick with it.

To Rick Barot: Thank you for bringing me out west to PLU and for trusting me to be part of Rainier Writing Workshop's beautiful community. Your reading of this novel came at a necessary time for its improvement, and I'm so grateful for your continuing mentorship.

To Alyson Sinclair and Stephanie Trott: Thank you both for making *The Rumpus* feel like a family and for working through so many of my half-baked ideas together. Thank you for your steadfast guidance and care. And a big shout-out to *The Rumpus*'s entire masthead who work so hard to keep the magazine going at a time when so many have shuttered.

Thank you to Morgan Talty for the literary friendship we've built over the years. Thank you to Vanessa Chan for advocating on my behalf, two of my favorite mugs, and tolerating all my bad puns. Thank you to Matt Bell for always offering career (and running) advice and Michigan camaraderie.

Thank you to Dustin Pearson for our never-ending conversation about art and literature. Thank you to all the writer friends who have kept me going in endless ways big and small (in no particular order): Kristen Arnett, Kayla Kumari Upadhyaya, LaTanya McQueen, Christopher Alonso, Christopher Gonzalez, Melissa Faliveno, Aaron Burch, Lindsey Drager, Megan Giddings, Isle McElroy, Annie Hartnett, Adam Dalva, Autumn Watts, Su Cho, Patrick Nathan, SJ Sindu, Marianne Chan, Clancy McGilligan, Colleen Mayo, Damian Caudill, Paul Hansen, Zach Linge, Jamie Ringleb, Carrie Muehle, Megan Stielstra, Adam Morgan, John Englehardt, Mac Crane, Allegra Hyde, Jenessa Abrams, Matthew Baker, Dina Relles, Robert James Russell, Mandana Chaffa, Walker Rutter-Bowman, and many more. If your name is missing, I promise it's mostly because my memory is terrible.

Ryan Miller, years ago I promised you a book shout-out if you grabbed me a beer from the fridge while I was not feeling my best. I have not forgotten—thank you!

Some hearty thanks to the debut book group who has offered invaluable advice and shared learnings throughout the publishing process. Thank you to all the contributors of *We Are All Armenian*, whose perspectives gave me the confidence to continue this project. Thank you to the institutions where I teach, the University of Michigan and the Rainier Writing Workshop, for supporting my art and keeping me (pun intended) above water. Thank you to the close friends from East Lansing, Scio Hills, Ann Arbor, Tacoma, Seattle, Tallahassee, and Chicago who are too numerous to list here. Lastly, thank you to my extended family for all the stories and wisdom, which are the inspiration behind so much of my work.

About the Author

ARAM MRJOIAN is a lecturer in the Department of English at the University of Michigan, where he serves as the managing editor of *Michigan Quarterly Review*. He is the editor-in-chief of The Rumpus and a 2022 Creative Armenia-AGBU Fellow. Aram has previously worked as an editor at the *Chicago Review of Books*, the *Southeast Review*, and *TriQuarterly*. He is also the editor of the anthology *We Are All Armenian: Voices from the Diaspora*, published by the University of Texas Press (March 2023). His writing has appeared in *The Guardian, Runner's World, Literary Hub, Catapult, West Branch, Electric Literature, Gulf Coast, Boulevard, Joyland, Longreads,* and many other publications. He holds an MFA in creative writing from Northwestern University and a PhD in creative writing from Florida State University. He lives in Michigan.

A Note on the Cover

The most striking aspect of *Waterline* to me as a reader was the duality of the symbolism water embodies throughout the novel; Gregor's mythical swim hovers in the background of each character, a reminder of their inherited trauma, but also of perseverance, hope, and new beginnings. Mari's swim into the depths of Lake Michigan pulls on the darker symbolisms of water; the unknown, the subconscious, danger, and death. I chose to create intentionally simple imagery to allow the feeling the cover gives to change as the novel is read. Is the swimmer swimming toward help or away from it? Is the water a refuge or a tomb? The pattern along the bottom is a traditional Armenian pattern. The red, blue, and orange used on the cover are the colors of the Armenian flag.

Stephanie Shafer

Here ends Aram Mrjoian's
Waterline.

The first edition of this book was printed
and bound at Lakeside Book Company
in Harrisonburg, Virginia, in May 2025.

A NOTE ON THE TYPE

The text of this novel was set in Arek Latin, a
powerful, multi-weight serif typeface. Designed by
Khajag Apelian, Arek melds clear-reading uprights
with kinetic italics to match Armenian cursive.
Originally designed for school books, Arek will
hold any reader's attention and handle any editorial
assignment with ease.

HARPERVIA

An imprint dedicated to publishing international voices,
offering readers a chance to encounter other lives and other
points of view via the language of the imagination.